MW01136437

THE WORKERS OF INIQUITY

A C.T. FERGUSON CRIME NOVEL (#3)

TOM FOWLER

WIDENINGGYREMEDIA

The Workers of Iniquity: A C.T. Ferguson Private Investigator Mystery is copyright (c) 2018 by Tom Fowler. All rights reserved. This book or parts thereof may not be reproduced in any form, stored in any retrieval system, or transmitted in any form by any means—electronic, mechanical, photocopy, recording, or otherwise— without prior written permission of the publisher, except as provided by United States of America copyright law. For permission requests, write to the publisher at tom@tomfowlerwrites.com.

Editing: Chase Nottingham. This book is at least 46% more readable because of his suggested fixes.

Cover Design: 100 Covers

Published by Widening Gyre Media, LLC. Silver Spring, MD.

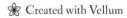 Created with Vellum

For Lisa and Isabel

CHAPTER 1

"Deliver me from the workers of iniquity, and save me from bloody men."

–Psalm 59:2

SOMEONE JACKHAMMERED THE FLOOR NEAR MY HEAD.

I had to be dreaming. I told myself no one could be using such a tool indoors. Then I heard it again. As the haze lifted, I realized it was my cell phone vibrating. I must have left it in the pocket of my jeans, which currently resided on the bedroom hardwood. It clattered again. I rolled out of bed, grabbed it, and looked at the number. Another one I didn't recognize. The alarm clock told me it was 2:30. I answered.

"Is this C.T. Ferguson?" a woman said.

"Yes."

"The private investigator?"

"Is there another C.T. Ferguson who would take your call at this beastly hour?"

"No," she said. "No, I . . . I suppose not." She sounded distracted. I sounded tired. This would be a great conversation.

"Is there a reason you called?" I said when she lapsed into silence.

"I'm worried about my husband," she said. "He's been gone for almost three days now."

"Do you know where he went?"

"Not exactly. That's part of the reason I'm concerned."

"What happened?" I said.

"We've . . . had some money problems. He wanted to put together a plan to get us out of debt. Do some quick buying and selling on the stock market, that sort of thing."

"Day trading."

"Whatever they call it. He said he didn't want to be bothered, so he checked into a hotel."

The behavior sounded odd. Why incur the expense of a hotel if you were having money problems? "Couldn't he have simply stayed home and locked the door?" I said.

"I tried to tell him." She sighed. Her voice cracked. "He's just so stubborn these days. I'm worried about him. I don't know what hotel he's staying at."

"You've called around?"

"To all the ones in the area, yes."

"Then either he went out of the area, or he's staying under an assumed name."

"Can you find him?"

"How?" I said. "All I could do is call hotels or show his picture around. And if he's sequestered himself in a room, showing a picture to the guy twiddling his thumbs on the night shift probably won't work. It's late, and we both need sleep. We can talk about it in the morning if you haven't heard from him."

"He might be dead." Her voice broke again. She paused. "He might be dead."

"If he is, he'll still be dead at a more respectable hour," I said.

"Come by after nine if you want to talk some more, but I'm going back to sleep."

She remained silent. I hung up.

* * *

THE NEXT MORNING, I woke up at eight o'clock without the benefit—or curse—of an alarm clock. As I approach twenty-nine, I've noticed myself rising earlier. I used to sleep until nine or ten, and only a bomb going off outside the window would rouse me from my slumber. Nowadays, eight was a typical time to wake. I threw on some jogging attire and shoes, stretched, and walked to Federal Hill Park for my morning run.

As usual, I wasn't the only one out for a constitutional. An attractive young lady in aggressively pink spandex trotted along with a dog of indeterminate breed. There were a few other walkers and joggers out, but I settled in behind her. If you're going to follow someone while you're running, make sure it's someone worth following. She stopped after one lap and walked back down Battery Avenue. I hoped she would take a short stroll up Warren and head to Riverside, where I lived, but she went the other way.

I completed a few more laps around the park, stretched against a tree, and returned home at a leisurely pace. My stomach rumbled before I walked in the door, so I worked on breakfast before I showered. I took some vegetables, cheese, and eggs out of the refrigerator and fixed an omelet. It had taken months—and many prospective breakfasts splatting on my kitchen floor—but I mastered the omelet flip. I flipped this one, poured tall glasses of milk and orange juice, and set them on the table. I slid the omelet onto a plate, covered it with mango salsa, and sat with it.

As soon as the first bite slid down, my cell phone rang. I looked at the number; it was the same woman who woke me with vague concerns about her husband. If I let it go to voicemail, she would only call back with more worries she couldn't articulate and I couldn't care about. I answered to get it over with. The omelet could always go in the microwave. "Hello?"

"Is now a better time for you?" she said. Annoyance danced with worry in her voice.

"Not really," I said. "I'm eating breakfast."

"My husband is still missing."

"When did you talk to him last?"

"A day and a half ago, I suppose," she said.

"Have you been to the police yet?"

"Why would I go to them?"

"He's been gone almost two days," I said. "You could ask them to open a missing persons case."

"No, no," she said. "They don't find too many lost people. I think I'd have better luck with you." Her voice quavered again. "Please. I'm worried about him. I want to be sure nothing's happened to him. Our . . . our children would be devastated. I would be devastated." She fell silent. Soft sobs came through the connection. She had to go and cry.

"Can you come by in about forty-five minutes?" I said.

She sniffed a few times. "I'll be there."

"See you then."

She hung up. I finished my omelet.

* * *

FORTY-THREE MINUTES LATER, someone knocked on my front door. Of course she would be early. I looked through the peep-hole at a woman who looked familiar, though I couldn't place from where. Gray hair sprang up in the center of her head. I remembered her with a head full of hair so black it looked like a crown pulled from the midnight sky. She was the only person I knew with hair so dark, though I'd fully suspected it came from some twit at a salon.

If the woman walking over the threshold recognized me, she didn't show it. Her eyes passed over me like another decoration to take in. I took her coat, hung it on my rack, and showed her to the office. Her clothes came from a department store. She strode like she hadn't yet gotten comfortable in her shoes. Her hips had no sashay to them, merely the steady back-and-forth of a business-woman. She sat in one of the guest chairs, and I took my place in the high-backed leather model behind my desk. I knew I knew this woman, but I couldn't come up with her name.

She spent a minute looking at my long desk. I had three 27-inch monitors atop it, arranged side-by-side. A printer sat at the far end. Two computers squatted on the floor, both to the left of my chair. The Windows machine used the two monitors on the left, and my Linux server connected to the one on the right. I also had a rarely-used paper notebook on the desk and a box of tissues I expected to receive a workout during this lady's visit.

"I told you about my husband," she said.

"You told me something," I said. "It's hardly enough to act on."

She looked at me as if seeing me for the first time. "You've probably heard of us. Stanley and Pauline Rodgers."

Now I had the name for the face. "I met you a few times, but I don't recall meeting your husband."

Pauline frowned. She stared at me so long I thought she had lapsed into a coma. "Ferguson," she said.

"Robert and June are my parents," I said.

"I thought you looked a little familiar. She offered a small smile. "I'm sorry you have to see me like this."

"What happened?"

"Like I told you yesterday, we encountered some money problems."

"At the risk of sounding indelicate, what happened to you sounds like more than some simple problems," I said.

She sighed. A weariness crept onto her face, highlighting the crow's feet near her eyes. She couldn't afford to mask them anymore. "You heard about that."

"Kind of hard not to."

"It was all a house of cards, basically. We took a bit of a hit when real estate first started struggling, but stayed afloat. Recently, it all collapsed. Bad advice, bad investments, the wrong stocks . . . you name it, it's kicked us over the last few months."

"Did your husband lose his job?" I said.

"He started his own fund." Pauline shook her head. "He had to shut it down." Her eyes glistened. "People lost money and jobs. I was forced to find work as a secretary." Now a tear slid down her left cheek. "I'm not even a good one, but I think the boss took pity on me."

"So now your husband is locked away in a hotel room?"

"As far as I know," Pauline said.

"And he's trying to regain the money he lost?"

"That's what he said. He thought up a plan. He needed to borrow some money to make ends meet for a while. I don't know where he got it, but I'm sure the payments are due. Even with his fund, we got bad advice before." Pauline sobbed now. "We can't go through it again. We just can't."

I pushed the box of tissues toward her. She nodded, grabbed one, and dabbed at her eyes. Her makeup already ran. Pauline spent a couple minutes composing herself before she said anything. "Anyway, I'd like you to find Stanley," she said. "I came to you because we can't pay for anything like this right now."

"Pauline, what if he lost more money?" I said.

She shook her head and cried a few more tears. "I just want him back. I want to know he's OK."

I nodded. "I'll see what I can do. In the meantime, I'll need to get some more information from you before you go."

"Anything I can give you. Will you let me know when you know something?"

"Of course," I said.

"Thank you, C.T." She wiped at her eyes again. "This has all been very humbling. The kids are taking it rougher than we are. We put them into public schools."

"Not an easy transition?"

"It was for Katherine," she said. "She's a senior at Goucher now. She had been studying at Brown." Pauline sighed. "It's been a lot harder on Zachary. He went to Calvert Hall before. Now he's in Loch Raven. He's already cut a few classes, gotten into a fight . . . this is really hitting him hard. It's not just the money."

"It's the loss of his father, at least figuratively," I said.

"Yes," said Pauline.

"I might need to talk to them at some point."

Pauline stared ahead. "I'd like to keep them out of it unless you really need them."

"I'll do my best," I said.

* * *

I CERTAINLY WOULD, once I figured out where to start. Pauline told me the family moved out of their swanky Fallston house, sold it for no gain, and ended up living in an apartment in Essex. This was like living in the royal palace, getting thrown from the roof, and landing in the stables right beside a giant bucket of horse turds. Even the smell was the same.

She checked all the hotels near their house. I discounted those right away—not because she had checked them but because he wouldn't stay there. If Stanley Rodgers wanted some time away from his wife, why stay someplace she could wander in and find him? No, he wouldn't be anywhere near their house, and he would probably use an assumed name to minimize the chances of being found.

It would make him hard to track. I'd have to come up with a list of possible places he might stay and show his picture around, then hope someone on duty at the time saw him. I might as well toss a penny into a fountain and wish for a pony, and I don't even like ponies. The alternative was cracking his assumed name. To do so, I would need to know an awful lot about him and get lucky making some guesses. Back to tossing pennies into fountains.

I liked my chances of figuring out a few places for him to stay better. So I'm Stanley Rodgers. I used to have the world on a silver plate, but now I had to eat a shit sandwich every day. I want my old life back, and I think I have a way to get it. To do it, I need to lock myself away from the wife for a few days and make money like I used to. Maybe I have a loan or two to pay off at the same time. So I go to a hotel and rent a room. A room? No, I rent a *suite*, I rent the penthouse, because I'm a big baller again, and regular rooms are for regular people.

Where do I go to do all of this, though? Not near my house— Pauline might find me and try to stop me. I have to get away from her. Do I go downtown? There's the PNC building, the World Trade Center, and I'd feel right at home amid all the money. It would be tempting. My business was in Towson. There's a lot of money in Towson, too, and it's county money, so it smells better. It's my old stomping grounds, the scene of my biggest success and my most harrowing failure. I'm going there to redeem myself.

Towson it was. At the least, I had a place to start. I went online and found a picture of Stanley Rodgers, then made a call to the Baltimore County police. I've done most of my work in the confines of the city—and my proper police detective cousin Rich has reaped the rewards—but I had a few cases take me into the county. During a couple of those, I worked with Sergeant

Gonzalez in Homicide. He answered the phone on the fourth ring. "Gonzalez."

"Nobody's dead in Baltimore County?" I said.

"You should know we sophisticated county dwellers don't have the crime problems you city folks do," he said.

"My ass. Give me your email address. I'm sending you a picture and some information."

"Do I want this information?"

"I'm trying to find someone," I said. "You heard of Stanley Rodgers?"

"Nope," said Gonzalez.

"He's a rich guy who lost his ass not long ago. His wife says he's locked himself in a hotel for three days trying to keep up with the Joneses again. I want to send you his picture in case he turns up somewhere."

"You think he's dead?"

"I have no reason to. As far as I know, he's trying to day trade his way back to a fortune."

"Tell the son of a bitch good luck," Gonzalez said. He gave me his email. "If he turns up, I'll call you."

"Thanks," I said.

Gonzalez hung up without saying goodbye. Rich always did, too. They must have taught it at the police academy.

* * *

I TOLD county law enforcement Stanley Rodgers was missing and provided them some information about him. I didn't expect them to find him, and if they did, I didn't anticipate it to be under positive circumstances. This all meant I still needed to discover what hotel he squirreled himself away in. Towson was the best bet; I felt sure of it. Towson also featured a lot of hotels, some better than others. Even eliminating the dives, Stanley would have several choices.

His brokerage had been in the heart of Towson. You couldn't drive through the traffic circle joining Joppa, York, and Dulaney Valley Roads without seeing it (and most people just plain couldn't drive in the circle at all). It still left the Sheraton and the Marriott of the nicer hotels in Towson. The Marriott was farther away and less likely, but I wanted to be more sure of my choice, so I grabbed my cell phone and called my parents' house.

"Dad, I need a little insight," I said.

"Sure, son," my father said. "Into what?"

"Into Stanley Rodgers. Remember him?"

"Haven't seen him in a couple years, but yeah, I remember him. We heard they fell on tough times."

"Fell hard, in fact," I said. "His wife is worried about him. He hid out in a hotel room trying to day trade his way to a new fortune."

"Sounds really risky."

"I think 'stupid' would be my adjective of choice, but 'risky' works. Anyway, I need to figure out what hotel he's in."

"How can I help?" said my father.

"His brokerage would hold parties and conferences. I never went, but I'm sure you did. Where did he have them?"

"The Sheraton."

As I calculated. "What I thought. Thanks, Dad."

"Glad I could help," he said.

This case would be easier than I expected.

* * *

I PARKED around the corner from the main marquee of the Sheraton and went in a side door. In the middle of the afternoon, hotels kept those open. I started on the first level and walked up and down the halls until I ran into someone in housekeeping. Morning rounds were long over, but a few of them wandered about working on things. It took me until the fourth floor to find someone, a petite lady in her forties whose name badge identified her as Graciela.

"Excuse me," I said to her *en Español*. My Spanish lagged behind my Chinese, but I could still have a simple conversation.

She smiled at me. "Did you lock yourself out of you room, sir?"

"No." I showed her my ID. "I'm trying to find someone, and I heard he might be here."

"I don't want to get anyone in trouble," she said.

"He's not in trouble." I endeavored to sound reassuring. It's not among my many strengths. "His wife is worried about him."

"Mr. Johansson is such a nice man," she said, then covered her mouth right away.

"I'm sure he is," I said. "It's why his wife worries. Thank you."

She frowned as I walked away.

From there, I went back to the main floor and out the same side door. Having found "Mr. Johansson," I would need to talk to him and tell him he should give up his foolishness and go home to his wife. First, I had to get into his room. Graciela wouldn't let me in, and I wouldn't expect any of the other housekeepers to, either. I would need to get a key from the front desk. Mr. Johansson had just acquired an assistant.

A few months ago, the Lexus I drove since my college years blew its engine. I replaced it with a last-generation Audi S4 which came with a manual transmission, drove better, and looked better still. I don't know if it looked like a car Mr. Johansson's assistant would drive, but I had a feeling it would. I parked in a spot visible from the front door, took a flash drive out of my pocket, and hoped I could play a harried assistant.

I ran a hand through my hair to mess it up, got out of the car with alacrity, slammed the door, and ran into the lobby. The cheery fellow behind the desk—Brent, his name tag said—didn't have a chance to finish his company-approved greeting before I broke in to my routine.

"My boss is upstairs," I said. I paced a few feet to either side. "He needs the information I have on this flash drive." I showed him. "But he didn't give me a key to his room."

"Sir, we could take it up for you if you—"

"Do you invest?" I said after rushing the counter and staring into Brent's eyes. "Do you?" He frowned. "No, you don't. You don't invest, and you don't understand investing. Mr. Johansson does. He can make a lot of money for a lot of people, but I have to get him this information. It's brand new and very important."

"I could call his room and—"

"He doesn't want to be disturbed with phone calls and knocks at the door. It's why he's had the sign on the door since he got here." A guess, but it seemed right, and I doubted Brent knew anything to the contrary. "Do you want to stand in the way of earning millions of dollars? Brent, front desk employee and impediment to financial progress." I pointed at him. "It'll be your fault. All. Your. Fault."

Brent's mouth hung open. He looked like he wanted to say something, but he closed his mouth, then gaped again. His eyes focused on me in the same way the guy who's on his sixth shot at the bar's eyes would. He looked at his computer screen and grabbed a blank key. "Mr. Johansson is in the penthouse."

"Of course he is. When a genius gets out of the office to work in peace and quiet, he doesn't stay with the commoners."

Brent chuckled, but I thought he did it to be polite. He didn't understand investing, and he didn't understand me now. He clicked a few keys, swiped the card, and handed it to me. "Good luck saving the financial world."

"You're a lifesaver, Brent," I said. "When's your shift over? I'm buying you a drink."

"Four o'clock, but that's OK. You have a good day, sir."

"You too." I dashed to the elevator and pushed the button. Why couldn't all my cases be this easy?

* * *

THE SHERATON PENTHOUSE didn't look like much of one from the outside. Those I've stayed in have been the only rooms on their floors. This top level had four alleged penthouses. "Suites" would have been a better name for them but also wouldn't carry the price tag associated with staying in the penthouse. Despite his financial woes, Stanley Rodgers couldn't resist its pull.

I walked to the door and slid in the keycard. The light turned green, the lock whirred, and I pushed. Something smelled like bad food. If Rodgers had locked himself in here for a few days, bad food probably wasn't the only stinky thing up here. The corridor inside the room at least boasted of a nice carpet. The gigantic bathroom featured a soaking tub, stand-up shower, two sinks, and marble floors. Despite its outward appearance, this suite might have deserved its lofty status. A flatscreen TV, muted and tuned to some financial network, hung on the wall in easy view of the king bed. I made a left at the bed and looked at Rodger's desk. His laptop, the screen saver active, sat on it. Beside the desk was a dorm-sized refrigerator which seemed small for the priciest room. A trash can full of food containers sat on the other side of the desk. I still hadn't seen Rodgers.

Past the office was a den with a leather couch, leather recliner, and another flatscreen TV. An ice bucket, now filled with water, rested atop the end table. I returned to the main room. Then I noticed the body on the far side of the bed against the wall. I shook my head and closed my eyes. It's never been easy for me to look at corpses, and I hope it never gets to be. The deceased was definitely Stanley Rodgers. He was older, grayer, and heavier than I remembered, but I harbored no doubts as to his identity. Rodgers had a single gunshot wound to his temple. A pistol with a suppressor screwed onto its muzzle lay on the floor close to his right hand.

It looked like a suicide. The corpse had stiffened, so Rodgers had been this way for a while. The "do not disturb" sign would have kept the hotel staff out. "Well, shit," I said to no one in particular. It was a good thing I brought my flash drive. While this looked like a suicide, I wanted to dig around more before I ruled out someone shooting Rodgers in the head. The contents of his important files could give me a place to start. I connected the drive and rebooted the laptop. It loaded into the Linux-based operating system on the drive, and I copied important-looking files. I put the drive back in my pocket, rebooted the computer again, and went into the bathroom. I grabbed a towel, retraced my steps through the penthouse, and wiped down anything I remembered touching. When I finished, I took a few pictures of the scene with my cell phone. Then I left with the towel.

Why did all my cases have to be this hard?

CHAPTER 2

At some point, I would have to let Pauline know what happened to her husband. She would ask me to keep investigating, and I would agree because it's how I am. I knew why Stanley Rodgers locked himself in the hotel room. Right now, one fact constituted the whole of my knowledge. Stanley Rodgers might have killed himself. Maybe he realized he couldn't recoup the money he and his family lost. Perhaps he figured eating a bullet would be better than facing his wife and kids again.

The suicide angle didn't feel right. He had a family. Pauline said theirs was a happy marriage despite the hard times. It meant someone killed Stanley Rodgers. Someone needed to know where he was, gain access to the room, and shoot him to stage a bogus scene. Oh, and do it all without drawing undue attention. It was possible. I knew Pauline would insist Stanley didn't commit suicide even if the evidence were overwhelming.

I captured Stanley's important files on my flash drive. I could get his cell phone records if I needed them. His brokerage account would be more complicated, but I could get it, too. Finding out how well (or how poorly) he was doing could be useful. Based on my visibility at the hotel, I needed a couple hours before Brent 's shift ended and I could call the police. I estimated it would be enough time.

It wasn't.

Sometimes, the bear gets you, and today, I was a bacon-covered snack for a ravenous grizzly. Stanley encrypted his hard drive and its contents. It made sense in hindsight, but most things make sense looking back on them. Movies depict people cracking complicated encryption schemes in a few minutes, often at gunpoint. The reality is deciphering good crypto takes a long time. Top-notch algorithms can take a lifetime to break. I owned good hardware and could farm out effort to the cloud, but time would still be a factor. I hadn't even started on the phone and brokerage account records.

Of course, my phone rang and of course, it was Pauline. I took a deep breath before answering.

"C.T., it's Pauline. I was wondering . . . if you'd made any progress."

This was the call I hoped to avoid. Soon I would have to tell this woman her husband had been shot, perhaps by himself. I couldn't tell her now. "I . . . have a lead," I said. "I'm working on it at the moment."

"Oh, that sounds promising." I heard her voice pick up. Optimism would only make the news I would give her later much worse. Some days, I hated my job. On a few of those days, I even disliked the way I went about working some of my cases. Today, both intersected.

"I hope it is. I'll let you know what I find."

"Please do," she said. "I don't want to keep you from your work. Let me know when you have more."

"I will," I said. "Take care, Pauline."

I tossed my phone onto the sofa. Lying to clients usually didn't bother me, but I rarely lied about something so important. Rich warned me my methods would catch up with me. This hadn't been the way he meant, but he was right nonetheless. I went back to Stanley's hard drive. Decrypting this would take a while. I looked at the clock. At least I could call the police soon.

* * *

I MADE the anonymous tip from a pay phone in Fells Point. Once I did it, I drove back home and kept working on the encrypted hard drive while waiting for the inevitable call from Sergeant Gonzalez. It marked twenty-five minutes of zero progress on the crypto.

"You might want to get down here," he said when I answered.

"What happened?" I said.

"The guy you told me about, Rodgers? He's dead. Has been for at least a day, is my guess. We'll know more when the ME finishes with him."

"I'm guessing he didn't die of natural causes."

"Gunshot to the head," Gonzalez said. "We found a gun near his right hand. Early tests show GSR on it."

"Ooh, an acronym. You're giving me credit for knowing gunshot residue."

"Yeah, I figured you watched CSI. Anyway, looks like a suicide."

"Or someone wants to make it look like one," I said.

"We think of this shit here, too, hotshot. We'll look into it. Everyone is still processing the room. You want to get down here, now's the time."

"Where are you?"

"Towson Sheraton, Penthouse B."

"I'll be there as soon as I can," I said.

Gonzalez hung up. I let out a deep breath I'd been holding. I could only hope I did a good job of playing ignorant.

* * *

WHEN I GOT to the Sheraton, the room looked like I remembered it with the addition of a dozen cops and the subtraction of any semblance of order. At least they were thorough. Drawers had been yanked out, sofa cushions strewn about the room, the bed dismantled. Gonzalez saw me and approached. "Looking like a suicide at this point," he said. He led me through the mess and showed me the gun, now in an evidence bag on the dresser.

"Suppressor," I said, pointing out the obvious.

"Probably means nobody heard anything," Gonzalez said.

"You have some men canvassing now?"

"Women, too," he said. We're progressive in the BCPD."

"Next you'll rename manhunt to 'personhunt,'" I said.

Gonzalez chuckled. "We ain't so fucking progressive yet." He looked around. "What do you make of this?"

I followed his gaze, trying to act as if I hadn't already seen the room today. "Nice place," I said. "I don't know if it counts as a penthouse, but it's much nicer than I'd expect someone with money problems to afford."

"Puzzles me, too," said Gonzalez. "If this guy was so poor, how's he drop five bills a night on a ritzy suite?"

"I think he wanted to stay here."

"Of course he did." Gonzalez gave me a look like I'd sprouted a second head.

"What I mean," I said, "is he wanted to stay here in this specific hotel, in an opulent penthouse. Maybe even in this particular penthouse." I walked to a window and threw open the curtain, flooding the area with late afternoon sunlight. "His old brokerage house was over there," I said, pointing. "He could see it from this window. He could see the site of his greatest success and failure."

"So he made sure he had enough saved up to get this room."

I nodded. "He wanted it," I said. "I think . . . he hoped for inspiration. Some of the old Rodgers magic he used to make a fortune before. Maybe he found it. Could be why someone killed him."

"You really think someone killed him?" Gonzalez said.

"I think he's an unlikely victim of suicide, though Emile Durkheim might disagree."

Gonzalez frowned. "You're going back to sociology class now?"

"I minored in philosophy," I said. "Sociology was right in there, too."

"You take it so you can make asshole quotes at parties?" said Gonzalez

"No, I took it because girls who major in sociology are easy."

Gonzalez looked at me for a moment, then nodded. Maybe he enjoyed similar experiences during his college years. "OK, maybe somebody did kill him," he said. "If so, we'll find evidence of it in this room."

"Can I do anything?"

"You can drive your fancy Lexus back to Baltimore and wait for my next phone call. We'll go talk to the widow."

"It's a fancy Audi now," I pointed out.

"Whatever," said Gonzalez.

* * *

RICH DROVE Gonzalez and me to talk to Pauline. She and Stanley lived in the city. How they sent their son to a county public school was not something I felt the need to ask about right now. I said I could drive Gonzalez myself, but Rich wanted to come along. Sometimes, his involvement in my cases puzzled me.

They lived in Waverly, near Hamilton, just inside the line between Baltimore and the county. The houses were single-family units older than any of us in the car and in various states of repair. The Rodgers' house featured a brick front in need of some work, shutters yearning for a fresh coat of paint, a slapdash roof longing for a hurricane to rip it free, and a garden grown by someone with a black thumb. It was a house a family of modest means could afford and one they were almost certain to hate.

We walked to their porch, and Gonzalez rang the bell. I stood beside him and Rich was behind us. After a moment, Pauline opened the door. Her eyes went to me, then to the other two. Hope drained from them when she guessed why we were here. Gonzalez and Rich showed their badges. Pauline looked back at me, her eyes welling. I needed to look away.

"Mrs. Rodgers, I'm Sergeant Gonzalez of the Baltimore County homicide unit," Gonzalez said. "This is Detective Ferguson of the Baltimore Police behind me. You know C.T. Ferguson already."

"He's dead," Pauline said. Tears started to roll down her cheeks. "He's dead, isn't he?" I could make an extensive list of things I hate about my job; telling people their loved ones were dead would be right at the top. I tried to do it as little as possible.

"I'm afraid so," Gonzalez said.

Pauline sagged onto the doorframe and cried. She tried to say something, but it only came out as gibberish around her sobs. We let her weep. There's really nothing else to do. I offered her a tissue, which she accepted. After a few minutes, her crying settled to the point she could talk. "What happened?" she said.

"We don't have to do this now," Gonzalez said.

"Just tell me what happened."

"Your husband was found dead in a hotel penthouse in Towson. He suffered a gunshot wound to his head."

"Someone killed him?" Pauline said. "Someone killed my Stanley?" Pauline sobbed anew. Gonzalez started to say something, then stopped when he realized it would be pointless.

"We don't know what happened yet," he said after a couple minutes. "We're considering all possibilities."

"Stanley didn't kill himself!" Pauline sniffed a few times. "There's no way. He wouldn't do that."

"Yes, ma'am," Gonzalez said.

"Don't you 'yes ma'am' me," Pauline jabbed Gonzalez in the chest with her finger. "You're patronizing me because you think Stanley killed himself."

"I think we're still early in the investigation, ma'am. We follow the evidence."

"Make sure you do."

"Yes, ma'am."

Pauline glared at Gonzalez. "Sorry," he said. "I'll need to talk to you more when it's a better time." He handed her a card. "Call me in a day or two. I hope to have more to tell you then."

She took the card, looked at it, and slipped it into the pocket of her jeans. "Thanks," she said. "Will you excuse me now? I have to call my children and tell them their father is dead."

"Of course," said Gonzalez. We turned to leave.

"C.T.," Pauline called as we walked away. I turned around. "Will you stay on the case and . . . and . . . "

"Yes, I will," I said.

* * *

WHEN I GOT HOME, I went back to work on Stanley Rodgers' encrypted files. I focused on what I might be able to do instead of how long it would take. I'd hacked good cryptography before, including the suite protecting the largest bank in Hong Kong. It took six fast computers in tandem fifteen days to crack. Today, I owned a faster computer, along with the ability to farm out some work to the cloud. Even if Stanley used better crypto, I knew I could get there in time.

The good thing about being a hacker nowadays is it's so easy to find and download any tool or code you need. The bad thing—at least from my perspective—is a lot of people can be hackers without the background knowledge once required. I coded my own encryption-breaker in Hong Kong, and I still have it. It's needed some tweaking over the years, but I trust it more than any similar program I could download.

I built five virtual machines with graphical processing units in the cloud. The GPUs would enable many more attempts per second. Once the VMs were operable, I uploaded and compiled my program on each, then tied the machines together to unify their efforts with my own computer. While my program worked its electronic voodoo, I went out for a run. Four miles later, I came home, showered, and made some spaghetti Bolognese with a nice leafy salad. I kept plenty of pasta for a lunch or dinner later in the week. Buying an expensive car meant I would need to eat leftovers more often.

After dinner, I went upstairs to find my bedroom door open. Here I was without a gun on my hip. As I got closer, I smelled a familiar whiff of expensive perfume. Gloria Reading lay on my bed watching TV with the volume turned down. I gave her a key a while ago when she feared for her safety during one of my cases. It struck me as odd she'd want to stick around under those circumstances, but she did. In the intervening time, I never asked for it back, and she hadn't offered to return it. Gloria's chestnut hair spilled around her head and shoulders. She smiled at me in her impossibly pretty way. The small nightgown she wore barely covered past her waist and drew my attention away from her smile.

"I saw you running when I was driving up," she said.

"I should have seen you when I got out of the shower," I said.

"I hid. The surprise on your face was worth it."

"You could have come down and joined me for dinner. There was plenty of it, and it was good. My compliments to the chef."

Gloria chuckled. "It smelled good, but I already ate. I have a tennis tournament this weekend and can't eat too much."

I sat beside Gloria on the bed, leaned down, and kissed her. "At least all those tennis lessons are paying off."

"It's only my second tournament," she said. "Don't sign me up for the WTA just yet."

"Can I sign you up for some vigorous exercise in the next few minutes?" I gave Gloria my best rakish smile even though I didn't need it. We were extremely compatible between the sheets. Outside the confines of a boudoir . . . well, we were still working on it.

She grinned and rolled on her side to face me. "You can even double-book me," she said.

* * *

THE NEXT MORNING, I made breakfast. I always cooked when Gloria stayed over because she was a walking debacle in the kitchen. If I stayed the night at her house, I made breakfast there, though I let her do more because I care a lot less if she ruins her own kitchen. Sometimes, we went out for the morning meal. I tend to favor diners, while Gloria prefers not to be seen with the kind of people who frequent them. This time, I decided to make a casserole with eggs, sausage, mushrooms, zucchini, spinach, and a sprinkling of cheese.

The zucchini sautéed in the pan when Gloria wandered in. I had everything else ready to go. The olive oil and basil crackled in the skillet as I turned the zucchini slices to cook them on the other side. Gloria wandered to my coffee maker—the only kitchen pseudo-appliance I trusted her to use—and whipped up a

Kona blend. While her java brewed, I added the zucchini to the casserole and put the whole thing in the oven.

"Smells good," Gloria said.

"The zucchini cooking or your coffee?" I said.

She thought about it for a moment. Gloria always needed a second or two to think about things before she had her coffee. "Both, actually. Do you use this Kona blend?"

"No," I said, "I buy it just for you."

"Really?" said Gloria.

"Yes."

"Why don't you use it?"

"Not strong enough," I said.

"Not strong enough?"

"My kitchen is pretty small. I know it's not big enough to have an echo."

"It's plenty strong," Gloria said.

I shrugged. "I've seen the coffee you make at your house."

"And?"

"And I could read a newspaper through it," I said.

"No one still reads the newspaper," Gloria said with a grin.

She bested me there. "Fine. I could read a news app on my phone through it. Either way, the coffee I buy you isn't as strong as I like. I want coffee rich enough to make a spoon stand at attention in the mug."

Gloria added enough sugar to energize a small child for an afternoon, then sufficient creamer to make her own ice cream. And she wondered why I didn't like my coffee the same way she did. "It's plenty strong for me," she said.

"To each her own."

While I waited for the casserole to finish, I steamed some milk and put some real coffee on to brew. While it percolated, I took the casserole from the oven, got down plates, and set the table. Gloria perked up when I put the casserole on the table. She closed her eyes and took a deep whiff. "Wow, it smells really good," she said with a smile.

"I aim to please," I said.

"You hit your mark, and not just in the kitchen."

If I were the type to blush, her compliment would have done it. I'm not, so I didn't. I spooned a medium-sized helping of the casserole and plopped it onto Gloria's plate, then gave myself a larger slice. I was about to take a sip of my latte when the doorbell rang.

Gloria shot me a quizzical look. I shrugged, got up, and walked to the door. Behind me, I heard Gloria pad up the stairs. Her nightgown, if it could be called one, was not appropriate for guests. I looked through the peephole and saw Pauline Rodgers standing on my doorstep. Her eyes looked red and puffy. I unlocked all three locks and opened the door.

"Hi, Pauline," I said.

"Did you mean it?" she said.

"Uh . . . yes, I meant to say hi to you."

"No, about staying on the case."

"I did," I said.

She closed her eyes and let out a deep breath. "Thank you. I don't know what's going to happen with the police investigation."

"Do you want to come in? I just made breakfast."

Pauline smiled, probably for the first time since she learned her husband had been shot. Or shot himself, which neither of us found very likely. "I'd like that," she said. "I probably need to eat something."

I showed her to the kitchen and put a slice of the casserole on a plate while she settled into a chair. "Do you want coffee?" I said.

"I think I need it more than I want it."

I fetched a mug and poured her a cup from the carafe I recently brewed. When it finished, I set it on the table and took my seat again. Pauline added a perfectly reasonable amount of sugar and enough creamer to make the coffee a medium brown. While she did, Gloria came downstairs, a silk robe covering her from the neck to the knees and slippers on her feet. Pauline looked at her and blinked a few times.

"Pauline, this is Gloria. Gloria, this is my client, Pauline."

Gloria smiled, which surprised me. Hell, her coming downstairs and associating with a commoner already shocked me. "Hello," Gloria said.

"Good morning," Pauline said. "I hope I'm not interrupting."

"Not at all," Gloria said. She took a swig of her coffee and then cut a piece of the casserole with her fork and ate it. I watched her for a reaction. She closed her eyes and sighed. "It's very good."

"Thank you," I said.

"Yes, this is really good," Pauline said as she finished chewing. "C.T., where did you learn to cook like this?"

"College. None of my roommates wanted to, so I taught myself. A cookbook here, an online recipe there, plus watching other people."

She nodded and went back to her breakfast. I couldn't blame her: it *was* good. I'd eaten about half of my slice and drank almost half my latte when Pauline broke the silence. "Can we talk about the case?"

"Of course," I said. "I presumed it's why you were here."

"I told the kids." She put her fork down and took a deep breath. "They're . . . coping. Right now, they're both home from school. None of us think Stanley killed himself."

"I think it's unlikely, too, but I don't have any evidence yet."

"Can you get some?" She obviously didn't mind discussing her husband's death in front of Gloria, who focused on her food and let us talk.

"I'm trying to," I said. "Do you know what your husband was working on?"

Pauline shook her head. "He stopped trying to tell me years ago," she said. "I can balance a checkbook, but that's as far as my head for finance goes. What he does is way beyond me."

I nodded. "It's beyond me, too, I'm sure. The reason I ask is I managed to . . . acquire some files from your husband's laptop before the police took it. I—"

"How did you do that?" she said. Gloria also looked up and now stared at me.

If I hadn't said anything, I wouldn't need to come up with a good lie now. But I ran my mouth, so I did. "They hadn't brought in any forensic people yet, only a couple of detectives," I said. "While they poked around the place, I snagged what looked like important files. I was hoping you might be able to give me some insight into them. Or the password to decrypt them."

"I wish I could." She paused and took another sip of her coffee. "Is what you did legal?"

"I prefer to think of it as going the extra mile for a client."

She smiled, and so did Gloria. "I'll think of it that way, too," Pauline said.

* * *

Pauline left after finishing her slice of casserole and having a second cup of coffee. She didn't tell me anything useful, but she did cry a couple more times as we kept talking about Stanley. To my continued surprise, Gloria got her a box of tissues and patted her on the arm a few times. I wondered who the pod person at my table was and what the comely stranger did with the Gloria Reading I knew.

"That poor woman," Gloria said as I cleaned up in the kitchen.

"You seem unusually sympathetic," I said.

Gloria looked at the tabletop for a few seconds before she answered. "I don't think I relate to people well. It's been a problem for years. I'm trying to work on it."

"I'm impressed," I said. "What brought this on?"

"A lot of people like me because I have money, or I'm pretty, or I get into good places." Her eyes welled. "Almost no one likes me for me. They don't like me for being a good person, and maybe I'm not." Gloria paused to cry. I put my casserole dish back into the sink, sat beside her at the table, and put my arms around her.

"I don't think you're a bad person," I said.

She looked up at me with tear-rimmed eyes. "You don't?"

"No. I think you have a sense of entitlement instilled in you by your parents, but I can relate to it. You have a good head, though, and a good heart."

Gloria smiled and wiped at her eyes. "Thanks, C.T.," she said. "It means a lot."

I kissed her forehead. "Anytime," I said.

"You're one of the few people who likes me for who I am."

"It's only because I'm a softie at heart."

"You're a good person, too," said Gloria. "I watched the way you talked with your client. You had genuine sympathy for her. When we first met, I thought what you did was silly. Now, I think you do good work. It's important."

"Wow," I said. "I have to make breakfast more often."

CHAPTER 3

My cracking of Stanley Rodgers' encrypted files continued. Even with the speed of my computer and the cloud virtual machines, it could take quite a while. I wondered if I would need to solve the case without the benefit of Stanley's data. What if it didn't tell me anything useful? Pauline didn't have his decryption key, but the kind of man who puts good encryption on his laptop is the kind of man who doesn't tell his wife the key or write it in an obvious location.

Gloria went home to change for her tennis lesson. I was alone with my thoughts on the case. Stanley Rodgers had been murdered. I didn't care how close the gun was to his hand, and I didn't give a damn about gunshot residue. He wouldn't eat a bullet. I felt so before talking to Pauline about it, but our conversation convinced me even more. There had not been a single shred of uncertainty in her voice or manner.

While I waited for the files, I could still try to get to the Rodgers' financials. I hoped Stanley maintained a separate account, but considering all their money problems, I figured they consolidated as much as possible. Breaking into banks was old hat for me by now. Their defenses were mostly geared to stop denial-of-service attacks or waves of hackers, not one clever detective worming his way past the firewall. I didn't know where the Rodgers did their banking, so I punched my way into the most common banks I could think of and nosed around.

The national banks with their larger databases returned results slower. I found several from local financial institutions, however, including a brokerage account for Stanley. He also kept a separate checking service with Rosedale Federal, the only account the Rodgers carried at the regional bank.

The brokerage transactions read like a Shakespearean tragedy. I was ready to cast the role of Falstaff by the end of it. Stanley maintained a very nice account worth a tidy sum for a long time, and then it all went to shit. He hadn't diversified enough—I wondered how he advised his clients on this front— and got caught holding the wrong stocks at the wrong time. His business lost almost all its value because he invested in a few companies whose use of smoke and mirrors rivaled the best magicians. I figured he would have known better. Why didn't he learn the lessons of Madoff and Enron?

Reading his investment history depressed me. Stanley made some decent gains in the last few weeks, but he still only put together a modest five-digit gain versus the healthy seven digits he'd enjoyed before. I moved on to the checking. I didn't see any checks for regular expenses. No cable bill, no electric payment, no gas receipts—why have a checking account if you're not going to use it for regular checks? This record showed only a couple of large influxes of cash and irregular payments of odd amounts. The payments were made out to "DR." I doubted the initials notated a doctor, but who the heck was it? Pauline wouldn't know; Stanley obviously hid this from her.

I had to find out somehow.

* * *

I DEDUCED I should talk to the kids, Katherine and Zachary. Calling Pauline to tell her I wanted to go there and visit with them would have been an option, but it would also give them a chance to get their stories straight. If they had them. Ambush people and stories go out the window. I got in the car and drove to their house. When I knocked, a young, pretty girl who looked a lot like Pauline answered. She had long blonde hair pulled back into a ponytail, a delicate nose, and bright blue eyes reddened from crying. "Can I help you?" she said.

"My name is C.T. Ferguson," I said, showing her my ID. "I'm working for your mom on . . . what happened to your dad."

"Oh, I think she mentioned it. She's lying down right now. Do you want to talk to her?"

"Actually," I said, "I'd rather see what you and your brother have to say."

Her eyes widened briefly and then she frowned. "Oh. Sure. I don't know what we'll be able to tell you, though."

"I don't know a lot right now, so anything you can think of could be useful."

She invited me in and directed me to the living room. "I'll get my brother," she said. I sat in a recliner which looked like it came straight from someone's yard sale. All of the furniture looked cheap and little of it matched. The end tables sported a few dings, and a dog's teeth pockmarked the leg on one. I imagined what the living room might have looked like before the Rodgers fell on hard times. Their furniture reflected their new economic reality.

A minute later, Katherine returned with her brother right behind her. He looked to be about five-ten but was built like a football player or wrestler. He wore a Calvert Hall sweatshirt despite the fact he no longer went there. Their tuition rivaled the rates many colleges charged. Katherine sat on the sofa; Zachary sat beside her, his thick arms crossed under his chest. His eyes went around the room, making a point of looking at anything other than me.

"Like I mentioned, I don't think we can give you very much information," Katherine said.

"At this point, anything you can tell me could be useful," I said.

"What if we tell you to get the hell out?" Zachary said. He finally looked at me, fixing me with a glare like I had killed his father and come into their house, twirling the murder weapon around on my finger.

"Dismissing me wouldn't be very useful," I said.

"Zach, he's trying to help," Katherine said.

"What's there to help with? Dad fucked us over and couldn't take it anymore. Gun, head, the end."

Katherine slapped her brother hard across the face. I winced from the sound of it. He closed his eyes, but otherwise didn't react. Tears welled in Katherine's eyes. "You don't know that," she said. "You don't know anything! He may not have killed himself." She looked at me, her eyes glistening. "Right?"

"Your mother doesn't think he did. For what it's worth, I don't think he did, either."

"What you say ain't worth anything," Zach said.

"Isn't," I said.

"What?"

"Isn't, not ain't. If you're going to wear a Calvert Hall sweatshirt, you should talk like you went there."

He leaned forward on the couch. "What do you know about The Hall?" he said.

"I played lacrosse for Boys Latin," I said. "I know I enjoyed beating your Cardinals."

Zach scoffed. He sat back on the couch. "Lacrosse is for pussies. Boys Latin is for pussies."

"What's public school for, then?" I said.

"What do you know about public school?" he said, leaning forward again. This time, he pointed at me when he spoke. Maybe it was supposed to scare me. I didn't want to antagonize him, but it seemed the only way to get anything out of him. Thankfully, Katherine was too wrapped up in her own tears to object.

"It's been a long time, so not much. I also don't know a lot about your father, which is why I came here today. I'm on your side."

"No one's on our side," Zach said, shaking his head. "As soon as she can't pay you anymore, you'll be gone."

"She's not paying me anything," I said.

"She's not?"

"Not a penny. I'm working pro bono." I didn't want to tell him I always worked my cases gratis. "I'm not going away, and I am on your side."

Zach leaned back on the couch and sighed. He looked at his sister and patted her shoulder. "I'm still not convinced."

"It's an improvement, at least," I said. "Your father was involved with someone whose initials are DR. I suppose it could be a doctor, but both letters were capitalized and there was no other name. Do you know who it could be?"

Katherine shook her head. "I didn't know many of Daddy's friends. After . . . he lost his job, a lot of them abandoned him."

"Assholes," Zach muttered.

"What about anyone he met recently?"

"He didn't really bring new friends around here," Katherine said. "I think he was embarrassed about where we lived."

"What about you?" I said, looking at Zack.

"He didn't say much about work." He frowned. "He mentioned someone named David once."

"In the context of money?"

"I think so," Zack said. "He talked a lot about money these

last few weeks. Some big idea he had." Zach shook his head. "For all the good it did him."

"A first name is more than I had before," I said.

"It's a clue?" Katherine said.

"It's something I can work with," I said as I stood. "I'll let myself out. Thanks for your time." I walked out the storm door and got in my car. When I looked back at the house, the interior door was closed, too.

* * *

WHO WAS DAVID? For all I knew, the David which Zach talked about may not have been the person Stanley referred to as "DR." While I ruminated on the possibilities, my phone rang. I answered it via the Audi's Bluetooth despite not knowing the number.

"You talked to my kids?" Pauline said. The anger in her voice still carried some weariness with it. Did the kids wake her to say I dropped in for a chat?

"I'll talk to anyone I think can help me understand what happened to your husband," I said.

"Well, not anymore."

"Not anymore?" I said.

"You don't talk to my children when I'm not around," she said. "You got it?"

"Pauline, like I said a minute ago, I'll talk to anyone I think might have something useful to tell me. Such a set of people might include your children at some point again."

"I don't want you talking to them alone."

"I don't want clients telling me how to do my job," I said. She fell silent for a minute. I decided to fill the gap in the conversation. "Pauline, this is how I work. I don't call you while you're at work and tell you what you should and shouldn't do. I don't expect you to do it to me. If you want someone who will bend to your every whim, then you should hire a patsy . . . if you can afford one."

She was silent another few seconds. "That was a cheap shot," she said.

"I needed to make sure I had your attention."

"You'd walk away from this case? From me?" Her voice sounded like she was about to cry.

"If you're going to keep trying to tell me how to do my job, yes," I said. "I don't work on contracts, and I don't charge for what I do. Those factors make it easy to walk away if the situation is wrong."

Pauline sighed into the phone. "All right. I guess I over-reacted."

"Apology accepted."

"Did my kids tell you anything?" she said.

"I'm not sure yet," I said. "I only left a few minutes ago."

"What are you off to do now?"

"Talk to someone about a name I got. I'll let you know if anything comes of it."

"All right. I'm sorry I got so angry there. This is a . . . difficult time."

"I understand," I said. "Don't worry about it."

"Take care, C.T., and good luck."

"Thanks." I hung up. All things considered, I couldn't really blame Pauline. I'd probably be upset if I were in her shoes. And my feet would really hurt from wearing them. Katherine was an adult, and Zach tried really hard to be one. Her kids could handle chatting with me.

I headed downtown. A restaurant awaited.

* * *

JOEY TROVATO and I always tried to dine at different eateries, but they were usually Italian. Joey liked other cuisines—I don't think he ever encountered a food he didn't like—but if I wanted his opinion on something, we met at an Italian place. Baltimore has a plentiful supply of them, even outside of Little Italy. I'd never been to this one before, but Joey assured me Mamma's Cucina would leave me salivating on my bib. I got a good spot in the parking lot on 41st Street and walked into the restaurant. I loved Hampden. It felt like the old Baltimore neighborhood it was, just with more character (and characters) than Fells Point or Federal Hill. If you came away without being called "hon" at least once, the fault rested with you.

When I walked in, Joey already secured us a table. This was typical. Joey would be late for his own funeral, but if food were involved, he was the most punctual person I knew. He was a black Sicilian of boundless humor and appetite. I'd known him since elementary school. Like me, he always had a knack for computers, but he used his skills to make new identities for people. We both ended up in jobs helping others, even if the legalities of our professions differed.

"Always good to try a new place," Joey said when I sat down. He already sipped from a soda in front of him. His menu was closed. I knew he'd picked out what he wanted, and I also knew it would go a long way toward feeding a basketball team.

"Variety is the spice of life," I said. I opened the menu and looked it over. Nothing jumped out at me to make this place special. Once you've seen a lot of Italian menus, a *ristorante* has to offer something different and interesting to capture your attention. Mamma stocked her cucina with standard Italian and sub shop fare. I hoped the tastiness of the food would make up for it.

"This place has the best pizza around," Joey said.

"Quite a compliment."

"Why?"

"You've probably eaten a whole pizza from every restaurant in the city," I said.

"You may be right," said Joey.

A waiter came to take our order. Joey let me go first. This way, when he ordered half the menu, I wouldn't be in shock and unable to talk. I ordered a cup of Italian wedding soup, a slice of pepperoni pizza, a slice of cheese pizza, and an unsweetened iced tea. The waiter turned to Joey. I winced in anticipation of the hit my wallet would take when the check came. Joey ordered fried calamari, gravy fries, and a meatball calzone. I thought about how revolting those sounded in combination.

"Who recommends the pizza and then doesn't order any?" I said.

"You'll see how good it is," Joey said.

"I think if you recommend something, you're supposed to order it."

Joey shrugged. "I'm not in a pizza mood."

"You're still getting the four major food groups, though."

"This should be good," he said. "What are those?"

"Grease, bread, gravy, and seafood," I said.

"The lunch of champions."

Despite his ability to put food away, Joey wasn't grossly overweight. He was heavy, and had always been, but some honest athleticism resided under all the cholesterol and grease. Joey ran a few 10K races in college when most people thought he would have a coronary before crossing the finish line. He probably still could today, even if he looked like he ate last year's winner. "I hope the food is championship-quality," I said. "I've seen the menu in a bunch of other places."

"Would I steer you wrong?" Joey said.

When it came to food, he wouldn't. I looked around. Even the décor reminded me of a dozen other Italian eateries I'd visited. Take a few rustic scenes of Italy, add several photos of the homeland, pipe in some music best left back in Italy, and there you had it. Hampden boasted of a lot of personality, but this restaurant must have missed the memo. The waiter came back with my tea and another soda for Joey. He drank the rest of his old one and transferred the straw to the new glass.

"I guess you asked me to lunch for my vast professional expertise?" Joey said.

"And your refreshing modesty," I said.

"I think as much of modesty as you do."

"I humbly submit I think less of it than you."

The waiter dropped off my soup and Joey's calamari. I added a bit of salt and a tad more pepper to the soup. Joey took the lemon wedge on his plate and squirted its juice over his calamari. He picked up a piece of it, immersed it in the marinara sauce like he were trying to win the NBA Dunk contest, and scarfed it down. I continually said I would never again watch Joey eat, yet I always did. It was kind of like a train wreck. Even though I knew there would be twisted metal and mutilated bodies, I still couldn't look away until witnessing him mangle his first bite.

I focused on the much more pleasing view of my soup. My impression of Mamma's Cucina brightened with my first bite. This was the best Italian wedding soup I ever tasted. I didn't consider myself a connoisseur of the stuff, but I'd sampled my share over the years, and Mamma made the best. Before long, I devoured the cup, spoonful by greedy spoonful. For the first time I could remember, I finished my appetizer before Joey. The fact he always ordered larger appetizers never held him back until today.

"What do you need to know?" Joey said when mostly finished with his calamari. I snagged a piece of squid while he wiped his mouth. Capitalizing on his brief moments of distraction (and hygiene) ensured I could steal some of his food now and then. I was paying for it anyway.

"A name," I said. I waited while the waiter cleared our appetizers and set out our entrees. My pizza arrived cooked to perfection. The cheese came out the perfect shade of golden brown with a few bubbles on top. The pepperonis got crispy on the outside edges. Exactly the right amount of grease sat atop the cheese, slowly coalescing into it. Joey's fries were submerged so far in their gravy a search party would be necessary to find them. His calzone looked like a large pizza folded in half and packed to the point of bursting. I hoped he would have the decency to use a knife and fork on it.

"You've never come to me for a name before." Joey plunged his fingers into the tin vat of gravy, extracted two fries dripping brown sauce, and devoured them both.

"I've never needed one until now," I said. "I don't know if you'll be able to help me, but you're the first person I thought of."

"For a meal at Mamma's, I'll do my best," said Joey.

"I'm working a case where a guy ended up dead. He experienced some money problems and thought he'd found a way back to the high life. I discovered a reference to someone initialed DR in his checking account."

"You got into his bank records?" Joey said.

"You could try not insulting me when I'm picking up the check," I said.

"Right. So money is involved, and you saw the initials DR." Joey paused in thought, and to eat another artery-clogging gravy fry. I was going to have a sympathy heart attack if I watched much more.

"I hoped a man in your line of work might know who DR is."

"I have a pretty good guess," Joey said. "David Rosenberg."

"David Rosenberg?" I said.

"You know him?"

"Never heard of him." I took a bite of my pepperoni pizza. It tasted even better than it looked.

"He's a loan shark," Joey said.

"He's Jewish?" I said.

"With a name like David Rosenberg, I think it's probably a law."

"I've never heard of a Jewish loan shark before," I said.

"These are more progressive times," Joey said. "They're not all Italian. Let go of your stereotypes."

"Like the fat Sicilian guy who loves food and has a shady career?"

"OK, maybe not all of them."

"Have you . . . dealt with Rosenberg before?" I said. I ate some more pizza. My tea ran low.

"I've helped someone get away from him," Joey said. He picked up the enormous calzone and bit off a massive chunk of the end. To my surprise, he didn't get sprayed with meatballs and sauce. I found the lack of mess a little disappointing. Eating like a barbarian should have consequences.

"What do you know about him?" I said.

"I've heard he's ruthless."

"Of course he is; he's a loan shark."

"And a Jew who works with money," Joey said.

"So much for more progressive attitudes," I said. I pondered the death of more enlightened times while I signaled the waiter. He brought me a new iced tea and Joey another soda.

"We can't all be as open-minded as you," Joey said.

"Everyone has a cross to bear," I said.

* * *

I NEEDED to have another restaurant conversation, but I wanted to wait until I felt hungry again. In the meantime, I called Gonzalez when I got home to see if he had anything new.

"Depends what you mean by new," he said.

"Whatever you learned since I was standing with you in the hotel room," I said.

"We know the guy died from a gunshot wound to the head."

"I can tell why you made sergeant."

"We know for sure GSR was on his hand." Gonzalez paused, as if about to ask me if I knew what GSR meant. Good thing we already established my *CSI* bona fides.

"So the suicide theory looks pretty good at this point?"

"It looks really good," Gonzalez said. "Guy down on his luck, having money problems, rents a nice room to live it up for a couple days, then puts a gun to his head."

"You realize it doesn't make a lot of sense as a theory, right?" I said.

"Why not?"

"If he's having money problems, why does he rent a penthouse? And if he's going to kill himself, why wait to do it until after he's already racked up a few days' worth of charges?"

"The guy used to be a high roller," said Gonzalez. "Now he's not. He wanted some of his old life back."

"I'm not buying it," I said.

"What a coincidence—I'm not trying to sell it to you," Gonzalez said. "It looks like we're going to call this one a suicide and close it. I get a case off my books."

"Maybe I can stop in, and we can compare notes before you banish this one to the archives."

"If you want. Come in tomorrow at nine."

"I'll be there," I said. This time, I hung up first. Rich and Gonzalez taught me well. I possessed no idea what I would share with him tomorrow morning—especially not without incriminating myself—but I could use the time to figure it out.

* * *

Il Buon Cibo has always been an aptly-named restaurant. They serve the good food. It's not the biggest restaurant in Little Italy, nor does it have the reputation—the honor goes to Sabatino's, which also is good but not spectacular—but the food is always great, the crowd plentiful, and the service friendly. The fact *Il Buon Cibo* is owned by Tony Rizzo, the head of organized crime in Baltimore, may help with all three of those.

Tony and my parents were friends forever, and I've known Tony since I was a kid. I don't think my parents knew what he did for a long time. I'd been aware for years, and it never kept me away. Guys like Tony are important for people like me to know. Since I told Tony I'd become a PI, he acted a little frostier toward me, but we were still friendly. I hope we remained so.

I walked in and nodded as I passed the maître d'. He'd become used to me by now. I think Tony's goons had, too, but they still were obliged to stand and look menacing when I approached. If you have no education and no neck, you do what you're good at. Tony always occupied the table near the fireplace, and there were never any other ones too close to his. The goons looked me over before Tony waved them off and beckoned me to sit.

"How are you, C.T.?" he said, and the smile he showed me reached his eyes. It's always good to receive sincere smiles from the mob boss.

"I'm doing well, Tony," I said. "How are you?"

"I can't complain."

"You're looking a little thinner. Your personal trainer must be riding your case pretty hard."

He snorted. "Shit. I don't need some big malook telling me what to do. It's all diet. All diet and no pasta."

I winced in sympathy. "Sorry to hear."

"Change is part of life." Tony swirled his red wine around in his glass and took a sip. "You hungry?"

"I am," I said.

A waitress I hadn't seen before walked past. Tony snapped his fingers, and she stopped in her tracks. "Holly, my friend would like some dinner."

I spied the reverent look she gave Tony. She nodded and looked at me. "Sir, what I can get you?" Tony usually hired pretty college girls as waitresses. Holly covered the pretty department but barely looked old enough to be in college. Her eyes were a rare bright blue.

"It's been a while since I looked at the menu," I said. "How about veal saltimbocca with a side salad and an unsweetened iced tea?"

Holly smiled. "Excellent choice, sir. I'll put it right in for you."

I watched her walk away with some interest until she turned a corner into the kitchen. "Please tell me she's in college," I said to Tony.

He chuckled at me. "My first thought, too," he said. "She's nineteen. You believe that shit? Girl doesn't look a day over sixteen. A sophomore at UB."

"Have I told you I've always admired your knack for hiring the prettiest college girls?"

"No, but I'll add you to the list of people who have."

"Fair enough," I said.

Holly brought my iced tea and salad. It looked like a large salad crammed onto a small plate and held there by nothing more than good fortune. Eating with Tony had its perks: I never paid for a meal, and the portions were enormous. I needed to run an extra mile after my meals with him, but they were always worth it.

"I know you don't need to mooch free meals, C.T.," Tony said. He leaned forward onto his elbows, the bones of which protruded from his sportscoat like I hadn't seen before. "What brings you by?"

I cut the large pieces of lettuce, tomato, and green pepper. A few spilled over the plate and landed on the table. Casualties like those were inevitable considering the size of the salad. "David Rosenberg," I said.

Tony's eyes narrowed. "What about him?"

"His name came up in a case. I don't know anything about him and hoped you could fill in some gaps for me."

"Is he shaking people down in my city?" Tony managed not to raise his voice, but his goons sat at attention now. He leaned forward a little, like a guy who held a great poker hand and didn't mind everyone else knowing.

"If he is, I don't know about it," I said. "My people live in the county. I understand he operates there."

"He knows better than to come into Baltimore," Tony said. Rosenberg didn't, but I saved the kernel of knowledge for a time it would be more beneficial. If I could finagle Tony into taking him out, everybody won—especially Pauline.

"I have no doubt," I said as I pushed my salad plate away. A busboy came so quickly I thought he materialized from thin air. Sitting with the man meant never having to wait for anything. When the busboy disappeared, Holly came back to freshen my iced tea, even though I'd only drunk about a third of it.

"Your food will be right out," she said with a smile. Looking at a girl like Holly made me miss being a college student. Someone my age could still chat her up now, but I'd feel a little creepy about it.

"Thanks, Holly," I said, giving her one of my best smiles in return. The high-wattage version kindled many a panty-peeling evening over the years. Holly merely went back to the kitchen. It was for the better anyway. I thought of Gloria, then wondered why she leaped to mind.

"What do you want to know about Rosenberg?" Tony said.

"Anything is useful," I said, glad for the distraction at the moment.

"Well, he's a Jew."

"I'm not sure why his heritage is important, but I managed to deduce it on my own."

"I figured," said Tony. "What you may not know is he's a real cutthroat son of a bitch."

Holly brought out my veal saltimbocca, and judging by the size of the veal, an entire family of calves had been wiped out to put it on my plate. I picked up my knife and fork. Tony continued talking after Holly left.

"Like I said, he's ruthless. He deals in money and thinks in terms of money. Whatever's best for the bottom line."

I blew on a piece of the veal to let it cool, then took a bite. I barely needed to chew it and the flavor was excellent. "You know anyone who works for him?" I said.

"Not by name, no," Tony said. "I'd know 'em if I saw 'em, though." Tony snapped his fingers again. "Bruno!"

One of the goons walked to our table. Tony waved him closer, and Bruno leaned down. He went away after Tony whispered something to him. I knew better than to ask.

"So you recommend watching my back around this guy," I said.

"Damn right," Tony said. "I'm not going to tell you not to talk to him, but I will tell you not to piss him off."

"Do I seem like the kind of guy who pisses people off?"

"You *are* a bit of an asshole."

"Maybe a little bit," I said.

CHAPTER 4

I CALLED RICH AFTER MY DINNER WITH TONY RIZZO, BUT he told me he was busy. The noise on the phone sounded like a bar in the background. Rich needed a night off here and there —even if it meant not helping me help him—and he said I should come by in the morning. I added it to my mental calendar along with my meeting with Gonzalez. Conferring with two cops in the same day is at least two more than I like to deal with.

When I got home, Gloria had come back. She lay on the couch, a thick blanket atop her, watching some reality show. I felt my brain spring a leak through my ears, but I soldiered on. "How was tennis?" I said.

She pulled back the blanket to reveal a bag of frozen peas pressed against the back of her leg. I didn't even know I had a bag of frozen peas. "I tweaked my hamstring," she said, pouting delicately.

"The tennis world will mourn your time on the disabled list." I put my keys on the small cherry table in my entryway. The keys almost toppled the impressive pile of junk mail accrued over the last week or so.

"I'm going to try and get back out there in a few days." Gloria held up the package of peas. "Can you put these back for me, please?"

"Sure." I took the bag to the kitchen. Once I opened the freezer door, I discovered I owned five packs of frozen peas I didn't recall buying. Gloria obviously intended to do her convalescence here. I'd hate to see what would happen if the poor dear broke her arm. I walked back into the living room. "Am I going to have to carry you upstairs, too?"

She cracked a smile. "I think I can manage."

She did.

* * *

IN THE MORNING, vanilla latte and coffee in hand, I went to see Gonzalez. I decided to visit him first; I could see Rich anytime. The sergeant on duty directed me to Gonzalez's desk, where I found him squinting at his flat-panel monitor. The BCPD had larger monitors than the BPD. "Need your eyes checked?" I said, taking a seat in the cheap faux leather guest chair Gonzalez kept on the other side of his desk. He looked to be hitting the age where glasses—specifically bifocals—became a necessity.

"I do my best thinking when I squint," he said.

I handed Gonzalez the coffee. The squadroom looked renovated within the last five years and painted more recently. The size of it belied the smallish appearance of the outside of the building. Desks were arranged neatly in rows with a few offices for the precinct brass along with the standard interrogation rooms. I was glad I came here first; talking about how much more I liked the BCPD's layout would make Rich nice and salty. "This is good coffee," Gonzalez said.

"All this new technology here and you don't have a good coffee maker?" I said.

"Shit, no police precinct does. It's like a curse. You put a coffee maker in a police station, and whatever it spits out tastes like warm piss."

I took another drink of my latte and gazed at the half-full mug of coffee on Gonzalez's desk. "Looks like I was too late to save you this morning," I said.

"Only makes me appreciate the good stuff more." He took another drink. "Anything new?"

"I was just about to ask you."

"We've seen nothing new come in," Gonzalez said as he leaned back in his chair and cradled the cup.

"So it's a suicide?" I said.

"Looks like it," he said.

"No one in his family thinks he killed himself."

Gonzalez spat out a mirthless chuckle. "I know you haven't been doing this a long time, so let me tell you something. The family *never* thinks their loved one did it. Never. This Stanley could have shot himself right in front of his family, then written a suicide note in blood on the wall, and they still wouldn't accept it. They can't accept it."

I knew he was right from a case Rich and I worked in Garrett County recently. Sometimes, the family's doubts were well-founded. "They probably can't," I said in acknowledgment, "but what if he really didn't kill himself?"

"He had a gunshot wound to the head," Gonzalez said, "GSR on his hand, and a gun right there. We're going to call it a suicide. It gets it off the books."

"But it doesn't actually solve the case."

"This ain't a perfect system."

"Could I see the case file?" I said.

"You don't give up do you?" said Gonzalez. I shook my head. Gonzalez put his cup on his desk. "I'm going to take a shit. Probably be about ten minutes or so. While I'm gone, make sure you don't look at my computer and read the case file I have pulled

up." Gonzalez clicked the mouse a few times, then stood.
"Clear?"

"Crystal," I said.

He walked away. I sat behind his desk and browsed the case
file. Everything he told me was in there. The medical examiner's
report was pending. Another gold star for the BCPD: they linked
their ME's reports and didn't force diligent and dashing PIs to
hack into a separate network to find them. I needed to work
county cases more often.

Before I got up, I made sure to jot down Gonzalez's IP and
hardware addresses on my coffee receipt. In case the BCPD
didn't close the case, I wanted to know what they knew. I left
before Gonzalez came back from the men's room.

* * *

ABOUT A HALF-HOUR LATER, I walked into Rich's precinct
house. It looked about as new as the one in the county, only with
more square footage and love for open-concept floor plans.
Armed with a new vanilla latte and coffee, I approached Rich's
desk. He sat behind it, one leg crossed over his opposite knee,
reading a file. I set his coffee between the piles of paper and other
detritus.

"You're late," Rich said.

I get accused of tardiness often, so I looked at my watch out of
habit. "We didn't have a set time to meet," I said.

"I needed coffee a while ago. You weren't here. Thus, you're
late." Rich picked up the coffee, raised the cup toward me in
thanks, and took a drink.

"I'll try to align my schedule to your needs in the future," I
said.

"Here's to the spirit of cooperation."

I sat in Rich's guest seat, a padded cloth task chair. It was more comfortable than Gonzalez's, but neither would win any points for aesthetics. "You ever hear of David Rosenberg?" I said.

He looked up and frowned. "I've never dealt with him," Rich said. "He's the county's problem."

"You know his name, though."

"And his reputation. C.T., this guy is no joke. He's ruthless when it comes to his money."

"I've heard the same," I said.

"Who told you?" said Rich.

"Tony."

Rich snorted. "How the hell would he know?" he said.

"He seems to think it stems from Rosenberg's ethnicity," I said. "But a man in Tony's position needs to know things. I don't ask how he learns what he knows."

"At any rate, he's right. Did Rosenberg come up in your case?"

"I think so," I said. I drank some of the latte. Having two in one morning dulled my taste for them. I would need a different fancy coffee drink to cleanse my palate. "The victim received money from someone identified as 'DR.'"

"How do you know?"

"His wife let me see their checking account," I said.

"Bullshit," Rich said, though I saw him fighting a smile. This was a BCPD case, so he couldn't get mad at me for employing my normal methods. "We talking serious money?"

"Twenty-five thousand, twice."

"Wow." Rich let out a breath. "Fifty grand is a lot of money. Sounds like it's probably Rosenberg. Why didn't you ask Gonzalez about him? He'd know more."

"BCPD thinks it's a suicide," I said. "They want the case off the books. If they're going to reopen it, I need to show them something."

"And you can't do it if you tip your hand." Rich frowned and shook his head.

"Now you're thinking like I do."

"Christ, I hope not," Rich said. "I think this will probably blow up in your face at some point. Gonzalez and the BCPD aren't likely to . . . indulge your peculiarities like we do. You might want to tread carefully here, and even tell them what you know."

"When it becomes important, I'll think about it."

"Be sure you do," Rich said.

"Can I call you to bail me out of a county jail?" I said.

"No," said Rich.

* * *

I ALMOST MADE it home when Pauline called me. Would I like to go to the funeral home for Stanley's viewings today? As a matter of fact, I would rather gargle with a bucket of thumbtacks, but I couldn't tell the poor lady no. I sucked it up and said of course I would be there. What else could I do? After I got home, I went for a run around Federal Hill Park. The girl with the small shorts was not jogging when I was. Add another disappointment to my day.

Four miles allowed me to sweat out most of my frustrations. I went back home, showered, and went downstairs to fix a quick lunch. Gloria left while I was talking to Gonzalez and Rich. I noticed I missed her when she left now. What this meant for our relationship, such as it was, would need to be a consideration for later. Lunch was the present priority. It consisted of a turkey sandwich, a couple handfuls of pretzels, and a glass of milk. After my meal, I put on a tailored black Armani suit and drove to the funeral home.

The last case requiring me to make a funeral home appearance ended up getting messy. I hoped this one didn't go down a similar road. I arrived three minutes into the first viewing, making me extremely prompt. Pauline talked to people, shook hands, cried some, and mingled. She didn't need me right now, so I looked at the trinkets set up to remember Stanley.

The Rodgers put together a picture collage, cramming more photos than I cared to count onto two large presentation boards. It didn't look very professional, but it served its intended purpose well enough. A video, assembled from the snapshots, played over soft music on a medium flatscreen TV. I scanned the photos and video, looking for any nugget on Stanley which might give insight as to who killed him. Several pictures showed him and his family on a boat, including one where Stanley and Zachary each held up an impressive fish. The name of the boat was Galaxy Class. Stanley had been a *Star Trek* fan. This fact didn't help me figure out who killed him, unless someone dressed like Spock did it.

"What are you doing here?" I heard a voice say behind me. Zachary wore a suit he obviously kept from the days the family had money to burn. It fit him as well as my Armani fit me, except his sleeves were a little too short. The suit grew well with him otherwise.

"Your mother invited me," I said.

"This is for friends and family."

"I guess I'm a friend of the family now."

He shook his head. "Whatever," he said. "Just try not to inter-rogate our guests."

"I'll do my best," I said.

He walked away, no doubt satisfied he headed off The Balti-more County Inquisition. I shrugged and made my way around the room. A few people shook my hand, asked me how I knew Stanley, and shared their own tales of his life. Everyone who talked to me had been a client of Stanley's at some point. No one identified themselves as his friends. I decided not to mention this depressing fact to Pauline.

After a circuit of the room, I found Pauline alone. She offered a tired smile. Her makeup, well applied though it had been, couldn't hide the lines under her eyes. I empathized.

"Thanks for coming," she said, giving me a quick hug.

"Of course," I said.

"Honestly, I don't know why I asked you to come. It's not like Stanley's killer is in the room." Her voice cracked toward the end. I offered her a tissue from the travel pack in my pocket.

"You need support. I understand."

Pauline nodded as she wiped at her eyes. "I'm trying to be strong for the kids, but it's hard," she said. "Zachary is even more quiet than normal. Katherine has been doing enough crying for all of us. She just went into the ladies' room again, the poor thing."

"It's a hard time for all of you." I looked around the hall again.

"Do you dislike funeral homes, C.T.?"

"Doesn't everyone?" I said. "Except funeral directors, I suppose."

"You've stayed on the outside most of the time you've been here," said Pauline. "Even now, you're looking around."

"Part of my constant vigilance as a private investigator."

"Or some discomfort at being here. It's OK. I understand. I'm just glad to have someone else in my support network right now."

"And I'll be a part of it again from seven to nine," I said.

* * *

WE HAD three hours between viewings. Pauline invited me to dinner with her and the kids, but I declined. They needed some time to themselves. She persisted, though, and then Katherine asked me, too, and got weepy when I hesitated, so I caved.

Zachary didn't seem too pleased, but little cheered him where I was concerned.

There are many good restaurants within a quick drive of Ruck's Funeral Home in Towson. We didn't go to any of them. Instead, we were the best dressed people at the Towson Diner on this day—and maybe in its history. Katherine said it became her favorite place since she transferred to Goucher, and she simply wanted comfort food. I couldn't argue with her logic.

The Towson Diner is shoehorned onto York Road in such a way to make getting in easy unless anyone else happens to be leaving when you're trying to pull in. Getting out is even worse. Making a left onto York Road at rush hour when we would be leaving is something best left to the Impossible Missions Force. The alternative would be to make a right out of the parking lot and use the York Road traffic circle to turn around. At the moment, I was glad I didn't drive to the diner.

After we ordered our food—a club sandwich and sweet potato fries for me—the Rodgers talked about Stanley. I felt like an outsider eavesdropping on a private conversation, only without the sense of titillation normally accompanying eavesdropping. I sat and nursed my iced tea; they needed the time to have a meaningful conversation, even if it took place in the middle of a diner. Finally, Pauline decided to include me. I would have preferred she hadn't. "What did you like to do with your dad, C.T.?" she said.

I was in a pickle here. My father and I got along very well, but we didn't do a lot of father-son things together now and never really did. My father encouraged me to continue martial arts (after my mother insisted I enroll), but he never stood there punching and kicking alongside me. I needed to come up with something. "Going to baseball games," I said. Which is true. My father likes to sit among the people in the bleachers. My mother, on the rare occasions she graced Camden Yards with her presence, sat in club level. "We still go a couple times a year."

"Lame," Zack said.

"Zachary!" Pauline glared at her son.

"We can't all go fishing," I said.

Pauline looked at me. "You're not helping," she said.

I shrugged. Why did they have to involve me?

* * *

WE MADE it back to the funeral home with only a minor adventure getting onto York Road. I returned to the viewing room while Pauline talked to the funeral director. Katherine and Zack followed me in. I paused at the collage, glanced at the boat picture again, and moved on. They stayed behind, looking at it for a while. My parents decided against having such a collage at my sister's viewings. Seeing this one made me more thankful for their restraint.

The evening crowd was a lot different than the afternoon visitors. They wore nicer suits, made more eye contact, and gave firmer handshakes. I didn't go out of my way to talk to anyone, but like in the afternoon viewing, a few people found me. This time, they introduced themselves as Stanley's friends, or friends of the family, not mere clients. I said I was a friend of Pauline's. She didn't have a lot of people there. Might as well even the scales.

About a half-hour into the second session, I saw a mousy man lurking near the photo collage. He wore a gray suit with a gray shirt and gray tie. If his hair were gray, it would have been the perfect camouflage. Instead it was brown. The suit looked at least a size too big for him. He pushed his glasses up on his nose often enough to make me think they needed to be re-fitted, too. He lingered at the collage, occasionally looking around the room like a wallflower uncomfortable leaving the corner at his first high school dance.

Being the gregarious fellow I am, I walked to him. He saw me approach and looked away quickly, though he didn't leave the photo collection. Normally, I would have offered him a handshake, but I suspected he didn't take part in social amenities. "How are you?" I said.

He swallowed hard before answering. "Not sure I should be here, really," he said. His tone sounded nervous, but his voice carried a surprising authority with it.

"Did you know Stanley?"

"Here's the thing." His voice dropped to a whisper. "I didn't know him at all."

"Then I'm not sure why you're here." I dropped my tone, too, figuring it would minimize his nervous looking around. It didn't. He scanned the room again before he answered.

"I stayed in the suite next to his," he said.

Now I understood his nervousness. I showed him my ID. "Wait here," I said. "I'm investigating this case, and I'm going to find a place we can talk in private."

I led the nervous man to an empty office down the hall and shut the door. The desk was way too crowded and messy for the funeral director to meet with the public in here. Papers, pamphlets, and books were scattered about in a system which must have made sense to someone. Gaudy decorations like plastic skulls filled the spaces not encroached upon by aggressive piles of paper. "OK, we can talk in here," I said.

He let out a long sigh. "Good," he said. "I didn't want to in there. Too many people . . . you never know who's around."

"I suppose. What's your name?"

"Marvin. Marvin Bernard." He didn't offer a handshake. I was neither offended nor surprised.

"C.T. Ferguson."

"You're investigating the case?"

I nodded. "I'm working for the widow," I said.

"Are the police calling it a suicide?" Marvin said.

"So far. They don't seem willing to come off it."

"It was no suicide." Marvin looked around the office, I guess out of habit. None of the tacky desk decorations threatened him.

"Did you see anything?" I said.

"No, no. I heard it happen, though. Our beds were on the same wall." He paused and reddened. "Please don't ask how I know."

I could guess, so I didn't. "What did you hear?"

"A couple of guys went in there. I heard two voices beside his. They talked for a while. From what I heard, it was about money. Then I heard someone get punched, then two muffled shots."

"Muffled?"

"Yes," said Marvin. "Maybe by a pillow or a silencer."

"Silencers don't really exist outside of Hollywood," I said. There had been a suppressor screwed onto the end of the gun, but only the county's ballistics tests could determine if it got added after the fact.

"Anyhow, whatever they used, the shots weren't very loud."

"But you definitely heard two."

Marvin nodded. "Absolutely."

Now I knew Stanley Rodgers hadn't killed himself. I needed a lot more to get Gonzalez and the BCPD to classify it as a homicide, though. "I'll keep you out of this as much as I can," I said. "But in case I need to reach you, do you have a card?"

He gave me a business card, and I handed him one of mine. Then he left the funeral home without going back into the viewing room. I looked at the business card. Marvin V. Bernard. Certified Public Accountant.

Of course he was.

CHAPTER 5

I NEEDED TO GO BACK AND SEE RODGERS' HOTEL ROOM AT the Sheraton. If Marvin told me the truth—and I had no reason to think otherwise—a second bullet hid somewhere. I couldn't get Gonzalez to take action on the case with a bunch of conjecture and a story about talking to a mousy accountant. If I could point to a second bullet hole in the suite, however, I'd be golden. I like being golden.

After locking the office, I walked back into the viewing room. Pauline talked to a few people and smiled as much as she could. Katherine and Zachary frowned and scowled rather than put on friendlier faces, but they still talked to some well-wishers. When no one stood near Pauline, I approached her. "I need to go," I said. "There might be something important about the case, and I need to check it out."

She looked wide-eyed at me for a second before nodding. "Sure, OK," she said. "Let me know if you discover anything."

"I will."

The Sheraton made for a very short drive from Ruck's. I parked along the side of the hotel and walked around to the front entrance. Being in a suit for the funeral would help me here, but I hoped my attire didn't look too nice. It should look like a cop's garb. I would settle for the outfit of a detective who cared how he dressed.

I walked through the front doors, over the giant, garish Sheraton rug, and into the lobby. Only one person stood in line at the front desk. Two people manned it, and the second one dressed in a pressed shirt and tie did paperwork while the other tended to the customer. I approached the well-dressed man.

"Detective Ferguson," I said, flashing my ID quickly enough he couldn't read it (I hoped). "Can we talk somewhere in private for a moment?"

"Do we need to?" His name tag identified him as Darren, assistant manager. His head was smoothly shaved, and a goatee circled his mouth. An unbuttoned shirt almost hid the very top of a tattoo on his chest. He glanced back at his paperwork. I could see Darren's priorities.

"Depends," I said.

He went back to the paperwork. "On what?"

"On whether you want your potential guest to know someone got murdered in this hotel recently." Darren and the other man behind the desk both looked up. The fellow in line stared at me and blanched. "Oops," I said. "I guess he knows now."

Darren stood and gestured for me to follow him behind the front desk, which I did. As we passed through a door into a series of offices, I heard the other associate try to talk the guest into staying at the Sheraton, saying he was sure I was mistaken. We went into a cubicle where four monitors on the wall displayed the outputs of eight security cameras. I wondered if Stanley's killers would be on camera. Gonzalez could request the video; it would sound a lot more official coming from him, anyway.

"Did you have to scare away my customer?" Darren said, slumping into a task chair. It was the only place to sit in the room. I leaned on the edge of the wraparound desk.

"I needed to break the hypnotic hold of your paperwork," I said.

"We all got shit to do, man."

"True, man. Right now, what I got to do is take another look at the penthouse where a guest got shot."

"I think we have someone staying there."

The BCPD must have said they were finished with the scene. "I'll be quiet," I said.

He frowned. "Shouldn't you have some dudes with you or something?" he said. "A CIS team?"

"CSI? No, not today. I'm only following up a lead. The CSI guys might come later."

"Oh," Darren said. "Do you think I could look around with them?"

"No," I said.

"Oh. So what do you need from me?"

A real police detective would offer a measured, even response, free of contempt. I kept this in mind as I answered. "I need to get into the penthouse."

Darren nodded. "Right. Let me call up there and see if anyone is inside." He consulted a guide sheet beside the phone and dialed 8902. Darren bobbed his foot up and down over his knee as he held the receiver to his ear. After about half a minute, he put it down. "No one's there," he said.

"Can you make me a key?" I said.

"Yeah, sure."

We went out to the front desk area again. Darren took a blank keycard, entered some numbers on the pad, and swiped the card through a reader. He handed it to me. "Good luck, Detective . . . what was your name?"

"Ferguson. And thank you." I left the front desk for the elevators before Darren used the rest of his brain and puzzled out I might not be who I implied I was. Once inside the elevator, I put my pass card into the slot to go to the penthouse level. A minute later, I got off the elevator and walked to the suite where Stanley Rodgers died. To make sure no one returned in the last few minutes, I knocked on the door. No answer. I swiped Sheraton-approved plastic and went into the room.

Someone was staying here. Whoever it was left an open suitcase on the bed. I saw men's clothes inside. Considering this fellow rented a suite, his knockoff Polo shirts looked cheap. I pictured where Stanley's body lay on the floor. He could have fallen from pretty much anywhere. Or maybe the guys who shot him moved him. Marvin said it sounded like someone had been hit before the gunshots. I didn't see any blood trails on the floor, though, so he was probably killed where he lay. Did the second shot come before or after?

If the bullet lodged anywhere normally visible in the room, the BCPD would have seen it. They would have unmade the bed and other basic things. The other bullet couldn't have left the area without damaging a door or window, which also would have been obvious. Wherever this bullet was, obviously was somewhere hard to see, somewhere the police wouldn't have looked when they processed the scene.

I poked around in the closet. The current guest hadn't hung up any of his clothes—none of them merited hangers—so the open space made my job easier. I used an LED flashlight to help me as I looked high and low, but I didn't see a bullet hole anywhere. Next, I looked under the king-size bed, but its frame was solid wood and flush against the floor all around, which cut down on the real estate I could search. What was left would be easily visible in a sweep of the area.

The two nightstands yielded the same results. The police could have shifted them easily. I needed something they were unlikely to move, something they would presume was there all along. This left the armoire against the wall. It contained several drawers, a shelf, and held the TV. I shined the flashlight along the floor near the upright wardrobe. Scuff marks—probably unremarkable in hotel rooms—were faint, but they were there. Those may have come from housekeeping two years ago, but right now, they were all I could go on.

I decided against moving the armoire with the TV and drawers intact. Even if it were light enough for me to budge, the process would make new scuff marks along the floor. I didn't know if it would count as ruining the crime scene, but doing so would certainly change it and make obvious the fact I came looking for something. While Gonzalez seemed like a decent fellow, he and his bosses wouldn't be as forgiving of my peccadilloes as the BPD. I took the drawers out of the cabinet, disconnected the TV, and put it onto the bed.

Now the armoire was light enough so I could lift a corner and swivel it out from the wall. I hefted one side of it, then went around and did the other side, then did the whole process again. When I finished, I could stand or crouch behind it. I looked at the wall, but only noticed a few spots of dirt the large dresser hid. When I crouched and used my flashlight, I found the bullet hole. It was maybe eighteen inches off the floor and the same distance inside the border of the furniture. Easy to miss without rearranging things. I snapped a picture of it with my phone. Once I had the photo, I moved the armoire back, reconnected the TV, and put the drawers back in.

As soon as I finished, I heard the lock whirr to life. I looked around. The bathroom was too far away, and I couldn't hide anywhere near where I was. I shook my head as the door opened into the room. A man in his mid-fifties escorted a much younger lady inside. They giggled and talked quietly among themselves, both of which they stopped when they saw me.

"Hotel security," I said, giving them a quick flash of my ID. "I think someone sent me to the wrong suite, though."

"They must have," the man said. "Can you leave now?"

Why keep a middle-aged man and his call girl of choice wait-ing? "Of course," I said. I left and headed for the elevator. When I heard the suite door close, I walked to the stairs. I didn't need them calling real hotel security. I went down to the second floor, then hurried to the steps running along the rear of the hotel. I exited via the back door, went to my car, and left.

* * *

I CALLED Rich on my way from the hotel and said I would bring carry-out if he'd be home. He said he would. I stopped at a conve-nience store for paper towels, then went to the best place for to-go food near Rich's house: Gil's Pizza. The shop looks like any other residence on Belair Road, save for the sign identifying it as a restaurant. They don't do eat-in or delivery: if you want one of their pies, you go there and pick it up. Gil's makes pizzas in only one size, and regardless of toppings, they always turned out perfectly greasy. It must have been the cheese. I used paper towels to cover the passenger's seat, so I could put the boxes there without worrying about the grease bleeding through. I loved Gil's pies, but I loved my leather more.

A few minutes later, I pulled into the driveway of Rich's Hamilton house. His parents died while he served in the Army, and he used some of the money they left him to pay cash for a nice Victorian. I like my place better, but it would have fit at least twice over inside Rich's, not to mention he had a driveway and a yard big enough to host a mean game of Wiffle Ball.

"Gil's," Rich said with a smile when he opened the door, "you must really want something."

"I happen to like Gil's," I said.

"Liking it isn't enough. Embrace the grease."

Rich brought plates and two bottles of beer into the living

room. We ate our pepperoni and sausage pizzas on TV trays. I only ate two slices, but Rich was halfway through his third when he got curious. "What brings you by, anyway?" he said.

"My case in the county," I said. "I'd like a second opinion."

"OK, shoot."

I told him the basics of the case, then about my conversation with Marvin at the funeral home. "I needed to check it out," I said.

Rich shook his head. "Or you could have told Gonzalez and asked the police to look into it."

"Your way is a lot more boring."

"It's also what you're supposed to do, C.T.," Rich said.

I shrugged. "I prefer to discover things for myself," I said.

"What did you learn?"

"He was murdered. Marvin's story checks out. There's a second bullet hole."

"So now what?" said Rich.

"Now I report some strong suspicions to Gonzalez," I said.

"You can't do it the way you're thinking. Even if he does take another look at the case, he'll wonder how you came to suspect everything. They're not going to go easy on you like we do."

Normally, I would have disputed the BPD goes easy on me, but this wasn't the time. "How should I do it, then?" I said.

"This requires me to think as you do." Rich chuckled. "I'm not sure I like it."

"You'll find my thought processes very liberating."

"I don't plan to do it very often," Rich said. He pursed his lips. I pondered giving him my best Darth Vader voice and encouraging him to come to the dark side but refrained. "I would tell him about your funeral home conversation with Marvin and you think he's telling the truth. Just leave off the part about your little investigation of the suite."

I nodded. "OK. Thanks for helping me put one over on the man."

"Shut up," Rich said, "and get me another beer."

* * *

IT WAS LATE when I left Rich's, but I called Gonzalez on his cell anyway. "This better be important," he said. His voice didn't sound sleepy.

"I knew a dedicated public servant like you would keep late hours," I said.

"So what's *your* explanation?"

"I still stay up late from my days as a player in college," I said.

"Sounds like the better career choice," Gonzalez said.

"It was. The actual reason I called is the Rodgers case."

"What case? He killed himself."

"I have a witness who disputes your theory," I said.

Gonzalez paused. "Someone saw him get shot?"

"Heard it happen. He was staying in the suite next door. Said he heard two muffled gunshots."

"And you think he's telling the truth," Gonzalez said, not in the form of a question.

"I do," I said. "He doesn't strike me as canny enough to tell a lie."

"What is he, an idiot savant?"

"A mousy accountant."

"Accountants lie," Gonzalez said with a snort.

"About money and the like, sure. I don't think he's lying about what he heard."

"What do you want me to do at eleven at night?"

"Find out how many bullets were missing from the gun you've already processed," I said.

"And if it's one?"

"Then I'll find my accountant and clobber him with a ledger book," I said.

"I'd pay to see you do it," Gonzalez said and hung up.

I needed to be quicker on the draw next time.

* * *

I ARRIVED home to find it empty. Gloria had taken her bag but left a scandalous dress in my closet and a small nightgown in a dresser drawer. While I admired her fondness for revealing clothes, I didn't know how I felt about her leaving them at my house. It felt very . . . official, and I wasn't sure how official I wanted things to be with Gloria. I enjoyed most of the time we spent together, but I also appreciated some time apart from her. She was too smart to have simply forgotten the sexy articles, and she put them where she knew I'd see them. We would have to discuss her clothing encroachment at some point.

After changing into a T-shirt and a pair of Polo sleeping shorts, I went into my office and logged in to my laptop. It only took a few minutes to use Gonzalez's IP address to break into the BCPD's network. Simple fingerprinting found an unused IP in the same range, and from there, convincing the BCPD my laptop owned the IP address and was one of its own computers was quick and easy work. The BCPD possessed no better security than the BPD. Most places didn't, which was good for me and sad for everyone else.

My quest for the case file was in its infancy when Gonzalez called me back. "What's the magic number?" I said.

"Your accountant was right," he said. He sounded like a little boy forced to return a puppy to the pet store.

"There were two bullets missing from the gun."

"Three," Gonzalez said, "but one was a test fire ballistics did. Two bullets were missing when they got it."

"Do you still think it's a suicide?" I said.

"I'm coming around to the idea someone might have killed this guy."

"The other option is he needed two bullets to kill himself."

"Most people don't," said Gonzalez.

"What's our next move?" I said.

"'Our?'"

"You'd still think this was a suicide if not for me. Just remember this when you collect a medal at the end."

Gonzalez chuckled. "You're a persistent son of a bitch," he said.

"Thanks."

"It's not really a compliment. Herpes is persistent, too."

"I don't come to you with my problems, do I?" I said.

"Touché. All right, meet me at the precinct tomorrow morning. We're going to look for the second bullet in the hotel room."

"I'll be there," I said. "What time?"

"Nine o'clock," Gonzalez said, "and bring some coffee."

I was about to say I would when Gonzalez hung up again. Bastard.

At least he was on board with the murder angle.

CHAPTER 6

At seven minutes after nine, I walked into the BCPD precinct house, carrying coffee for Gonzalez and a vanilla latte for me in a drink holder, along with a bag of goodies in my other hand. I saw him at his desk, squinting at something on his monitor. I sat in his guest chair without waiting for an invitation. His eyes slid over to me. "You're late," he said.

"It's acceptable to be up to fifteen minutes late for a social event," I said.

Gonzalez swept his hand to take in the room. "This look like cocktail hour at the Ritz Carlton to you?"

"I certainly hope not. It would be a dreadfully boring crowd." I freed his coffee cup from the drink holder and set it on his side of the desk. "Maybe this will make you a little less crabby."

He took a long drink of it. "It's a start. What's in the bag?"

"Donuts for you . . . a breakfast sandwich for me."

"What if I want the sandwich?"

I reached into the bag, taking out a smaller paper bag holding my turkey bacon, egg, and Monterey jack breakfast sandwich. "Then you should move faster. Besides, you're a cop. Eating a breakfast sandwich would break a stereotype."

"I guess we can't have that." Gonzalez grabbed the bag and looked inside. "A variety. I'm starting to like you."

"I'm good at plying public servants with sugary breakfasts."

He took a bite of a chocolate glazed confection. "Don't put it on your business cards."

"I'm surprised you think I have business cards."

Gonzalez seemed happy to eat his donuts—he selected a blueberry next—so I ate my sandwich. When he finished the fruity one and drank about two-thirds of the coffee, he looked more awake. "The gun in the room is definitely the one someone used to shoot our guy," he said.

"It's 'our' now, is it?"

"Your medal speech was stirring."

"Any prints on it?"

"Only his." Gonzalez shook his head. "Whoever shot him went to some trouble to make it look like a suicide."

"Good thing you had a brilliant private investigator working the case."

"Yeah, sure," Gonzalez said with a roll of his eyes. He grabbed the third donut, a raspberry jelly filled, out of the bag. "We'll see how brilliant you are when we get to the crime scene."

"I'll try to shine just brightly enough to be impressive," I said.

* * *

A DIFFERENT DESK clerk happened to be on duty at the Sheraton. Gonzalez flashed his badge, and I showed my ID. The CSI technician adjusted his impressive bag of crime scene investigative voodoo. The manager on duty appeared a minute later. I lucked out; it was a different person. Gonzalez did the talking. This manager voiced the same objection about the room being occupied but still gave us a key when he could tell we didn't give a damn.

Gonzalez opened the penthouse door without knocking. Thankfully, we didn't walk in on an orgy, but we did wake up the guy I saw the night before. The call girl was gone. I guess he didn't pay enough to get her to stay. "What the hell?" he said, pulling the sheet and blanket up to cover himself to the neck.

"BCPD," Gonzalez said, showing him his badge. "We need to look around the room."

"Why do you have hotel security with you?" the man said. He stared at me. "I thought you said this wasn't the right room."

Gonzalez now looked at me in much the same way Rich often does. I shrugged. "Turns out it was after all."

"We're going to look around now, if you don't mind," Gonzalez said.

"Sure. I'll just stay here."

"Good idea."

"I wasn't involved in whatever it is you're looking for," the man said.

"I certainly hope not."

The CSI tech already poked around. Gonzalez followed him. I leaned against the deck and tried to look inconspicuous. "You mind pointing us in the right direction?" Gonzalez said.

"If I were you, I'd look behind the armoire," I said.

"A hunch?"

"A pretty strong one."

"Whatever, I'm not taking the fucking thing apart. You've been here before, so you must know how it's done."

I nodded and moved toward the armoire. "The curse of fore-knowledge," I said as I removed the drawers.

"Or of lying by omission."

"You never asked if I'd been here before."

"I guess you have me there."

I disconnected the TV again and moved it off the armoire. The CSI tech pushed the large dresser out and found the bullet hole right away. Gonzalez nodded at him, and he took pictures of the hole and everything around it, then got some measurements. We walked away to let him work.

"You came here last night?" Gonzalez said.

"Perhaps there's a fellow in hotel security almost as handsome as I," I said. "It's hard to believe, but it might be true."

"Or perhaps you came here last night."

"It's a possibility."

"I don't know how things normally work in Baltimore," said Gonzalez, "but we don't like it when people play fast and loose in the county."

"They tend to the say the same thing in Baltimore, too."

"Then I don't feel so bad. Obviously, you don't listen very well."

I said, "I prefer to think of it as being results-driven."

"Any other results you'd like to come forward about now?"

"None."

"You sure?"

"Positive. I'm not holding out on you."

"This time." Gonzalez checked with his CSI. "You almost done, Miller?"

"Just about," Miller said.

"Good. We'll process everything and see what we know later today." He looked at me again. "I'm going to take a risk by sharing this information with you. Don't be an asshole with it."

"I'll do my best."

"Maybe you already did."

"There's no maybe about it," I said.

* * *

AFTER LUNCH, Pauline Rodgers called me and sounded frantic, so I drove to her house. When I knocked, she made sure to ask who it was, then I heard her undo two locks and a chain before she opened the door. Worry lines creased her face. "Thanks for coming," she said.

"It sounded important."

"It is. Come in." I entered, and she reset both locks and slid a chain in place behind me. The chain was new. It wouldn't stop a charging toddler jonesing for a lollipop, but I didn't have the heart to tell Pauline in her condition. She led me into the kitchen where we both sat at the light brown table. It looked like it came from a thrift store. Scratches marred the surface, and a dog had taken a liking to one of the legs. Pauline took a drink of coffee. I got the feeling it wasn't her first cup.

"This was in my mailbox this morning," she said, handing me a folded piece of paper. I took it from her trembling hand and read:

Dear Pauline,

I am sorry to hear of Stanley's passing. This has to be a diffi-cult time for you. At the risk of adding to the difficulty, your husband owed me a rather sizable sum of money, which I now must collect from you. I will contact you tomorrow to make arrangements for payment. You do not want my bill collectors at your door.

DR

I looked up at Pauline. Her hands still shook, and she inter-mittently bit her lip. "What does it mean?" she said.

I really didn't want to do this, but the letter winnowed my options. "Your husband borrowed money to fund his . . . money-making plans," I said.

She shook the paper. "Who the hell did he borrow money from, the devil?"

"Close. A loan shark."

Tears flowed. I looked around for a box of tissues but didn't see any. I settled for a napkin and handed it to her. She took it and dabbed at her eyes. "What the hell am I going to do about a loan shark?"

"He's not going to go away unless you can pay him."

"I can't pay him," she shouted, then sobbed.

I let her cry for a few minutes. When her weeping got quieter and sobs less frequent, Pauline wiped her eyes and set the napkin atop the table. "I can't pay him," she said again. "There's no way."

"Stanley didn't have any money to leave you?"

She snorted at me.

"Life insurance?"

"He wasn't working. We cashed out his only policy a while ago. That money's long gone."

"Then I think you need to talk to the loan shark."

"What am I going to say to him?"

"I'll be there when you meet with him. Tell him the truth. He's not going to be sympathetic, but he might give you some time."

"What would I do with more time? Work three jobs?"

"We'll figure something out."

"You'd better."

I left a few minutes later. Pauline was disconsolate, and I didn't see the point of staying only to have her reiterate she couldn't pay David Rosenberg. As I walked back to my car, a red Mustang with a white racing stripe and extremely shiny chrome wheels drove slowly past. Two shady characters eyed me up and down, and one pointed a camera. After they snapped the picture, the Mustang sped off. With a head start, I could never catch them on all the side streets.

Either I'd been followed, or those guys were casing Pauline's place. Regardless, David Rosenberg would soon know who I was.

Fantastic.

* * *

THE INFORMATION AGE has made searching for data about someone much easier. I can't imagine going to the library, looking in phone books, standing in rain-soaked doorways, and all the sundry methods my past counterparts used to learn about someone. Now, I could comb through a bunch of tweets and blog posts about someone. More data doesn't make it better, though. Any idiot can post a tweet or a blog update, and many have. If David Rosenberg could learn about me, I could find out about him. All I'd learned from Tony Rizzo was Rosenberg was ruthless and Jewish, and I could have guessed the latter for myself. I started with basic searches and narrowed my criteria until I concentrated on the right David Rosenberg. The first thing I saw was a blog called "David Rosenberg Sucks." I figured I would discover this fact on my own and skipped the blog. Ditto another journal proclaiming his status as an asshole.

I saw several pictures of Rosenberg. He was blessed with a round face, a prominent nose, and eyes appearing too small for his head. His hair was long gone from the top of his head but was full everywhere else and a mix of brown and gray. The pictures of him standing made him look a little paunchy but not seriously overweight. I guessed him to be in his early sixties. The small, dark eyes lent him a sinister quality.

Rosenberg's legitimate business was in restaurant supply. I wondered if he sold anything to *Il Buon Cibo*. He posted a location in the county—Pikesville. I didn't know exactly where it was, but I could hazard a good guess. Pauline and I would need to talk to Rosenberg soon. I hoped we could avoid doing it there. Meeting a loan shark didn't rank high on my list of things to do, but if I needed to, I'd just as soon not hand him home-field advantage.

I saw a few pictures of Rosenberg's goons, including the two who drove past me outside Pauline's. His stable was smaller than Tony's, but they looked just as menacing as the Baltimore crew. I wondered what jobs they performed at Rosenberg's restaurant supply business. Meet Brutus, the oven specialist. For all your cleaning needs, see Clubber in the back left of the store. He specializes in removing blood from tile floors.

Nothing else of note came up on my basic searches. I decided to put off a more advanced search for now. Those two clowns in the car concerned me. Rosenberg would acquaint himself with me sooner or later; I preferred later. How did he know about me already? Or were those two just sticking with Pauline to see what happened? What if they went back?

If they returned, I couldn't do much about it now. I didn't think they would, though. Rosenberg wanted his money, no doubt, but he worked a process for getting it back. Sending two goons to menace a widow right away didn't seem like a play in his playbook. Rosenberg first sent a letter reading as nice on the surface. He would contact her again.

I spent the rest of the day getting ready for Rosenberg and his crew. I hit the dojo for a sparring session and then the shooting range, where I fired all my handguns. Practice is something I'm often lazy about. This case wouldn't give me such a luxury. I needed to be prepared.

* * *

THE NEXT MORNING, I made a breakfast for one. Two eggs over hard, wheat toast with butter and jelly, and a cup of Greek yogurt. The kitchen still smelled like the pepper I heated in the pan before adding the eggs. Pauline called right when I was about to cut into the second delicious egg. They had to be the best I ever made. I hoped this one would still be good lukewarm. "Hello?"

"C.T., it's Pauline."

I loved it when people announce themselves on the phone.

Like I haven't had caller ID since it became a thing. "Hi, Pauline."

"I got a phone call." I waited for her to elaborate, but she didn't.

"So did I."

"You did?"

"Yes, only a moment ago. A woman who hired me decided to call and have a cryptic conversation. It was very strange."

She was silent for a second, then chuckled. "I guess I deserved that. I got a call from . . . him."

"Rosenberg?" I said.

"Uh-huh. What do I do?"

"We're going to meet with him."

"You sure it's a good idea?" Pauline said.

"It's better than any of the alternatives."

Pauline sighed. "All right."

"Did he offer a time and place?"

"His restaurant supply business at one-thirty."

"All right," I said. "I'll pick you up at one."

"Thanks, C.T. I think this is more than you signed up for, but I'm glad you're sticking with me."

"I like to see things through."

Now, I hoped the tendency didn't get me killed.

CHAPTER 7

How does one dress when visiting a loan shark? Does it change the algorithm if the usurious moneylender is known to be ruthless? I didn't want to announce to David Rosenberg and his crew I was a private investigator. In the past, when required to accompany clients and not wanting to appear in my official capacity, I've gone with a cover of Trent (my middle name), a dashing gentleman who works in finance. I took enough business classes in college to fake the basics, which is all I've ever needed.

I chose a nice blue pinstriped Armani suit, paired with a yellow Ralph Lauren shirt and a striped blue Armani tie. I skimped on the shoes: Nunn Bush. Trent the finance guy should look good, but not perfect. He skimps on his shoes because the market is uncertain and clients even moreso. I accessorized the suit with a .32 revolver holstered on my left side near my back. It was the smallest gun I owned, and while I didn't trust its stopping power, I did trust it to fit under a suit jacket and buy us time to make an escape if we needed to.

About six months ago, I went off the grid for a challenging case and bought a late-1980s Caprice from an "automotive reconfiguration engineer," as he liked to call himself. The Caprice was big, blue, and ugly, so I got it painted, souped up, and fortified against small arms fire. If we needed to make an escape, the Caprice was the best choice. I guess Trent skimped on his car, too. At least he wore a killer suit.

I picked Pauline up promptly at five after one. She looked at her watch after she got in the car. I didn't say anything. "Where's your other car?" she said.

"This one can take a bullet and keep going," I said.

She blanched. Perhaps I shouldn't have mentioned this feature. "They're going to shoot at us?"

"I doubt it," I said, trying my best reassuring tone. "Rosenberg merely wants to talk. It always helps to be prepared, though."

"I guess."

I drove to Rosenberg's Restaurant Supply. We pulled up at one-thirty-three, which was very prompt for me. I would blame it on traffic if asked. The business featured an adjacent lot off Reisterstown Road, so I parked the Caprice there. I checked the gun one more time as Pauline and I walked to the building. We went inside and to the reception desk to the left of the door. A pretty redhead behind the desk smiled at us. "Can I help you folks?" she said.

"We're here for Mr. Rosenberg," I said. "He should be expecting us."

"Let me check for you." She smiled again and worked the intercom. I looked around. Restaurant supply was boring. Salt shakers, mops, tablecloths, and silverware didn't excite me. The shelves were well-stocked everywhere I looked. As far as I could tell, this was a legitimate business. "Mr. Rosenberg will see you," the receptionist said. I wondered how much she knew.

"Thank you," I said.

Pauline hadn't said a word since we arrived. She did nothing but stare at the floor but finally lifted her head to look at me. Her expression was so morose I thought she entered a contest to find the most downtrodden woman in Maryland. I gave her a quick smile. "Let's go."

"All right," she said with a nod.

A tall, medium-built man came up to meet us. He had about five inches on me, putting him at six-seven, but he looked athletic, not brawny. Rosenberg had different standards for his goons than Tony Rizzo. This fellow moved with the easy confidence, of one who knew how to take care of himself in a fight. Hair as dark and glittery as coal was pulled back into a ponytail. His gray eyes matched his shirt. If he were a woman, I might have said he looked exotic, like he showed some Asian ancestry. "Mr. Rosenberg will see you now," he said. "Please follow me."

We walked behind him to the back of the building where a large black door blocked access to something important. A standard ten-key keypad restricted access. Our guide's tall frame blocked my view, so I couldn't see the access code. I heard four beeps before the door opened. "This way," he said, leading us down a hallway wide enough for one person at a time. The walls were plain, and the passage contained only a single door dead ahead.

The tall fellow knocked twice, then three more times. "Come in," called a voice from the other side. Our escort entered and showed us inside with a sweep of his arm. I walked in first in case anyone tried to waylay us. It was the chivalrous thing to do, even if it clashed with my otherwise well-developed sense of self-preservation.

Rosenberg sat behind an uncluttered mahogany desk. It would have been too high for him if he hadn't maxed out the upper adjustment on his chair. To his right, a man built more like a typical goon stared at us as we walked in. He didn't look like either of the guys who snapped my picture; I was oh-for-two on finding them so far. Rosenberg's guest chairs were borrowed from a cheap hotel. Pauline sat in the one on the left, and I took the other one. The tall fellow closed the door behind us, then leaned against the wall beside it.

"Who the fuck are you?" Rosenberg said, looking at me. Pauline inhaled sharply.

"He asked in a warm and friendly tone," I said. Pauline was already frightened, so I tried to keep the mood light so I didn't get scared, too.

"A comedian," Rosenberg said, shaking his head. "What's your name, funny man?"

"Trent. I work in finance. I'm Mrs. Rodgers' consultant."

"She needs a financial consultant?"

"Everyone could use one. If you come by our office, I'm sure we could make your money work better for you, too."

"You hear that, Jasper?" Rosenberg said to the tall man who guarded the door. ""They'll make my money work better." Rosenberg, Jasper, and the goon all enjoyed a good chuckle. "Let me tell you something, ace. I don't need a fucking consultant. My money works damn well. Other people's money works even better."

"All right."

"Pauline Rodgers." Rosenberg turned to face her. She threatened to cry. "Nice to meet you."

"You . . . uh, you, too," she said.

"Sorry to hear about Stanley's death."

"Th . . . thank you."

"Let's get down to brass tacks. Your husband owes me money. A good amount of money."

"He . . . he was investing it."

"I don't give a shit. He borrowed money. He used said money. He did not repay it. He still owes it. He's dead. Now you owe it."

"How much are we talking about?" I said when Pauline went speechless.

"He borrowed seventy-six large." Pauline gasped. I continued to look at Rosenberg. "There's interest and other fees. With those, you owe me eighty-five."

"Eighty-five thousand?" Pauline said. Only her liberally-applied blush kept her from looking as white as a sheet.

"Yeah, eighty-five thousand. I'd pay fast. Interest adds up quick."

"Mrs. Rodgers intends to pay this debt," I said. "Due to what happened to her husband, though, she can't pay it off at once."

"You want a payment plan?" Rosenberg said.

"Please," Pauline said.

"She wants a payment plan," he said to the goon sitting to his right. I guess Jasper got excluded from financial jokes. Maybe he failed Accounting 101. Then again, I doubted the guy sharing a chuckle with Rosenberg could spell "college" if I spotted him the first four letters.

"This ain't a damn credit union." Rosenberg looked at Pauline again. "You ain't financing a car. You don't get six years."

"I need . . . some time," Pauline said.

"I can give you six months," Rosenberg said. "About a third up front. So thirty large ASAP. Then you get five payments. Twelve thousand each."

"You're asking for ninety thousand," I said.

"You're in the right field, ace," Rosenberg said. "Five thousand is the inconvenience fee. I hate payment plans."

"I . . . I don't—" Pauline started talking, but I cut her off.

"Mrs. Rodgers will get you your first payment. She needs a few days to assemble the money."

"Assemble the money? What is it, fucking Legos?" I almost laughed at his quip. Rosenberg was an asshole who cussed too much to sound intimidating, but I gave him credit for *un bon mot*. Instead of laughing, I flashed a winning smile.

"Considering the circumstances, Mrs. Rodgers just needs a little time."

"She has forty-eight hours." Pauline started to weep. "Tears ain't changing it, lady. Forty-eight hours. You don't wanna miss a payment."

Pauline nodded but didn't say anything. "Forty-eight hours it is," I said.

"Good, it's settled." Rosenberg looked back at the paper on his desk. A few seconds later, he looked up at us again. "Why the hell you still here? Jasper, show them out."

"I think we can manage on our own," I said. I stood and helped a teary Pauline to her feet. She wobbled once she stood, but I steadied her with a hand on her forearm. "Let's go, Pauline."

"Forty-eight hours," the goon sitting with Rosenberg said.

"Your echo is a little late," I said.

"You a smartass?" Rosenberg said.

"Better than a dumbass. I don't like limiting my career choices to retail and thuggery."

The bodyguard stood and put on his best scowl. I wondered if I'd pushed things too far. I became aware of my heart beating in my chest and the weight of the gun near my back. "Jasper, get them out of here," Rosenberg said. "Spare the jokes next time, ace."

"They're just one more free service I offer," I said. Pauline and I walked out of the room, with Jasper close behind. He led us toward the front of the store without a word.

"Have a nice day," he said when we got to the point where he met us before. "Please avoid collection procedures." Jasper flashed a brief smile, then walked toward the back of the store. The receptionist smiled at us as we walked past, even though Pauline still cried. I grew tired of smiles. I felt weary of this case.

Pauline and I walked back to the Caprice. I pondered our next move, and none of the choices turning over in my head struck me as solid.

* * *

WHEN I GOT HOME, I discovered one thing went well: Stanley's hard drive finished decrypting. At the moment, it was the entirety of the list of things right with the world—this and the fact I wore a damn sharp suit. I changed out of said sharp suit into more comfortable clothes, then grabbed an IPA from the fridge. After the meeting with Rosenberg and his crew, I needed it.

As soon as I looked at Stanley's data, I wished I paid more attention in accounting class. I only took it because it was required and only showed up often enough to get a B-plus, but it was basic accounting and what downloaded was way beyond that. Stanley's day-trading plan involved a lot of option exchanges and short sales on volatile stocks. It looked like his plan—if it could be called one—was to catch them on an upward trend. I would have to break into his brokerage account to see the fruits of those efforts.

I didn't find much else of use on Stanley's hard drive. He composed few love letters, presumably to Pauline, and I read about a third of the first one before my arteries clogged with saccharine. Stanley was better off sticking to stocks, and I didn't even think he ran a solid scheme there. He rode a good wave for a while—a lot of investment types did—but based on what I could see of his financial acumen, he wasn't going to recapture the magic anytime soon.

In my final sweep of Stanley's hard drive, I found a spreadsheet buried in a random folder. It showed an initial balance of seventy-five thousand. Rosenberg said Stanley borrowed seventy-six. A single grand of the sum would have paid for his hotel suite for a few nights. The original seventy-five had been whittled well below its original value. Based on Stanley's hourly returns—to use a technical Wall Street term—he'd lost his ass. His initial funds sat at thirteen thousand, based on the last figure he entered.

If he did so poorly in such a brief time, I wondered how much of the remaining balance was eaten away without him there to cash it out.

Pauline could use the money. I went back through Stanley's documents and found information about his brokerage account. I tried to log into it with his user ID, entered one of my email addresses in lieu of his, and clicked on the link for a forgotten password. A minute later, I obtained a temporary password and logged in. This process was easier than setting a password cracker loose. A brute force attack would probably lock his account. I might have made some reasonable guesses as to the password, but doing so also ran the risk of locking everything. This way was more low-tech, but it got me in without any complications.

I went to the balance sheet and cringed. Stanley's remaining thirteen large had been eaten away to just over nine. I chose the cash-out option and selected the existing account he linked. It wouldn't even cover the down payment to Rosenberg, but it helped. I could brainstorm some ways to raise the rest and buy us time to take on the loan shark and his organization.

Nothing else on Stanley's computer proved useful. I'd already struck gold, so to speak, and I couldn't complain. Pauline could, but the only person who could really listen would be lowered into the ground tomorrow. I informed her I would be skipping the funeral. Slogging through the viewing proved enough. I was about to get another beer when Gloria called. "Hey, what are you up to?"

"I finished doing something for the case," I said. "Right now, I'm staring into an empty beer bottle."

"Don't stare too hard. You might go cross-eyed." I heard her giggle.

"I'll do my best."

"Do you want to go out later?" she said "There's a new restaurant I want to try."

If Gloria discovered a new restaurant, it would be expensive and would struggle to live up to whatever hype her socialite friends bestowed upon it. The last one boasted of small plates, which people like for some reason, but also took pride in prices inversely proportional to the plate size. One of these nights, I would make Gloria pick up the check. As often as I paid, we might as well be dating. "Sure, sounds good," I said.

"Great," said Gloria. "We have a seven-thirty reservation. I'll come by around six."

I smiled. "Sounds good."

* * *

GLORIA and I freshened up before our dinner reservation. I could probably call it a date, and maybe Gloria even thought of it as one. Someday, we would sit down and have a conversation. It wouldn't be today. I put on a black blazer over a black T-shirt and a nice pair of blue jeans. Gloria, who usually wrinkled her nose if I put on jeans, didn't say anything. She busied herself with making sure her ensemble fit well. Like all her dresses, this one clung to her curves in exactly the right places. For someone who said she didn't spend a lot of time shopping, Gloria always wore fashionable clothes that walked the line between appropriate and scandalous.

"We're going to be late," she said as she put on eyeshadow.

"Then you should call and make it for later," I said.

"Oh, I should, should I?" Gloria winked at me, then frowned because doing it mussed her makeup. She went back to it with a determined look.

"We're late because you're insatiable."

Gloria finished putting makeup on her right eye. "Guilty as charged," she said. "But if you're complaining. . . ."

"None here." I smacked her magnificent bottom. "Just

pointing it out." I splashed on some cologne, then checked my hair in the mirror to have something to do while Gloria completed getting ready. All my hairs were the same dark brown as always, and they were still where I left them.

"Fine, I'll call when we're en route. The way you drive, it shouldn't take longer than ten minutes to get there."

"I can make the drive in nine minutes."

"But not eight?"

"Can't account for the lights."

"That's what they all say." This time, Gloria smacked me on the butt.

I sat on the disheveled bed and watched her. Gloria didn't need makeup, but if she were going somewhere she could run into other people, she always wore it. It was like a Vanity Express Card. I had one in my wallet, too, so I couldn't fault her. Sometimes, Gloria noticed me watching her, but she always focused on her makeup like a sword swallower would the point of a blade.

A few minutes later, she put her makeup back into the bag and set it down in my bathroom. I wondered if she planned on leaving it here, too. She must have enough at her house to furnish an army of women for a year. "Ready to go?" she said.

"Let's eat," I said. "I hope this isn't a small plate place. I've worked up an appetite."

"See," said Gloria, "there are perks to being late."

"You're preaching to the choir," I said.

* * *

GLORIA LIED. We didn't go to a new place, and it wasn't ten minutes away. She heard about a Szechuan restaurant called Mr. Chan's from a vegan friend and made up the other story because she feared my objection on dedicated carnivore grounds. Already, I dreaded going there. General Tso's sprouts didn't appeal to me.

Gloria insisted the restaurant catered to carnivores and herbivores alike. Pikesville was a lot longer than ten minutes from downtown, but I sped up I-83 to the Beltway and we parked in a lot across the street at eight-sixteen. As we got out of the car, I realized we weren't far from Rosenberg's. I hoped he didn't care for the food.

We walked in the double doors, past the wind chimes and indoor fish pond. Swirls of colors swam in the water. I hoped nothing in there got used to make sushi. A banquet room on the right held at least a dozen people, and they made enough noise for half again as many. The main dining room was about half full. Booths ringed the perimeter with four-seat tables filling up the center space. A Chinese woman in her forties sat Gloria and me at the last available booth. It was on the other side of the dining room from the banquet hall, but the voices still carried. Aimee Mann knew her stuff.

I looked over the menu and saw why vegetarians and vegans loved the place so much. I never witnessed so many options and so many fake meats. They featured the standard fare of tofu and tempeh, but also stuff not heard of before like healmey. If I hadn't heard of it and could only guess how to pronounce it, I wasn't going to order it. I focused on the meat options, which took up three pages of the menu. Mr. Chan loved variety.

A Chinese girl in her twenties came to take our order. We both asked for iced tea. The waitress returned a minute later with the two drinks, along with a bowl of noodles, complemented with duck sauce and hot mustard. Gloria pondered options while the waitress waited. She finally settled on a spring roll and a yuba red curry—whatever the hell yuba was. I ordered eel nigiri from the sushi menu and the salmon and shiitake stir-fry from the main menu. The waitress raised eyebrows when I chose foods in Cantonese. She complimented me on my accent (in her native tongue, of course) before disappearing into the kitchen.

"What did she say?" Gloria said, putting sugar in her tea.

"She said you're a very lucky woman to be out with such a handsome man," I said.

Gloria stirred her tea. "Really?"

"Actually, she complimented me on my accent."

She smiled. "That's too bad. I liked the other one better."

"So did I."

We ate noodles until Gloria's spring roll and my nigiri arrived. Gloria frowned at the strips of fresh eel covering small blocks of white rice. I mixed my wasabi into a small dish of soy sauce. "You eat eel?" said Gloria.

"I've been known to on occasion."

She wrinkled her nose. I couldn't help but notice how cute she looked doing it. "I don't get the appeal of sushi."

I gestured toward my plate. "You can try a piece of mine."

"I'm not feeling that adventurous," she said, shaking her head. "Whatever happened with the woman who came to see you?"

"Her husband got killed."

"That's terrible. Do you know who did it?"

"I have an idea who," I said, "but not why yet. I need a motive."

"Who do you think did it?"

"Her husband was in hock to a loan shark for a pretty good sum. I don't know why the loan shark or his cronies would kill him without giving him a chance to pay up. It seems like bad business." The realization took me back to my first case. One of my old buddies, Vinnie Serrano, set himself up as a bookie and budding loan shark. He made the point how killing whoever wrote the checks was unwise.

"It seems like awful business," Gloria said.

"Yeah, it is."

"Aren't you worried? If this loan shark killed someone who owed him a lot of money, what stops him from going after you?"

She posed a very good question. I watched concern furrow Gloria's brows. "I don't know," I said. "Right now, he doesn't know who I am. He thinks I'm Pauline's finance guy. If he guesses I can help her pay him off, he'll want to keep me around."

Before we could converse further, the waitress returned with our entrees. My stir fry looked and smelled delicious. The salmon, mushrooms, and vegetables combined for a dish boasting of more colors than a rainbow. Gloria's looked like many red curries I've seen with the yuba standing in for chicken. The waitress wished us a happy meal in Cantonese before she left again.

We tabled talk of the case while we ate. The stir fry was amazing. I barely needed to chew it before it dissolved in my mouth, especially the salmon. It could have been a tick or two spicier, but I hadn't asked for extra spice, so I couldn't complain. Nor would I complain about a meal this good. Gloria cut her pieces of yuba into more manageable bites. Seeing it cut in half shed no light on its nature for me.

"Do you want to try this?" Gloria said.

I shook my head. "My body is a temple," I said.

"A temple to whom?"

"Depends on my mood. Dionysus sometimes . . . Athena other times."

Gloria laughed around her bite of food, covering her mouth with a napkin. "I can see those," she said.

We finished our dinners and declined dessert. A petite sweet came in the form of fortune cookies and orange slices. I reached for the check but Gloria grabbed it first. "This one is on me," she said.

"Who are you, pod person," I said, "and what have you done with Gloria Reading?"

She smiled. "A pod person?"

"You eat like a vegan, you seem interested in my case, and now you're paying the tab. You've been body snatched."

"Maybe you can do other things with my body later. Unless you still think I'm a pod person."

"I'll have to inspect you closely," I said. "We can't risk having an alien on the loose."

"Sounds like we can't be too careful," Gloria said. "We'd better take our time."

* * *

GLORIA WAS quiet on the drive home. It stood as a marked contrast from the end of our meal. I looked over at her a few times in an effort to draw her out, but I got nothing. Finally, when we were most of the way down I-83, she found her voice. "I'm going to court soon." If my Audi's engine had eight cylinders instead of six, I wouldn't have heard her over it.

"For what?"

After a few seconds of silence, she said, "My old tennis coach."

I sucked in a deep breath and gripped the wheel hard enough to turn my knuckles white. "What happened?"

"He's been accused of a lot."

"Did he—"

"No," Gloria broke in. "Not to me, at least." She paused and collected herself with a sigh. "He propositioned me. More than once. Said he could get me better pairings in the tournaments." Another deep breath. "Sorry. I didn't mean to unload on you."

I grabbed her hand and smiled. "Don't apologize," I said. "You need me to go beat his ass?"

She smiled. "Thanks, but no. We'll get him in court."

"I'm sure you will." I squeezed Gloria's hand. She squeezed mine. Neither of us pulled back. A couple minutes later, I parked a few houses up from mine. Gloria and I walked down Riverside Avenue. As I fished my keys out of my pockets again, I saw a red Mustang with a distinctive racing stripe cruise the street. Whoever drove made sure to go slow enough to be noticed. The windows never lowered, and the car sped up past my house and was gone. I watched it for a few seconds.

"Everything OK?" Gloria said from my top step.

"Yeah," I said after a second. "Just watching the Mustang. Nice car."

"I like your car better."

I grinned and hoped it didn't look forced. "Me, too."

CHAPTER 8

I woke up a bit after 8:30 the next morning. My venetian blinds, which I meant to replace since the first time I saw them, barely restrained the sunlight outside the bedroom window. Gloria lay on her side, facing away from me, and she breathed the rhythmic sighs of a happy sleeper. I got out of bed, swirled some mouthwash around in my mouth, put on my running shorts, shirt, and jacket, and went downstairs to stretch. When I felt as limber as a dancer, I headed outside.

If I owned any grass, I might have seen dew glistening on it. I zipped the jacket up a little higher, walked briskly for two minutes, then ran toward Federal Hill Park. When I got there, I confirmed the grass did, in fact, have dew on it. Being right about the little things mattered. At eight-forty on a weekday morning, Federal Hill Park cannot boast of many joggers. People with regular jobs are already at work or on their way, and hipsters aren't awake yet, so it only leaves people like me. Me and my two running compatriots for the day. I noticed with some disappointment neither was the girl I loved to follow on my laps.

I ran my second lap around the park when I noticed the red Mustang again. My left hand went for a gun, but a void on my left hip reminded me I hadn't worn one. The Mustang pulled to the curb. I kept a close eye on it behind my sunglasses. The passenger's window went down. Someone got out of the driver's side. Both men held revolvers. I saw a bench about thirty feet away. All I needed was to make it there.

They thumbed hammers back, the mechanisms clicking to break the quiet morning calm. A zig-zagging sprint carried me to the long wooden seat as the first shot blasted. It shredded the air as it whistled past me. The second shot tore up a divot near my feet. A finish-line dive put me behind the bench, and I landed in a belly flop. I moved to a low crouch. The shots thundered in and my heart beat just as loud. My two fellow runners took off in the opposite direction. I could only hope one of them would call 9-1-1, and I wouldn't need a hearse.

A bullet splintered the backrest near my head, sending wood shrapnel into the left side of my face. "Shit!" I closed my eyes and turned away. Blood ran down my cheek. I opened my right eye first, then the left and hoped it still worked. It did. Thick wood and metal hardware saved me so far, but I couldn't count on the scanty protection forever. I looked around for something I could use. Under a nearby tree was a branch I could use for a club if I got the chance. I looked back to my assailants, saw more muzzle blasts, then their revolvers clicked on empty chambers.

I sprang toward the branch and picked it up on the run. Wiping blood out of my eye, I dashed toward the car. The man crouched outside the driver's door—a short and dumpy fellow who looked like shooting a gun was the only exercise he took—tried to reload his revolver as I bore down on him. He looked down at the gun, then up at me, and I swung the club at his head like Manny Machado going after a hanging curveball. The crunch sounded more like a home run than I expected.

Without breaking stride or watching the first man fall, I ran around the car to confront the second gunman. He finished reloading and snapped the cylinder shut. I couldn't get close enough to club him in the head, so I settled for his shooting hand. He yelled in pain as the gun bounced off the car door, then the curb before skidding to rest under the car somewhere. We both glanced down and looked back up at the same time.

This guy sported more of a traditional goonish build than his friend, like he spent most of his mornings admiring his reflection in the Downtown Athletic Club mirror as he did another set of bicep curls. His upper body looked like it came from the pages of a comic book.

He grunted and lunged at me. I sidestepped and swung the tree branch. He turned enough to take it on his massive back, which broke the club in two but didn't even stagger my assailant. He turned to face me and tried to grab me in a bear hug. I stepped to the rear. A siren pierced the morning in the distance; I hoped it headed this way. I watched the musclebound goon as he tried to hit me again. His legs, not as cartoonish as his torso and arms, moved stiffly with no grace at all. He lunged once more. This time, I dodged and delivered a side kick to the front of his knee. The bone cracking sounded like when the stick splintered across his back. He fell forward, away from the car, and I gave him a wide berth as he crashed to the grass.

I hoped it would take the fight out of him, but it didn't. He tried to punch me from the ground. I blunted the ineffective blow with my leg, then kicked him under the chin. The goon's head snapped back, and he collapsed forward. It didn't knock him out, but it did take the wind out of his sails. I walked back toward the Mustang. The driver lay on the street, an impressive pool of blood forming near his head. I wondered if I'd killed him until I saw the rise and fall of his chest.

The sirens got closer. I leaned against the car, wiped some more blood from my face, and waited.

* * *

I TOLD Officers Jennings and Brennan exactly what happened while a paramedic looked at my face. His very attractive partner tended to the assailant with the broken leg. What did I do to get stuck with the male EMT? He used tweezers to dig slivers of wood out of my skin. A couple narrowly missed my eye. "You could have been blinded," he told me as he worked.

"I could have been killed," I said. My comment shut him up.

I told the truth, and neither attacker could counter my story. "The one with the head wound is in pretty bad shape," Jennings said after EMTs loaded him into an ambulance and whisked him away.

"I'd be in worse shape if he shot me," I said.

"Understood. We're not charging you with anything."

"The state's attorney will want to look it over, I'm sure," Brennan said.

"And here I thought my donation to the State's Attorney's Office covered parking tickets and assaults," I said.

Brennan chuckled. "You didn't donate to her," he said.

"Would you?"

"I can't comment on an elected official such as herself," he said while shaking his head hard enough to unscrew it from his shoulders.

"Of course not."

"You seen these guys before?" Jennings said.

I winced as the paramedic dug a splinter out. "Sorry," he said. "It was in there pretty good."

"Do I need stitches?"

"No. I'll clean these up for you and put a bandage on top. You should wear one for a few days to make sure everything stays clean."

"I will."

"So now your healthcare is established," Jennings said, "you ever seen these two before?"

"I've seen the car twice." This must be a record with respect to my truth-telling to the police. "Both times, it drove past me like whoever was inside followed me. But you can see the windows. Too dark to make out who's inside. Could have been these two clowns. Who knows?"

"You've never seen them away from the car?"

"Not before today."

Jennings made a few notes. "Any idea what you might've done to draw their attention?"

"I'm just a guy trying to make a living."

"Uh-huh. You know who they work for?"

"Nope." So much for my truth-telling. Though I didn't *know* who sent them, I could hazard a pretty damned good guess.

"Why do I get the feeling you're holding out on me?"

The female paramedic bent to treat the wounded man's knee. "Maybe my reputation precedes me," I said without looking away from the nice view.

"It does," Brennan said. "But we know you a little. Maybe you don't need to hold out on us."

If I told them these two clowns worked for David Rosenberg, the BPD would sniff around his whole operation. They'd need the BCPD to help, so two police departments could muck around in my investigation and endanger Pauline. Rosenberg couldn't want the cops involved, and twice the cops meant twice the chance he would catch on and do something to Pauline. Or to me. "I don't know who they work for," I said.

Jennings shook his head and flipped his notebook shut. "All right . . . . If you . . . uh, happen to find out at some point, let us know."

"You'll be the first," I said. "I mean, the second. No, the fourth."

"Fourth?"

"Their employer would know. They would. I'd be third, and when I told you, you'd be fourth."

"You're not nearly as funny as you think you are," Jennings said, though he fought a grin while he said it.

"Everyone's a critic," I said.

* * *

I WALKED BACK HOME, checking for shooters, ne'er-do-wells, and all manners of miscreants along the way. I didn't find any. My face still hurt from the wood shrapnel, and the paramedic digging said shrapnel out. It could have been a lot worse. The shooters could have been in a less obvious car. I stopped thinking about these things and unlocked the door. I always took care to lock it behind me, but this time, I triple-checked all three locks. Note to self: add a fourth.

Gloria walked out of the kitchen and frowned when she saw me. "What happened?" she said. "I was worried." I told her. She ran toward me and squeezed me tighter than I thought she could. "I got the feeling something bad went down."

"I'm OK," I said, hugging her and letting out a slow breath. It felt good to wrap my arms around her after what I went through.

"This is the second time you've been shot at near your house," she said. The first time happened just a couple months ago. Gloria had been with me. Two gang members tried to take me out drive-by style with a shotgun. If I hadn't seen the reflection in an SUV side mirror, both of us would have been hit.

"I know. I think I need to separate my office from my house. I can't have these kinds of people buzzing around here."

Gloria finally released me. She peered at me with wet eyes.. I didn't know she'd been crying. "I think that's a very good idea."

"And there are plenty of empty offices around the city."

She smiled. "Maybe you can get an office in the World Trade Center." Her eyes brightened.

"Something to work towards, maybe" I said. "For now, I simply need a door, some locks, and a landlord who doesn't care about my computing habits."

"I think you'll be able to find one."

* * *

"WHAT'S WITH YOUR FACE, SON?" my father said as we settled for lunch at Chiaparelli's in Little Italy. There was a time we all would have gone to *Il Buon Cibo*, but my parents and Tony experienced a falling-out about a year ago. One of these days, I would ask why, and someone would give me an answer. It wouldn't be today. I took a deep breath. My father asked the question glibly, but concern furrowed his brows. My mother wore a similar expression.

"I got shot at," I said in a lowered voice.

"Coningsby!" my mother said loud enough for everyone in the restaurant to take notice. Yes, fellow diners, it's my real name; would it help if I explained I went by my initials? "My goodness. Why did you come out to lunch with such a face?"

"I took some wood bits in the face, so I'll wear a bandage for a few days. Other than superficial wounds and being shaken up, I'm OK. I can't live my life looking over my shoulder."

"What happened, son?" my father said.

I relayed the events of my aborted morning jog around Federal Hill Park to include the gunfire and the sturdy tree branch which allowed me to escape with my life. My mother listened with a white-knuckled grip on the table. "Coningsby, you're lucky to be alive," she said.

"The thought occurred to me."

Before she could answer, a waiter introduced himself as Jay

and took our drink orders. My mother asked for a glass of wine, even though I rarely saw her drink in public. My father and I both wanted tea. Jay left, and my mother picked up where she left off. "This job is dangerous. When we wanted you to help people, we were surprised when you chose to be a private investigator. We knew it could be dangerous, but we thought you would avoid those cases."

"So did I," I said. "I thought I could sit behind my computer and solve people's problems. Occasionally, I can. More often than not, though, I have to get my hands dirty. Hell, I saw a dead body and got knocked silly on my first case. It's been an eventful ride."

"If you want to do something else, we'll understand."

I gave my mother a funny look. My father did, too. "Why would I quit?"

"Because this is so much more dangerous than any of us thought it would be."

Jay returned with our drinks. Despite the fact we'd barely looked at our menus, we each knew what we wanted to eat. When you've been to one good restaurant in Little Italy—and Chiaparelli's is among the very best—you can order at any of them. Only the specials change. My mother chose eggplant parmesan, my father spaghetti Bolognese, and I requested spinach ravioli.

"I'm not a quitter, Mom," I said when Jay departed again. "I'm a loafer sometimes, but not a quitter. I can't walk away from this now. It's been almost a year. A lot of people have depended on me. Pauline Rodgers counts on me now. I'm trying to see to it she comes out of this alive."

"Make sure you do the same, son," my father said.

"It's always my goal."

"What are you going to do to make sure it happens?"

"I plan to wave a gun around wherever I go. It should discourage people from coming up to me."

My mother rolled her eyes. My father chuckled. He could always see the humor in a situation. My mother was usually too busy being concerned and making sure everyone knew she was concerned. "You need to be serious, Coningsby," she said. "Your life could still be in danger. Just because you stopped those two men doesn't mean someone else won't try again."

"I know, Mom."

"Is there anyone you can call?"

"You mean like a bodyguard?" I said.

"Maybe," she said. "Something like that would be good, I think."

"I haven't really thought about it."

"Maybe you need to."

"In the meantime, I'm going to get an actual office. This has shown me I can't keep running my business out of my house. There needs to be some separation."

"Another good idea, son," my father said.

Jay brought our food on a large tray. The perk of Little Italy for lunch is food always came faster. He set everything before us, checked on our drinks, and disappeared again. "Right now, eating is a good idea," I said.

"Look into protecting yourself, Coningsby," my mother said. "You can't keep taking these awful cases and coming away unscathed."

I nodded. "I'll see what I can do."

* * *

AFTER I GOT BACK from dining with my concerned parents, I did what I said I would. I didn't want to hire a bodyguard. I could take care of myself. My training in Hong Kong, and the black belt conferred on me, proved the fact. Bodyguards were for people who couldn't defend themselves. I shook my head at my outmoded way of thinking. The fact I'd studied advanced martial arts didn't matter to the two shooters this morning, and it wouldn't matter to the next asshole with a gun Rosenberg sent after me.

A quick online search gave me some local options, but who would I be getting? Private security companies could boast about nebulous awards and standards. One said all their people were bonded. Did they need to advertise this? Another touted the protection of several pop stars during local concerts. I thought I could fend off the kinds of kooks who would menace Taylor Swift. I could call a few of these companies and make inquiries, but the whole thing struck me as a crapshoot.

I thought about people I knew. None really fit the bill. Joey was big and could pull off looking like a legbreaker, but when it came down to it, he didn't have the skills. I knew a few guys from the dojo, and while they were proficient at breaking boards with fists and feet, those feats alone did not a bodyguard make. I needed someone with real experience in security, could handle threats to me as well as himself or herself, could be invisible when necessary, and didn't object to shooting someone if the situation required it.

An idea came to me, and I picked up the phone and called Colonel Stevens. The colonel was a family friend who retired from the Army a few years ago. I helped him out by taking on a cold case back in the spring. Now I hoped he could return the favor. As usual, the colonel let the phone ring for a while before he answered in his familiar gravelly voice.

"Colonel, it's C.T."

"C.T., how are you?"

"I'm well, sir. How are you?"

"Hell, I can't complain, but sometimes, I do it anyway just to see if anyone is listening."

"Are they?" I said.

"Not usually. What can I do for you?"

I explained the situation this case put me in. "I think I need a bodyguard," I said to wrap it all up. "I could call some company, but who knows what I'll get? I figured you'd know a few good people to recommend."

"As a matter of fact," he said, "I do. Let me make a few calls, and I'll get back to you."

"Great. Thanks, Colonel."

"Give my best to your parents."

"I will, sir."

He hung up. I waited for his call by making a trip to the grocery store. I checked for rapscallions on the way there, in each aisle of the store, and on my return. As I drove home, I reminded myself to start looking for a real office.

* * *

ABOUT AN HOUR after I got home, Colonel Stevens called back with a recommendation. The fellow's name was Rollins, and I should meet him at 1800 hours at Illusions Magic Bar. I thanked him and said I would be there. I spent the next two hours looking into office spaces near Federal Hill. Plenty were available, ranging from renting a house to a real office in a building designed to host real offices. I favored the latter as long as I could setup my computers how I wanted.

I could walk to Illusions in a few minutes, so I did. The evening was cool enough for me to wear my leather jacket and holster the .45 under it. If anyone took a shot at me, I would blast a manhole-sized fissure in them in exchange. Peace through superior firepower and all. I kept a close eye out for any more of Rosenberg's henchmen, but I didn't see anyone too suspicious on my stroll through the streets of Federal Hill.

I strode into Illusions promptly at 6:05. The place packed

them in for their magic shows, but at other times, you could easily find a seat at the bar. A family of magicians owned Illusions, and if they weren't busy, the proprietors would often regale their patrons with tales and demonstrations of magic. Watching your cell phone disappear inside an inflated balloon while enjoying an adult beverage is a unique experience.

Colonel Stevens informed me the man I would meet was black. He didn't give me many other details. Illusions hosted four people at the bar: a man and a woman, both white, at the far end, a black man in the middle, and another at the near end of the bar. The man sitting at the middle of the bar was paunchy and shoveled peanuts into his mouth as if they were coated in ambrosia. The one closer to the door had a military buzz cut with not a single hair out of place. He wore a white button-down shirt, dark jeans, and boots suggesting he won a fight with an alligator. He nodded as I let the door close behind me.

I pulled out the barstool beside his. "Not here," he said, and got up to head toward one of the many unused tables. At least he had his own drink. I ordered an IPA, paid for it, and followed him. Rollins' build reminded me of Rich's—a little shorter and more compact than mine but always conveying the threat of violence.

"The colonel tells me you're in a bad spot," he said.

"Sounds about right."

Rollins pulled pink liquid through a straw with an equally pink umbrella beside it. "Tell me about it."

"My client owes a loan shark through no fault of her own. Because I've been advising her, I'm on his radar, too." I pointed to the bandage on my face. "Wood via gunshot from a bench in Federal Hill Park."

"How many were there?" he said.

"Two."

"You take them both out?"

"Using a tree branch I could have taken to the plate in a softball game."

He nodded. "Not bad. Sounds like you don't have great need of a bodyguard, though."

"But," I said, "I can't also be vigilant for every threat and still try and get my client out of the fire at the same time." I took another sip of the IPA. It was hoppy and a little citrusy. "I'm good at multitasking, but even I have my limits."

"And this is where I come in," said Rollins.

"Hopefully, yes."

Rollins pulled more pink concoction from his straw. I didn't know what it was. I'd seen girls in bars drinking similar stuff, but I never asked them about boring things like what's in the glass when I chatted them up. It smelled pretty strong from across the table, whatever it was. "The colonel said you're a family friend. Said I should give you a good rate. You dress like you don't need a discount. Armani jacket, right?" I nodded even though I knew it would be superfluous. "Your jeans are Calvins, shirt is Ralph, and I can see the Tommy logo peeking out on your belt buckle."

"Would you believe I shop at outlet stores?"

"Not for a second."

He stared, which compelled me to talk. "Too bad, because I do. I have some money, but I put it into my house and some investments. Now I need to get an office."

"You been running your business out of your house?"

"It seemed like a good idea at the time." Rollins shook his head. "I never expected to get caught up in a bunch of dangerous cases. Getting shot at was for detectives on TV, not me."

"Find an office."

"I'm working on it."

Rollins finished his drink and put it down on the table. I could see his bicep flex under his shirt as he straightened and bent his arm. "Here's the deal. Two hundred a day, plus expenses."

"What about the discounted rate?"

"You're getting a nice discount."

Oof. "All right," I said. "What does this usury get me?"

"Me. I'll be around as often or as little as you want. I can follow you on foot, by car, whatever. You won't know I'm there, and the assholes trying to shoot you won't know I'm there, either, until it matters. I don't do vendettas, and I don't shoot first unless one of us is in danger."

"Sounds fine."

"Good, because those terms aren't negotiable." Rollins went back to the bar. I heard him ask for another bay breeze.. A minute later, he returned with it. "What's the word?"

"You're my bodyguard," I said, "but I'm not writing a song about you."

He cracked a small smile. "You probably can't sing anyway."

"Guilty as charged."

"All right. I'll start tomorrow. What time do you get up?"

"It fluctuates but normally between eight-thirty and nine."

Rollins stared at me. "Eight-thirty and nine?"

"Yes."

"Eight-thirty and nine?" He grimaced like someone had just pulled his spleen out through his navel. "What the hell do you do if you need to wake up early?"

"If I need to, I do. I just don't like to."

He took a drink of his bay breeze and shook his head. "You wouldn't have made it in the Army."

"Did you?"

"Did I what?"

"Make it in the Army?"

"I did all right. Started doing private security when I got out."

I sized him up long enough to make him frown. "You enlist right after high school?"

"Shit," he said with something approximating a laugh. "College first. Once I had my degree, I could go down the officers' path."

"So you started at twenty-two. I'd say you look about thirty-six now. It gives you fourteen years in, tops. Retirement starts at twenty, so unless I've really missed my guess, something doesn't add up."

Rollins kept staring at me, but I didn't wilt under his gaze. I simply gazed back at him like a man who knows he has the best hand at the table. "I'm starting to see why the loan shark took a shot at you," he finally said.

"You're dodging the issue."

"There's an issue?"

"I'll only find out anyway. I like to know who I'm hiring. Maybe the colonel didn't tell you, but I do a lot of my detective work by hacking into things. I can get your Army file, your credit report, your phone records . . . all it takes is talent, a little patience, and time. Fortunately, I have all three."

This elevated Rollins' stare to a glare. "I'm thirty-eight," he said. "I spent just shy of fifteen years in the Army. Since my discharge, I've worked in private security. I learned a lot in there."

"Why'd you get discharged?"

"I'm going to keep some secrets for myself. You want to try and look it up, I can't stop you. But I can stop working for you."

"Fair enough," I said. "Tomorrow morning, then. I'm going to go running around Federal Hill Park again."

"Back to the scene of the crime right away?"

"Why change my life just because one asshole wants to hire goons to take a shot at me? Besides, I have you watching my back now."

A curt nod. "You do. How long's your run?"

"About three, four miles."

"I guess I'll run with you."

"So much for not seeing you, then."

"My camouflage jogging suit doesn't work in a park," Rollins said.

* * *

I MADE it home without incident. I meant what I said to Rollins: I didn't want to change my life because David Rosenberg didn't like me. The fact I looked over my shoulder anywhere I went constituted more than enough change for me. When I got home, Gloria was already upstairs sprawled on my bed. What I could see of her evening wear past the blanket made me eager to climb in with her.

She woke up briefly after I eased in but sacked out again as quickly. In the morning, I got up, checked the bandage on my face, put on my running attire, and hit the streets. When I got to Federal Hill Park, it was eight-forty-three. A few industrious joggers made their way around, including the girl I liked to run behind. I made sure to stretch and walk long enough so I could fall in at an appreciable distance.

I saw Rollins in a bright yellow and blue track suit about half a lap ahead. In that getup, anyone could see him. I noticed a small bulge at the back of his jacket. It reminded me I still didn't wear a gun to my morning constitutional. Having a bodyguard made for a good excuse not to, I supposed, but I still needed to get into the habit. There would be other cases, other assholes like Rosenberg, and other attempts on my life.

I finished about forty minutes later, the girl I enjoyed following packing it in about five minutes before. At least she smiled at me as she jogged past. I hoped my next case involved a runaway dog. No one would get mad enough to want to kill me over it, unless I incurred the wrath of a salty dogcatcher. I didn't know if dogcatchers were still a thing. Rollins jogged behind me on the opposite side of the street. He moved like he could have gone another hour without needing water or rest. To be safe, I waited until he was passing my house before I unlocked the door and went inside.

I headed upstairs to shower. I applied a new bandage, hoping I would only need to wear one for a few more days. When I came out, Gloria stirred, and she joined me downstairs after freshening up. I opened the refrigerator and pondered breakfast options. One casualty of my run-in with the pair of assassins had been my stock of groceries. Of all the ways to check out, getting shot while buying toilet paper ranks near the top of the lame scale. I found enough turkey bacon for two, plus all the ingredients for waffles.

While I worked on my waffle mix, Gloria sat at the kitchen table, drinking a glass of orange juice. "I hired a bodyguard," I said.

Her eyes widened, but she nodded and smiled. "I'm glad to hear it," she said. "Where is he?"

"Hell if I know. Outside somewhere, I guess, watching the house. Except when I'm out running, I don't expect to see him unless I need to."

"Then how do you know he's doing his job?"

"He came highly recommended by someone I trust."

She frowned but shrugged when she saw I was OK with the arrangement. "I hope you don't need to see him, then."

"Me, too," I said, even though a feeling in my gut told me I would.

CHAPTER 9

I WAS ABOUT TO EAT LUNCH WHEN PAULINE CALLED. "CAN you talk to Zachary?" she said.

"I don't think he's a big fan. He didn't even like my Facebook page."

"He's been so . . . withdrawn since this all started," she said, ignoring my joke. "I can't get through to him. Katherine can't. Stanley usually could, but he's . . . " Her voice cracked as she trailed off. "You're a man, and you're at least a little close to his age. Can you try?"

"I can try, but this isn't my area of expertise."

"I understand."

"And my fees double for counseling services."

I heard a light chuckle come through the connection. "I think I can afford to pay those rates," Pauline said.

A bit later, Pauline let me in when I got to her house. "He's in the den," she said, "glued to some video game." She shook her head. "He spends more time with it than he does with any of us."

"Maybe it's a good game," I said. Pauline gave me a look. I smiled. She shook her head again. I got this reaction a lot. "Did you tell him I was coming?"

"No. I didn't want him to run away."

"Touché." I looked in the den. Zachary sat on the couch, his back to us, shoulders and head showing over the backrest. He played *Halo 3*. I didn't notice him wearing a headset. "He doesn't play online?" I whispered.

"No, we never let the consoles online," Pauline said.

"All right. I'll see what I can do."

"Thanks, C.T."

I walked in and watched Zachary play for a minute. If he noticed me, he didn't give any indication. He leaned forward as his character approached a slew of enemies. A few seconds later, he'd dispatched them all and not even taken a shot in return. I stopped playing the *Halo* series after the first one, and while I got good, I never approached those skills. Of course, I made up for it by having chops in more important areas. Zachary sat engrossed in the game. I walked around the sofa and sat on the opposite end. It took him a minute and another two encounters to notice I was there. "What are you doing here?" he said.

"Watching you play *Halo 3*," I said.

He smiled a little. "I'm good at it."

"Yes, you are."

Another enemy bit the dust. "Did my mother ask you to come?"

"She did."

"And talk to me?"

"She didn't ask me to watch you play video games," I said.

He snorted and shook his head. "She worries too much."

"Because you don't need any help."

"Damn right," he said. Our conversation, such as it was, didn't detract from his Halo prowess.

"You have it all figured out," I said. "Must be nice."

"I'm a lot smarter than she gives me credit for."

"I was like you when I was your age. I thought I knew everything and didn't need help with anything." Maybe I hadn't changed a lot in those respects, but I kept the reality to myself.

"Yeah? What happened?"

"Then I lost someone I cared about, too."

He finally gave me more than just a sideways glance. I saw the veneer crack. The hard look in his eyes—probably practiced in a mirror—yielded to a genuine curiosity. For the first time, I think he saw me as something other than an adversary. "What happened?" Zachary said in a small voice.

"My sister died. I was sixteen. She was nineteen and in college."

"Did someone kill her?"

I shook my head. "Heart defect. No one noticed it before. They didn't have the technology to look for it when she was a kid, I guess." I saw things shimmer and blur in my peripheral vision.

"Wow. That sucks, man. I'm sorry."

"Thanks. I won't pretend I know what you're going through. Even if my father died, everyone's loss is different, and everyone grieves differently."

"What did you do after . . . after it happened?"

"I walled myself off," I said. "Didn't want to talk to anyone or deal with anything. I didn't care about school or sports."

"Were you close?"

"Closer than I would have admitted. We were really tight." My eyes welled up more. Even now, over a dozen years after Samantha died, talking about her death still hit me like a brass-knuckled punch in the solar plexus. "I had my share of friends, but Samantha was probably my best. I talked to her about anything and everything."

"Did she confide in you, too?"

"Some. Not as much as I did in her, but she was three years older and had been through a lot more. She didn't need to talk as much."

"How did you get through it?" I saw Zachary's eyes brimming now. I wondered if he had allowed himself to cry since the mess with his father went down.

"I tried to be tough. My parents were destroyed. I wanted to be the strong one." I paused for a couple of measured breaths. "The reality is I shouldn't have been. I needed to grieve right along with them. My grades suffered for a quarter before I came to my senses and got myself back on track."

"And you're OK now?"

I nodded. "It's been a while, but it's also taken a while, in some respects. It's supposed to."

A tear slid down Zachary's cheek. He made no move to stop it. He simply nodded, and then the tears flowed. The controller hit the floor, and he drew his knees to his chest and sobbed. I wiped my eyes and stood. Pauline dashed into the room. She knelt on the floor in front of Zachary. He saw her and collapsed into her arms. She told him it would be OK as he wept on her shoulder. Pauline cried, too.

I let myself out.

I NEEDED TO KNOW MORE, a common theme in my cases. People don't tell me enough, or I don't gather enough information at first, or people lie, and what have you. In this case, I wanted to know more about David Rosenberg. How deep were his pockets? Did he have a cache of backup goons to replace the two I had taken out of commission? How soon would he come after someone in my situation—or someone in Pauline's—and how hard would he pursue?

As usual, I started my searches online. This time, I wanted to find people who had dealt with the seedier side of Rosenberg. I meticulously organize my bookmarks (one of the few things in my life to get such treatment), and in my "Active Case" folder, I saw the link for the blog with the wonderful title "David Rosenberg is an Asshole." Unless the founder already tried on a pair of cement shoes, I figured Rosenberg's reported ruthlessness did not extend to carrying out a Google search.

The post wasn't particularly well-written, but I found the speculation interesting. A woman created the blog to spread the word David Rosenberg is, in fact, an asshole, especially because he might be involved in kidnapping in addition to loan sharking. The woman and her husband borrowed from Rosenberg for home improvements. Stuff happened, and they were unable to pay. A couple weeks later, their daughter went missing, never to be seen again. The blogger provided few other details. I hunted for them anyway.

Most people are not nearly as anonymous online as they think. This woman registered an actual website, not just a random blog. It made finding her easier. Within a few minutes, I'd gathered all her contact information. It didn't involve any underhanded methods, either—the information is freely available via WHOIS records. I might know how to find it quicker, but anyone could have looked it up with a little bit of know-how—including David Rosenberg.

I called the phone number listed on the registration. When a pleasant female voice answered, I said, "Is this Anne Horton?"

"Yes, this is she." Ah, an educated woman.

"Mrs. Horton, my name is C.T. Ferguson. I came across your website dedicated to David Rosenberg today."

She paused. "How did you find me?"

"I'm a private investigator who shares your sentiments about Mr. Rosenberg."

"You're investigating him?" she said.

"Sort of. I'd rather explain it to you in person. Could we meet somewhere?"

"How well do you know Harford County?"

"My GPS fills in the gaps for me," I said.

"Can it find Java by the Bay in Havre de Grace?"

"I'm sure it can."

"I can meet you in an hour," she said.

"I'll be there. Thank you."

* * *

AN HOUR and four minutes later, I walked into the front door of Java by the Bay. It was more wide than deep, with a counter toward the back, several coffee pots, a menu that would shame a national coffee chain, and a basket of fresh baked items near the register. The small lunch I inhaled before I left needed a delicious slice of carrot cake to be complete, so I ordered one to go along with my vanilla latte. The girl who rang up my purchase appeared to have just finished high school. The woman who sat at a table along the left wall resembled a high school teacher.

She had a serious face, but it became friendlier as she offered me a tentative smile. Her white blouse was buttoned high enough to give her trouble breathing if she leaned forward. She paired it with blue business slacks and brown flats. I carried my coffee and carrot cake to the table. "Anne Horton?" I said.

"You must be Mr. Ferguson," she said. Her smile broadened. "Please, have a seat." She gestured with a sweep of her hand.

"Please, call me C.T."

"Well, C.T., I must say, you're a little younger than I thought you'd be."

"I have an old soul and a healthy love of classic rock."

She chuckled. "I hate to sound so . . . official, but do you have any ID?"

"Sure." I set my license out for her to see. After a sharp bob of her head, I put it away. "Thanks for meeting with me."

"You say you're investigating Rosenberg?" She sneered when uttering his name, making it sound like she snarled it. I understood.

"My client is in a similar situation to yours. The difference is her husband has died, and she can't make the payments."

"That's terrible." Anne Horton shook her head this time. "We weren't able to because Peter lost his job. I work part-time, and we live paycheck-to-paycheck as it is."

"How did you hear about Rosenberg?"

"One of Peter's coworkers borrowed from him. Said it was easy." She snorted. "Nothing was easy about it, except getting the money. The bastard makes that part real easy."

"How long before . . . uh—"

"Before Amy disappeared?" She spared me asking it; I couldn't think of a way without coming off as indelicate. "Two months. We missed our first payment, told them it would be a little late. Rosenberg's people said they understood. We paid what we could. And then . . ." She trailed off, sighed, and took a drink of her coffee. I wished I had something stronger to offer her.

"How old was she when it happened?"

Anne looked at her coffee lid as if the answer were written on it. "Sixteen. She just started her junior year at Havre de Grace High."

"I have to ask, but I presume you never got any proof Rosenberg had anything to do with it?"

"Of course not." Anne laughed a bitter laugh. "He didn't know anything about lending money, either. Absolutely no idea who we were or what our story was about."

"And the police believed him?"

"The sheriff's office up here worked with Baltimore County on it. They didn't get anywhere. Either he has a good cover story or some cops on the payroll."

"Did they take a report?"

"No." She attempted another bitter laugh but this one died at a chuckle. "They told us they talked to Rosenberg and couldn't find any basis for a case. One of them even said I'm lucky they didn't go after me for filing a false report." Anne took a slow, measured breath. I was almost surprised it didn't set the table aflame.

"How long has it been?"

"Two years. Amy's eighteen now." She wiped at her eyes. "Though I don't know where she is . . . or if she's even alive." Her eyes closed; when they opened, they were wet with tears and pointed right at me. "Do you think you could find her?"

I had a feeling she would ask at some point and really hoped she wouldn't. Antarctic passes trod by penguins would be warmer than the trail of Amy Horton. "Honestly, I doubt it," I said. "But I'll see what I can do."

"That's all I can ask," she said. "It's certainly more than the police did."

"I aim to please," I said.

* * *

Now I NEEDED to warn Pauline, as if she didn't have enough on her mind. *Yes, I know your husband got killed, and a loan shark is looking to sink his teeth into you, and by the way, your daughter might get kidnapped if you can't pay up.* I didn't even have to say it aloud to know how it sounded and how it would be received. Pauline had enough on her mind. Maybe I could talk to Katherine directly.

Pauline gave me her kids' cell phone numbers in case I needed them in an emergency. This certainly counted. I called Katherine's cell phone. "Hello?" she said after three rings.

"Katherine, this is C.T. Ferguson. I'm the P.I. your mom hired."

"Oh, hey. What's up?"

"Do you have a few minutes? I need to talk to you about something."

"Can you talk to my mom about it?"

"Not really. This is something I should discuss with you."

She sighed. *Sorry to inconvenience you, Katherine. Let me know how the duct tape and windowless cargo van feel.* "Like, I could meet you later. I have a break now, then a lab, then a study group."

"What time?" I said.

"How about seven?"

"Sure. Barnes and Noble café not far from your campus?"

"I'll be there."

* * *

She wasn't.

I surprised myself by being a couple minutes early. Traffic hadn't been as bad as I expected, leading to a surplus in my time budget. I used it for watching coeds as they came and went. Some of them could be felons. I needed to make sure they weren't carrying guns, and verifying this required diligent inspection. Some may call it a burden, but I'm happy to serve.

On my second vanilla latte, I got the inkling Katherine wasn't going to make it. It was already seven-thirty and not a peep from her. Her lab or study group could have run late, but she would have been raised with the good manners to call in such a case. I tried her cell phone, and it went directly to voicemail. I hung up without leaving a message.

At quarter of eight, I tossed my cup away and started for the door when I saw Katherine walking through the store toward the café. She held out her hands. "I'm so sorry," she said. "My lab ran over, then my study group did, too. And then my phone battery died, so I couldn't call you. I'm sorry."

"It's OK," I said. I didn't add my concern for her well-being and my fears she had been abducted from Goucher's campus by a cadre of hooded Rosenberg henchmen. "As you may have learned in a philosophy class, shit happens."

She smiled. "I'm going to get a coffee. You want anything?"

"I've already had two, but thank you."

I watched Katherine as she got in line. She moved with a confidence college boys—and men past the age of higher learning—would find attractive. It helped she was quite pretty on top of it all. If she were to get kidnapped, I didn't want to speculate what might happen to her. Unfortunately, I figured I would need to once we got into the meat of our conversation.

Katherine sat opposite me a couple minutes later, armed with a drink smelling faintly of caramel. She brushed golden hair off her shoulder. It took all of my miniscule professionalism not to peek at her chest. If she turned away to look at something, the professionalism may crumble under the strain. "So, what's going on?" she said. "It sounded important."

"It might be," I said, "and I don't want to pile on your mom with everything she's already been through."

"I'm sure she would appreciate that."

I lowered my voice. The café wasn't crowded, but I valued discretion for something like this. "I've done additional investigation into Rosenberg, the man your father borrowed the money from. One couple found themselves unable to repay the loan when the husband lost his job. Not long after, their sixteen-year-old daughter got kidnapped."

Her cup stopped in mid-trip to her lips. "That's terrible." She frowned. "What happened to her?"

"I don't know," I said. "The parents never heard anything. It's been two years."

"Wow. I don't know how they go on in a situation like that."

"Hope sustains them, I'm sure, but it has to be fading with every passing day."

"Are you concerned something like that will happen to me?" she said.

"I think the possibility has to be acknowledged," I said. "It's a very small sample size, of course, but you need to be aware you could be a target."

Katherine stared at the table for a minute before she found her voice again. "My mother can't pay him, can she?"

"Not all the money, no. He's allowing her to use a payment plan, but it's not exactly the kind with a fifty-dollar minimum each month."

She picked up her coffee again, swirled it, watched a little spill out the hole at the top, and frowned. "What should I do?" she said as she blotted the tiny mess with a napkin.

"Be alert. Be cautious. Try to go out in groups. Minimize the time you're by yourself, even if it's only walking to or from your car on campus. I don't know if you're going to be a target, but I think you need to be vigilant for the possibility."

"Yeah, I should." She still hadn't drunk any of her coffee. "I'll try to carpool. If I can't, I'll park near other people going to the same building."

"I know it sucks to change your life around," I said, "but hopefully, it won't be for long."

"You're still looking into this guy?"

I nodded. "There's not a lot out there about him. He's done a good job of staying under the radar, which I'm sure is the way he wants it."

"You'll get him." She smiled for the first time since we'd started talking. I would have been a sucker for her smile in college. It was the kind to reach into your gut and light a fire burning in both directions. "You seem like you know what you're doing."

"It doesn't mean I actually do," I said.

"I know." She took the first sip and smiled again. "But I have faith in you."

"Thank you." I gave her my most polished grin. She deserved it for giving me a mini-pep talk after I dropped some lousy news on her. "I'll do my best to earn it."

"I think you'll earn it just fine."

A few minutes later, I walked Katherine to her car. She parked in the nearby Bahama Breeze garage, belonging to an island-themed restaurant, but the building boasted of a convenient Towson location and never closed. In an area begging for more parking, this made the garage popular with far more people than only restaurant patrons. She drove a Saturn of indeterminate year looking to be in good condition. I hoped the car and Katherine both remained untouched by Rosenberg.

* * *

BECAUSE SLIMEBALLS HIRE EXPERTS, Rosenberg naturally employed an accountant. I needed to know who he used. The books were probably cooked, but I could glean something from them. In the meantime, I would settle for his bank records. Like a good paranoid loan shark, Rosenberg stashed his money with a small local bank. The good news for him was it would take a while for someone to think of looking there. The bad news was smaller banks didn't have the security of larger banks. Once I unearthed his accounts, it didn't take me long to get the details.

I printed information for Rosenberg's personal and business accounts, going back three years. If he used another account tied to the loan sharking business, it could take some time to find. I didn't even know where to start looking. It's not like "Rosenberg Usury LLC" would be on an account in a bank somewhere.

I collected the printouts and looked them over. While I took an accounting class in college, I couldn't claim to be much of a specialist in it. I spent most of the class time checking out a few girls, and a good bit of my study time doing things other than studying with those girls. The B-plus I got in the course stood as a monument to the ease of basic accounting more than the work put into it.

Rosenberg's business account looked legitimate as far as I could tell. Expenses were clearly categorized and went with matching invoice or check numbers. Revenues accompanied invoice numbers, as well. Nothing jumped out as a bogus charge or expense. Maybe I would need an accountant to look this over. Maybe Rollins minored in accounting before he went into the Army.

Maybe I would win the lottery based solely on my charm and good looks.

I dealt with overseas banks before, so I knew a few ways to go snooping around over there. It took a while of careful looking and more judicious footprint-erasing, but I found an account for Rosenberg. Even though the US government made it illegal for American citizens to have overseas accounts, it doesn't deter someone who is enough of a scofflaw to be a loan shark. Banks in places like Grand Cayman offer discretion, which is better for their clients, and upgraded security, which is worse for dashing, enterprising hackers. I hacked the Chinese national bank during my time in Hong Kong, though; I could tackle this.

After some trial and error, I got in. Rosenberg made semi-regular deposits here, presumably the profits from his illicit lending operation. I looked at his statement and watched those deposits get smaller and less frequent over time. Several transactions caught my eye, including the occasional deposits of twenty thousand dollars. Those stood out among the nickels and dimes composing Rosenberg's other transactions.

As I put all these boring printouts and spreadsheets away, I realized I still didn't know who Rosenberg's accountant was. I went back to his business account and perused the expenses. Every month, he wrote a check to Eisenberg Accounting LLC. Despite his apparently flagging profits, Rosenberg paid Eisenberg the same amount. I wondered how much Eisenberg knew. If he were cooking the books, why would they show declining profits? Was Rosenberg stashing the money someplace else?

Tomorrow, I would talk to Eisenberg to discover these things, and I would take Rollins with me.

CHAPTER 10

AFTER I WOKE UP THE NEXT MORNING, I LEFT GLORIA
sleeping and went downstairs to call Rollins. He sounded more
awake than I felt. "Top of the morning to you," he said.

"I have a couple things I want to do today," I said, "and I may
need your help with them."

"What'd you have in mind?"

"The loan shark I'm looking into has an accountant. I want to
find out some things from him. If my usual powers of persuasion
let me down, I'll need you to step in and do a little extra
convincing."

"I think I can manage. Accountants scare easy."

"There's more."

"Shoot."

I said, "I might have a chat with the shark, too, depending on
how things go with the accountant."

Rollins paused for a deep breath. "You sure your plan is
wise?"

"I'm not proposing we jump into his tank without looking
first and coming up with a strategy."

"So you'd like to use my tactical expertise?" said Rollins.

"You charge extra?"

"No, I just like to say it. When are we starting all this?"

I looked at my watch: eight-fifty. "Come by at ten-thirty. We'll take my car."

"I'm not sure you driving is a good idea," he cautioned.

"You haven't seen this car yet," I said.

* * *

"WHERE THE HELL did you get this?" Rollins said from the passenger's seat.

"I've gotten used to people asking," I said, "though rarely with such envy in their voices."

Rollins sipped coconut water through a straw from a pink sports bottle. "I'm pretty sure it wasn't envy."

We rode in my blue Caprice Classic. It looked unlike any other car I owned, mainly because it was a car I wouldn't be caught dead in. If my corpse were found in the trunk of a Caprice, mine would be a restless spirit. "I took a difficult case a few months ago," I said. "I needed a car on a budget, so I called an automotive reconfiguration engineer, and he happened to have this ready to go."

"Automotive reconfiguration engineer?" Rollins said with an amused smile.

"I think he needs to put it on his business cards."

"So you got it from a chop shop."

I nodded. "And in the intervening time, I've contracted for a few improvements."

"Like what?"

"They added bullet-resistant glass and redid the body to be close to bulletproof. The stock engine couldn't handle the added weight, so it's got a newer and stronger one."

"Its windows check handgun fire, then, and the body's level three reinforced with Kevlar."

"You and your fancy Army terms."

"Sounds useful. Let's hope you never have to see how well it works. Where are we going first?"

"The accountant's office."

"Why?" said Rollins.

"I think we'll be more successful there," I said. "Might as well start the day on a good note."

"Norman Vincent Peale would be proud."

"I think Leibniz would see through my façade, though, and Voltaire might shake my hand."

Rollins shook his head. "You and your fancy philosophers," he said.

* * *

EISENBERG ACCOUNTING LLC occupied a tiny office in Fells Point. It was crammed into a house with a couple of other businesses who shared the space because none could afford even half the rent alone. At least Eisenberg made up for it by having a professional-looking name placard on his door. He left it slightly ajar. I peeked in and saw someone at the desk, so I knocked. "Come in," he said.

Rollins barred his arm to block my path, then entered first. I would need to get used to certain aspects of having a bodyguard. The fortyish man behind the desk wore the kind of suit sharing a rowhouse four ways would suggest. He maintained a cluttered desk stacked with ledger books, random papers, and a large calculator. So much for Excel. Rollins sat in one of the two task chairs. I sat in the other.

"Can I help you?" the man behind the desk said.

"Are you Mr. Eisenberg?" I said.

He somehow found a business card and a small clear path on

top and slid the card toward me. "That's me. What can I help you with?"

"I think my desk is too neat. I could use some advice on disorganizing it."

Eisenberg looked at me and frowned. "I'm a busy man. Jokes aren't on the calendar."

"You might also be able to help me with some accounting."

"Now we're talking," he said. "What kind of help do you need?"

"My friend here is an . . . independent loan consultant." Rollins gave me a look, but I kept going. "We need someone of your expertise to make sure his books appear on the up-and-up."

"Well," Eisenberg said with a forced chuckle, "I'm not sure what you've heard, but I'm not that kind of accountant." He added a forced smile to try and look sincere. I didn't buy it.

"You have a good reference from David Rosenberg," I said.

The forced smile fled. "Would it help if I said I don't know who he is?"

"Not at all," Rollins said. He shifted in the chair, allowing Eisenberg a view of the gun under his fashionable tan suede jacket. "I think we need to have a conversation."

"Maybe over brunch?" Eisenberg said. "My treat." If the gun scared him, he did an excellent job of hiding it.

"As long as you don't make a scene or do something stupid," Rollins said.

"We're not after you," I said. "I don't care if you're a good or bad accountant or if you cook everyone's books. You're a means to an end, and the end is Rosenberg."

Eisenberg's head bobbed. Some of the color left his face, chasing the smile. I think he realized the situation he was in. "No tricks. Just brunch."

"Name your place," Rollins said.

* * *

BRUNCH HAS BECOME trendy in Baltimore. Even taverns which shouldn't venture beyond serving alcohol and peanuts manage to find a way to cram in some tables and pack the menu with omelets, bacon, and danishes. It's become a competitive cottage industry. Most of those places only served food at traditional brunch times on Sundays. During the week, if they were open, the menu only held liquid lunch choices. Eisenberg chose Brick Oven Pizzeria. I liked the place, so I didn't bother arguing the technicalities.

Neither Rollins nor I were particularly hungry, so Eisenberg ordered a large pizza with tomatoes, green peppers, and mushrooms. We said we would each eat a slice or two. After Eisenberg paid cash for lunch, we all got our beverages and walked across the uncrowded restaurant to a table as far from the counter as possible. I wondered when the lunch crowd would roll in. At least I could amuse myself by looking at the Baltimore-themed table toppers if Eisenberg started droning on about accounting principles.

"What is it you need to know about . . . one client of mine?" he said.

"I've seen his financials," I said. "All of them."

Eisenberg's eyes went wide. "How did you do that?"

"Let's just say I have a problem with electronic boundaries. Regardless, I looked at the numbers. I admit I'm not an accountant, but something doesn't look right."

"Meaning what?" Eisenberg moved his straw around in the lid.

"I think you know what he's getting at," Rollins said. His jacket remained zipped up about two thirds of the way. No gun visible.

"The books are cooked."

"Maybe even better than the pizza we're about to eat," I said. "Though I admit it would be a challenge."

Eisenberg pursed his lips. "My client isn't really profitable anymore," he said after a moment. "His legitimate business is struggling. Restaurant supply is dependent upon a base of thriving restaurants. It's not there anymore for a few reasons." He stopped to take a drink of his soda but didn't elaborate on the eatery challenges. It was just as well because our pizza came out then. The lady behind the counter dropped it off with a friendly smile as a few lunch eaters trickled in.

"What about his illegitimate business?" I said after a bite of pizza. I'd never sampled a vegetarian pizza from Brick Oven before. I would have one again.

"As you can imagine, this economy isn't the most fertile playground for . . . a man in his profession. With interest rates up, you'd think people would seek more . . . independent loans, but they're not. They're finding ways to save, cut back on expenses, things like that." He took a large bite of pizza.

"Or simply not paying their mortgages," Rollins said.

"It's better now. I advise people against it, regardless of the value of their home versus its loan."

"So you're saying Rosenberg isn't exactly raking in the dough in either business," I said.

"Yes."

"He's getting income from somewhere, though. I've seen it but I can't figure out where it's coming from."

"I know what you're talking about." Eisenberg grabbed another slice and tore into it. He talked around the food in his mouth and managed not to be gross. He must have been well-practiced in the art. "I don't know the source of it, either. He hasn't told me."

"Have you asked?" said Rollins.

"Not directly. You learn not to pose such questions to a man like him directly."

"I'm sure you do."

"Any speculation on where it may have come from?" I said. I finished my slice. This was early for lunch, but I grabbed a second. I could always have something small later in the afternoon.

"Speculation is all it would be," Eisenberg said.

"You know the man and his situation. Your insight could be valuable."

"I really don't have any good ideas. Obviously, he found a way to make some money he doesn't want many people to know about."

"So it has to be more unsavory than what he already does," I said.

"Why?"

"Otherwise, I presume he would tell you. You know what his . . . second job is, after all. Why not tell you about a third?"

"Your suspicion may be valid," he said. "I danced around it a little and tried to get him to say something about it, but he tends to play things close to the vest."

"If you find out where the money's coming from, I'd appreciate a call." I showed him a business card but didn't give it to him. "Your client knows who I am," I said when I saw his puzzled expression, "and he doesn't like me. It's better for you if you don't have one on you."

"Then it's fortunate I have a good memory for numbers."

"Sounds useful in your line of work," I said.

Eisenberg smiled before taking a bite. "Very much so."

* * *

I FELT Rollins staring at me in the car as we made the short drive back to Federal Hill. "Something on your mind?" I said.

"You don't think you played it a little loose in there?" he said.

"Not really. I might have been able to hold back some, but I wanted him to know what was going on."

He looked at me again before saying anything. "You think he knows more than he's telling you."

"Of course he does. You don't work for a guy like Rosenberg and run off at the mouth about it."

"And you think he's eventually going to run off at the mouth?"

"Probably not. I don't think he knows everything, but he knows some things, and now he's curious to know more."

"And you'll learn it from him . . . how?"

"You heard him say he does everything on his computer."

"Yeah, so?"

I smiled. "Computers are often easier to learn from than people."

"You're going to hack him?"

"If I need to."

"Man," Rollins said with a chuckle, "the colonel was right about you. You are one unconventional cat."

"Colonel Stevens called me a cat?"

"I'm paraphrasing."

"I thought you might be," I said.

* * *

WE SAT outside Rosenberg's Restaurant Supply. I wanted to discover more about his operation and where the money came from. Staking out the place didn't have the best odds of helping with those, but it couldn't hurt. Besides, I was at a loss for anything else to do. Rollins sat shotgun most of the time. Occasionally, he got out and walked around, always heading closer to

Rosenberg's. It looked like a normal operation when I visited, and nothing I saw while sitting outside made me change this impression.

Rollins walked to a coffee shop and fetched us some hot drinks. He wrinkled his nose at my usual vanilla latte but got me one anyway. His smelled so strongly of caramel I thought he dipped his hands in it. "Your macchiato is sickeningly sweet," I said.

"Just how I like it," he said.

I was getting a sugar rush just sitting in the Caprice. "I might have to go for a longer run tomorrow. You'll have eight hundred calories of caramel to burn off."

Rollins smiled and took another sip. "I'll be OK." I harbored no doubt. Rollins looked like a guy with a negative body fat percentage. He wasn't muscle-bound, but anyone could see he kept himself in peak condition. His metabolism could probably burn off the caramel drink with an hour of vigorous blinking. I envied him.

A little while later, Jasper ambled out and got into a silver Mercedes sedan. "He's one of Rosenberg's big men," I said.

"You gonna follow him?"

"Seems more exciting than sitting here watching birds congregate on the roofs."

I pulled out after Jasper drove by. Rich had given me some pointers on following other cars before, but I learned a lot from movies and TV shows. Rollins didn't criticize me, so I must have been doing something right. I kept two or three cars between Jasper and me the whole time. His silver Mercedes proved easy to play tag with.

"What if he's picking up lunch?" Rollins said.

"Then we will have followed for nothing," I said. "Though I guess learning where Rosenberg and his crew eat might be useful."

"Sure. You wanna poison their food, you know who to give the powder to." Rollins finished with a chuckle. I decided not to tell him about the time I "poisoned" Vinny Serrano's food to make him suffer and coax a pointless confession.

"You never know; we might have to." Rollins shook his head and smirked. "What's funny?" I said. "Does poisoning someone's food cost me extra?"

"Depends on how well you want it done."

Jasper pulled into a deli. A lunch run. Great. I kept going along the side street and picked up Reisterstown Road again two blocks down. Before Jasper returned, we reclaimed our spot watching Rosenberg's business. Jasper got out of his car and walked in carrying an unwieldy bag of food in his arms. He used an RFID badge to open a side door. I made a mental note of it. It was the only useful memo added to my mental notepad.

* * *

LATER IN THE EVENING, I got a call on my cell phone from a number I didn't recognize. Before I became a private investigator, it used to bother me. Now I've gotten used to it. I always hope for a breathy female voice to be on the other end of the call, and I am frequently disappointed. "Hello?"

"They got her," said a male voice. He sounded more breathless than breathy. Disappointed again.

"Got whom? Who is this?"

"Zachary. They got her, man. They got my sister." His voice cracked as he spoke. "I tried to stop them, but . . ."

"Slow down," I said, sitting up fully in the chair. "Who took your sister?"

"Some guys. I don't know them. They got her right in front of our house."

Rosenberg was definitely involved. What if I'd pressed and

looked harder and longer into his enterprise? What if I'd let
Rollins bounce his accountant off the pavement a few times?
None of those thoughts did Katherine Rodgers any good at the
moment. I expelled them from my head. "Is your mom home?"

"No, I haven't called her yet."

Why the hell not? "OK, I'm on my way over there. Call your
mom when we hang up. Don't call the cops. Tell her not to,
either. Make sure she understands."

"I will. Oh, man, why couldn't I stop them? Now they've got
her and who knows what . . ." Zachary's voice cracked and broke
again as he dissolved into tears. I sympathized.

"Zach, listen to me. Your father's gone. You're the man now.
Hold it together for your mother." He sniffled on the other end of
the connection. "Can you do it?"

"Yeah," he said in a small voice, then cleared his throat.
"Yeah, I can." He sounded better in control.

"All right, I'll be there as soon as I can." I hung up and called
Rollins.

"What's happening?" he said.

"My client's daughter just got kidnapped," I said.

"Shit. Who called you?"

"Her little brother. He said he tried to stop them."

"It's getting real now. Your loan shark smells blood in the
water."

"Yeah, thanks for the update."

"Just sayin'," he said. "He couldn't kill you, so he takes the
girl. You keeping cops out of it?"

"As long as I have to. Where are you?"

"Half a block from your house."

"Meet me at the Caprice," I said.

CHAPTER 11

I CALLED RICH AS ROLLINS AND I DROVE TOWARD THE Rodgers house. He answered in a tired voice. "Hello?"

"Rich, I might need your help with something," I said.

"Color me surprised. What's up?"

I let the slight pass. Katherine Rodgers was more important than my ego, at least for now. "The loan shark, Rosenberg, might be dabbling in kidnapping."

"What?" The weariness fled Rich's voice. "What happened?"

"My client's son called me," I said. "His sister got taken from in front of their house."

"Rosenberg did it?"

"Don't know yet, but who else is a good candidate?"

"Fair point," said Rich. "Have you called the police yet?"

"Does calling you count?"

"What do you think?" I heard agitation creep into Rich's tone. It happened often when we talked.

"I think having a bunch of cops sniffing around Rosenberg's operation isn't going to help Katherine Rodgers."

Rich didn't say anything for a few seconds. "You might be right. We don't even know for sure he took her, though it seems likely. Look, I just worked a long shift, and now I'm off for two days. I'll meet you at the Rodgers house."

I was stunned, and it made me pause for a second. "All right . . . great."

"But if we're not hot on this girl's trail quickly," he said, "we're going to get more people involved."

I figured as much. "I guess we will."

"We will. What's their address again?"

I gave it to him.

* * *

By the time Rollins and I got there, Pauline was home and looked like she wanted to jump off a bridge. Zachary tried to comfort her, but there was none to be found. His face sported a couple of bruises—one would turn into a hell of a shiner—and a laceration he should probably get stitched. Haunted eyes reflected sadness and failure. He thought he let his sister down when he couldn't stop Rosenberg's toughs from taking her. I would need to talk to him, but I needed to talk to Pauline first.

As I sat beside her, she gaped at me and sobbed. Before I could say anything, she sagged against me, head on my shoulder and arms wrapped loosely around me. I patted her back and let her cry. Rollins took stock inside, then went outside and searched some more. Pauline's bawling slowed when he returned. I caught his eye, and he shook his head.

Pauline sat up and stared at Rollins. "Who's he?" she said through her tears.

"His name is Rollins," I said. "I hired him to help me after I got shot at a few days ago."

Her acknowledgement was lost in a couple of final sobs, and I handed Pauline a box of tissues from the end table. She took one without comment and wiped her eyes, then blew her nose loudly enough to stop traffic two blocks over. As if on cue, I heard a car door slam out front. Rollins turned toward the sound and looked out the window. "Looks like a cop, whoever it is," he said.

"My cousin," I said, "and he is a cop. We can trust him."

"Are you sure we should have the police here?" Pauline said, composing herself.

"We're not going to ignore what happened," I said. "But we're not going to spook Rosenberg by having a SWAT team descend on him, either. At least, not yet."

"I really don't want to involve the police."

"I don't blame you. I try to involve them as little as possible."

Rollins let Rich in, and he looked around before sitting on the ottoman. "What's the situation?" he said.

"Katherine is missing," Pauline said. She burst into tears again.

"Any word from whoever took her?"

"Nothing," I said.

Rich looked at Zachary. "Could you identify the men?"

The kid stepped forward. "They wore ski masks, but I could see their eyes. They looked Asian."

"Asian?" Rich and I said in unison.

"Yeah. Definitely turned up at the corner. The right complexion to be Asian, too."

"I didn't see any Asians at Rosenberg's place," I said. Jasper's face showed Asian ancestry, but not enough to count in Zachary's scenario.

"Of course you went to his place," Rich said.

"Not now, Rich. He might have replaced the two guys I took out. Asian goons need jobs, too."

"We need eyes on Rosenberg," Rich said.

"You and I can stake it out tomorrow," I said. "We'll take your car. They might've noticed the Caprice."

"What about tonight?" Pauline said. Makeup had run down

her face, giving her the effect of wearing a sinister mask. It made her voice rising to a shriek much more potent. "My daughter is missing right now! Who knows what those guys are doing to her?" She glared at all of us. Zachary tried to console her, but she shoved his arm away and stormed out of the room.

"The lady raises a point," Rollins said after everyone digested Pauline's rampage. "What about tonight? Staking out Rosenberg's place tomorrow is great, but we got ten hours or so until anyone shows up there. Lot of time."

"We'll do what we can," Rich said. He frowned. "Maybe we shouldn't keep this off the books. Maybe we should lean on Rosenberg."

"And if it gets Katherine killed?" I said.

Rich sighed.

"I know you don't like doing things my way," I went on, "but I think keeping this unofficial is in her best interests right now."

"What if we get a ransom demand?" Zachary said.

"Then we make it official," Rich said. "Even if he says no cops. They all say it."

"Until then, we're looking into this on our own," I said. "Let's start with where it happened. Zach, come outside with us."

He brightened a little. "Can I go on the stakeout with you guys?"

"No," we all said at once.

He frowned. We went outside.

* * *

RICH AND ROLLINS pored over the sidewalk and the patch of grass between it and the curb. I left them to it. They had training in this I didn't. They crouched, studied the grass, whispered back and forth, and eventually moved into the street, doing the whole thing again from a different angle. I tried a more direct approach.

"Tell me what happened," I said to Zachary, keeping my voice low so as not to disturb the masters at work.

"We parked there," he said, pointing to a gray Supra parked at the curb. "There was another car parked in front of the house. When we walked past it, these two guys got out and told Katherine to get in." Zachary shook frustrated fists. "She told them to fuck off. So did I. They tried to grab her, and I tried to fight them." He sighed. "I couldn't. I'm on the wrestling team . . . I should be good at fighting off a couple of guys like them."

"It's not your fault," I told him.

"If I could have protected her, she'd be in our house right now."

"These guys got hired because teenaged brothers can't take them down. They're good at what they do."

"I guess," he said.

"They are," I said. "It's why assholes like Rosenberg hire them. Look, I know good wrestlers can overpower the average person. These guys are pros. They were probably bigger more experienced."

"Yeah."

"Don't beat yourself up over it." I clapped him on the shoulder. "You did your best."

"Now you guys need to do your best," he said.

"We will."

"Can I come along?"

I declined. "Your mom needs you. If you're gone, she's all alone, and I don't think it's a good idea right now."

Zachary offered a small smile. "You're right. I have to be here for her."

Rich and Rollins joined us. "Did you put your ears to the ground?" I said.

"Just tried to get a feel for what happened," Rollins said.

"I got one, too, by talking to Zachary. Easier than counting broken blades of grass."

Rollins continued like he didn't hear me. "Looks like two guys walked up. There was a struggle. Two people hit the ground. Someone tried to make a break for it but only got a couple steps away. Then there are long strides toward the car."

"I could have told you all that shit," Zachary said.

"Sometimes, it's good to find things out for yourself," Rollins said.

"At least you took one of them down," Rich said.

"Yeah," Zachary said. He turned around and walked back into the house.

"Poor kid," said Rich. "He thinks he could've stopped them."

"Let's make sure he's not a poor kid because he has to bury his sister," I said. "I would rather spare him the pain." I knew all too well how it felt, and I was Zachary's age when it happened.

"What's the move, then?" Rich said.

"We need to know who these Asian guys are. Do they work for Rosenberg? Can you ask around discreetly and see what you get?"

Rich gave a rare gesture of agreement. "Discretion will be my middle name."

"I'm going to look more into Rosenberg," I said. "I've done a lot of digging already. Obviously I need to go deeper. I'll try and track Katherine's phone, too, but I'm sure it'll be a dead-end."

"What about me?" Rollins said.

"Keep an eye on Rosenberg. His house, his work, wherever. If he takes a shit, you should know what he ate for breakfast."

"I'm on it."

"We'll all check in with each other in the morning, see where we stand," I said. "How about seven? Then we can all keep an eye on Rosenberg for whatever turns up. Sound good?"

They both nodded. Rich left. I drove Rollins back to my house.

A busy night loomed ahead of us.

* * *

KATHERINE'S PHONE gave me nothing. The last location it reported to a cell tower was about a hundred feet from her front door. Her kidnappers must have destroyed the phone as they drove away. Smart. They'd done this before. Amateurs may have turned it off, which wasn't enough. We were dealing with a pro team.

With the cell tower a dead end, I looked for some ties between Rosenberg and the Asian community. Trying to find this kind of information online was like trying to navigate a labyrinth with a dying flashlight. I could uncover a lot of things in cyber-space, but data like this eluded me. Goons of any persuasion, Asian or otherwise, didn't exactly maintain message boards talking about good opportunities. I needed boots on the ground, so I got in the Caprice and took a drive.

On my way into town, I called Mouse, an informant who worked for the police and sometimes fed me miscellaneous data. "I need some information," I said when he picked up

"Good thing I'm in the business," he said in his squeaky voice. Despite being older than me, Mouse sounded like he got stuck in the middle of puberty. "What do you need?"

"Can we meet somewhere? I'm on my way into downtown."

"Meet me at the Harbor. I'm tired of the bars."

"Where? It's a big area."

"Outside of McCormick and Schmick's," he said. "I'll be there in ten minutes."

"Me, too," I said.

* * *

ELEVEN MINUTES LATER, I walked toward the Pratt Street
Pavilion. I always found it surprising how Harborplace and its
pavilions were older than me. They don't look especially modern,
and the selection of stores and restaurants seemed chosen by
tossing darts at a list, but the area is the centerpiece of Baltimore's
tourism industry. If only the harbor itself could be cleaned up to
resemble the pavilions. What possessed the ducks to stick around
was a mystery to me. I guess the amount of available bread
outweighed the used condoms, occasional corpses, and other
detritus.

Mouse sat on the pavilion steps leading up to Tir Na Nog in
front of McCormick and Schmick. Both restaurants were as dark
and quiet as graveyards. As usual, Mouse wore all gray. His plain
features, small stature, brown hair, and perpetually drab clothes
earned him his trademark nick. Mouse worked for informant
money and not much else. I didn't even know if he kept a place to
sleep every night.

"You're late," he said as I sat on the stairs beside him. Mouse
scooted to the railing.

"You still expect me to be on time?" I said.

"I'm optimistic. What are you looking for?"

I told Mouse about Katherine Rodgers, giving him a little
background on the case without telling him everything. "Now the
girl is missing. We obviously think Rosenberg did it. Her brother
said the guys who took his sister were Asian."

"And you think it's odd."

I nodded. "He's got one partially Asian guy, but he doesn't
strike me as a goon. The others were either Jewish or Italian."

"You want me to see what people are saying about Rosenberg
and the Asians."

"I knew you'd catch on." I handed Mouse two pictures of

Benjamin Franklin. "Three more for information I can use."

Mouse pocketed the hundreds. "How soon do you need to know?"

"Every hour Katherine is missing makes things worse for her," I said. "The sooner you know something, the better."

"All right." Mouse stood. "Pleasure doing business with you. You pay way better than the cops."

"The perks of not being a public servant are many," I said.

* * *

THE MONEY SITUATION with Rosenberg still bothered me. His accountant wasn't very helpful. I might need to find another bean-counter, but first I needed all of Rosenberg's financial information. A closer look at data on hand would be enough to start. Who could I have look it over once I'd collected all of the books? I realized I knew a lot of people in very disreputable fields, but I didn't really know any accountants.

Then I remembered the funeral home. The man who first tipped me off to the gunshots was a CPA according to his business card. I made a note to call him in the morning. I wrote actual memos at this point because I didn't trust myself to remember mental notes on the menial amount of sleep I expected to get. In my college days, a two-liter of soda, a textbook, and a computer was enough to keep me up all night and straight on 'til morning. Now I would never drink so much carbonated crap in one sitting, and I paid a heavier price for all-nighters. I must be the only person in the world who got old before turning twenty-nine, let alone thirty.

I did more digging into Rosenberg and loan sharks in general. Many supplemented their income with other illegal rackets. If Rosenberg did, I couldn't find any evidence of it. On a lark, I went prowling around the BPD's network to see if they discovered anything unsavory about Rosenberg. Only one arrest on the books for conspiracy to commit kidnapping, but the charges were dropped and nothing further happened with it. I figured a similar charge would show up on every good loan shark's rap sheet.

Having found something on the BPD's network, I next went poking around the BCPD's. How did gentlemen in my profession get information from the police before networks and hacking? The BCPD had an identical complaint against Rosenberg about a year earlier than the BPD's. Just like in the other one, the charges got dropped and nothing else transpired. I frowned. Two kidnapping complaints. Even though they didn't get pursued, the police twice found enough to get Rosenberg arrested.

Was there fire behind this smoke, or was this just sine qua non to being a loan shark?

I looked at the clock. My bedtime long since vanished in the rearview mirror. We would need to start our stakeout tomorrow. The clock ticked for Katherine Rodgers. My eyelids grew heavier. I downloaded what I could find of the case files for Rosenberg's two arrests and started reading them. At some point, they bored me until the ol' lids got heavy enough I studied the insides of them for a while.

* * *

I AWOKE WITH A START. Sleeping in a chair, even a comfortable leather executive chair, is never the same as sleeping in a bed. My neck felt stiff and hurt when I moved it. My left arm hung useless and tingly from my shoulder. I collected myself for a minute as feeling returned. It was just before seven. Rich and Rollins should be checking in with me soon or waiting for me to check in with them. I picked up the reports dropped during my nap, went upstairs, and swished mouthwash. When I came back downstairs, my phone rang. It was Rich. "Find out anything?" I said.

""Not really. I asked a few people in a few different departments. They all have some feelers out but nothing else."

"They didn't know anything ?"

"The gang folks said there's little if any Asian presence in street organizations. Blacks and Hispanics don't like them or trust them enough, and their numbers are too small to start their own."

"And no one has much on Rosenberg?"

"Right. Just some suspicions, nothing concrete."

"And a kidnapping charge a few years ago," I said. "Didn't go anywhere."

"Where did you see his record?" said Rich.

"Where do you think?"

Rich sighed. "Of course."

"Don't feel bad, Rich. The BCPD network has as little information as yours and probably worse security. If that's possible."

"Now I can sleep well when this is over. Any word from your bodyguard?"

"Not yet. Why don't you come by the house, and we'll meet him somewhere?"

"All right. I'll be there in about twenty minutes."

"Bring some breakfast."

"You get breakfast. You can afford a bodyguard . . . you can afford a box of donuts."

I had a clever retort all ready to go, but Rich hung up. I decided to save it for the next time it might be useful. I went upstairs to brush my teeth and change into clean clothes. A shower would have to wait. I was picking out my duds for the day when Rollins called.

"You find out anything?" I said.

"Pretty quiet night," Rollins said. "Rosenberg had a few of his cronies over. I followed one, but all he did was go home. Then I went back to Rosenberg's house. Looked like he was asleep."

"Rich didn't find much, either."

"What about you?"

I told Rollins about the two kidnapping arrests. "There's a saying about smoke and fire," he said.

"True. We need to find less smoke and more fire."

"Let's do it today, then. I'm getting a shower. I'll come by your house in a half-hour."

"Rich and I will be waiting," I said.

* * *

AFTER I GOT off the phone with Rollins, I went to Dunkin Donuts. I got a half-dozen donuts, three different breakfast sandwiches, a latte for myself, and a box of coffee for Rich and Rollins. When I got back, Rich sat in his blue Camaro. He walked up to the house behind me. "I really need some coffee," he said. Red streaks floated in his eyes, complementing the dark circles beneath.

"I have cups and some thermii inside," I said.

"Thermii?"

"It should be the plural of thermos."

"I'm not sure Webster agrees," Rich said.

I took out my keys and unlocked the door. "I'm trying to win Merriam over instead. She's easier."

Rich chuckled and followed me inside. I got down a coffee cup. No sooner did the cup hit the table than Rich opened the box of coffee and poured. "It's not ambrosia," I said.

"Closest thing we'll find," he said, then took a slug. Even though steam rose from the mug, the heat didn't seem to bother Rich.

I took the egg white veggie sandwich out of the bag. "There are two sandwiches still in here, plus a six-pack of donuts."

Rich raided the bag like it contained the fountain of youth. He took out one of the sandwiches and chomped about a quarter of it in one bite. I didn't know which one he grabbed and as quickly as he ate it, I don't think he did either.

"Hungry?" I said.

"Just a little."

I heard a knock at the door and then Rollins announced himself. "Try not to eat all the donuts while I'm answering the door," I said. I let Rollins in and came back to see Rich had devoured the rest of the breakfast sandwich. "You two might need to throw down for the rest of the food."

"He can have the other sandwich," Rich said. "The dunkers might lead to a scrum."

"Take it outside, boys," I said.

Rollins grabbed the sandwich and took a normal-sized bite of it. "We can take the donuts with us," he said. "You have thermoses?"

"I have at least three thermii," I said.

"Thermii?"

"Don't ask," said Rich.

Rollins thought about it and shrugged. "The sooner we get to Rosenberg's, the better. His business opens at eight."

I looked at my watch. Seven twenty-five. "We'll be there in time. I'll get the coffee."

"What about traffic?" Rollins said.

"We'll have a police detective in the car," I said. "I'll drive on the shoulder as much as I have to."

Rich rolled his eyes. "Tell me you won't."

"Only when necessary," I said.

* * *

It wasn't. I only passed on the right via the shoulder once, and even then, only for a few hundred yards. Rollins cracked a smile as I sped around a couple of people who forgot which pedal made their cars go forward. Rich's expression suggested he'd gargled with lemon juice. Traffic on the Baltimore Beltway sucks in the morning no matter which direction you go. Heading toward Pikesville added gridlock on Reisterstown Road after exiting the Beltway.

Thanks to some professional-grade driving, we got to Rosenberg's before eight. I brought the Caprice even though they might recognize it. If they decided to show us their recognition by opening fire, the Caprice would offer the most protection. Besides, I didn't want to get the Audi scratched, shot, or otherwise maimed. I parked around where I had the last time we camped out. I hoped it looked like normal residential or business parking. To help with the illusion, we all sat as low in the seats as we could.

People started rolling into Rosenberg's right at eight o'clock. Jasper and a couple of donkeys went in first. Rosenberg himself, accompanied by the stocky goon who chauffeured his car, walked in a few ticks after eight. People we estimated to be customers went in and out over the course of the morning. Rich and Rollins drank coffee and shared stories about their days in the Army. I long ago ran out of vanilla latte, so I turned to coffee to force my eyelids open. Most of the Army stories were boring to someone who never served. The others threatened to splash me with runaway machismo.

At about nine-thirty, Jasper and two goons—one of whom was Rosenberg's chauffeur—ambled out and got into Jasper's car. "I wonder where they're going?" I said.

"Doesn't matter," said Rollins. "Once they roll out, we can march in there and talk to the man a lot easier."

Jasper and the other guys pulled away. We waited three minutes for them to come back, then got out of the Caprice and walked toward the building. When we were inside, I saw a few customers milling about and picking up supplies. The path to the door at the rear was unobstructed, and we walked toward it. I kept an eye out for goons, as I'm sure Rich and Rollins did.

When we got there, we stopped. "I'll wait out here," Rich whispered.

"Why?" I said, keeping my voice to a whisper.

"I'm off duty. It's better this way. Don't worry. I'll barge in if you guys need help."

"We'll be fine," Rollins said. He drew his gun with one hand and tested the knob with the other. "Unlocked."

I took out my .45. No point in taking anything smaller to a potential firefight. Rich unholstered his gun and stood to the side. No one in the store noticed us yet. I signaled to Rollins, and he thrust the door open.

Rosenberg stood from behind his desk. A guard seated just inside the threshold stood, too. Rollins punched him in the mouth, and he fell backwards, moaning and covering his face. Another shot up and took a step toward me. I kicked him in the solar plexus, driving the breath from his lungs and causing him to slump forward, making it easier to kick him in the face. His head snapped back and thudded into the side wall before he sagged to the floor. He wasn't getting up anytime soon. I looked at Rollins pouncing on his foe and knocking him before he glared at Rosenberg and flashed a threatening smile. It conveyed menace and a general lack of interest in the viewer's well-being at the same time.

"What's the meaning of this?" Rosenberg said. He still stood, but his brows formed a deep frown. He looked between Rollins and me.

"We can start with your attempt on my life," I said.

"I don't know what—"

"Shut up," I broke in. "We're really here for Katherine Rodgers."

"Who?"

"The daughter of Stanley and Pauline Rodgers."

Recognition flashed in Rosenberg's eyes. "Don't know her," he said.

"I'm tired of this." I walked close and punched Rosenberg in his paunchy stomach. The air whooshing from him as my fist drove home proved a very satisfying sound. He staggered into his seat and coughed a few times. "Let's try again. Katherine Rodgers was kidnapped. We know you've been accused of kidnapping before. Where is she?"

Rosenberg shook his head as a few more coughs escaped. "I don't know," he managed to say.

I pulled my fist back again. He winced and hid behind his raised hands. "I don't know where she is," he said, some power returning to his voice.

"Her mother owes you money. You threaten me, then her. Then her daughter disappears. I stopped believing in coincidences a while ago."

"I don't know where she is," he said again.

"You saying you had nothing to do with kidnapping her?" Rollins said. He strode to Rosenberg and glared down.

"Yes," Rosenberg said after looking away from Rollins.

"I'm not sure I believe you."

"We should go," Rich said from outside the door.

Rollins slapped Rosenberg hard across the face. If I only heard it, I may have thought he shot the bastard. "We're gonna find out you're lying and come back for you," he said. "Count on it."

Rosenberg swallowed hard and didn't say anything. Rollins and I left the room. We kept our guns ready under our jackets. "Jasper and the other guy are coming back," Rich said. We went out the front and walked briskly around to the Caprice. Jasper and his co-goon had gone inside. They didn't come out. I fired up the Caprice, turned it around, and stomped on the gas.

CHAPTER 12

"HOW'D YOU LIKE TO HIRE AN ACCOUNTANT?" I SAID TO Rich on the way back to Baltimore.

"I think I'm OK," he said.

"Let me ask again. How would you like to meet Rosenberg's accountant under the guise of hiring him while Rollins and I burgle his office and look for incriminating information?"

"How could I refuse?"

"You need me for a B and E?" Rollins said.

"No, I just need you to make sure no one Es behind me," I said.

He chuckled. "You stretch my job description, but it's cool. This is fun."

We got back to my house. I gave Rich the number for Eliot Eisenberg's business. He walked into the other room to make the call. I sat behind my desk and took a deep breath. We needed to keep moving. Katherine Rodgers might not have a lot of time, depending on who took her and what they planned to do with her. Even though we were all tired, we had to push past it and keep going. Rich walked back in a minute later. "We have a meeting set up for forty-five minutes," he said.

"Where?" I said.

"Miss Shirley's. I have no idea what we're going to talk about, but I'll keep him there for the duration of breakfast."

"We should have enough time," I said. "Meanwhile, I'm going to dig some more. Rich, can you look into who worked the case and made the arrest? Knowing what he knew could help us."

Rich nodded. "I'll check with the county, too."

"I'll sit here and look pretty," Rollins said, "unless you have something more productive in mind."

I thought about it for a moment. "Yes. Use my laptop in the other room and research human trafficking. The sex trade in particular."

"You think this girl is being trafficked?"

"I think we can't ignore the possibility. Rosenberg said he didn't grab her. Let's assume he's telling the truth. It means someone else did for their own reasons. If she is being trafficked, it makes what we do today even more important."

"I'm on it," Rollins said and walked out of the room.

We were all on our various projects.

* * *

RICH TEXTED to let me know Eisenberg entered Miss Shirley's. I felt a brief pang of envy at not getting to eat there. Rollins and I were parked a block away from Eisenberg's building, waiting to hear the good word. The exterior door was open, but Eisenberg locked his inner office before he left. Rollins pulled the outer door shut. Our space shrank to the size of a typical elevator. "Keep an eye out," I whispered as I took out my special keyring.

"Where did you get the tools?" Rollins said.

"Hong Kong." I looked at the lock—a Schlage with some wear on it. This would be easy.

"How long were you over there?" Rollins said as I chose the appropriate tension wrench.

"Of my own volition? Three and a half years. Then I spent nineteen days under the watchful eye and loving care of the Chinese penal system."

"Wow. Must've been shitty."

"Yes, it was." I worked on the lock using the tension wrench and a slender steel rod.

"You speak Chinese?"

"Yes, but I didn't let them know."

"They torture you?" he said.

I didn't answer. After a few seconds, Rollins nodded. I kept massaging the tumblers. Within another minute, I had it open. Rollins jumped in front of me, opened the door, and went in. One of these days, we might find a bomb, a lion, or at least a gunman behind a door when he did his bodyguard bit. Not today. We walked into Eliot Eisenberg's messy office. Ledger books and other desk detritus threatened to assault us as we walked in.

"How we doing this?" Rollins said.

"He must keep secret books on Rosenberg," I said. "Even if they're cooked. We probably have forty minutes. Rich can only bullshit this guy for so long. We'll try to be organized about it."

Rollins looked around. "Hard to be organized in here."

"He has a process. I think I recognize the animal, vegetable, mineral system at work."

"I'm worried we'll knock a pile over by looking at it funny," he said.

"We'll need to be careful." I examined a heap stacked with a nominal degree of care. Eisenberg helpfully wrote on the covers of the books. If he wanted to protect Rosenberg, he may have written a fake name. It would complicate our search. I flipped through the first few pages to see if anything in the ledger looked familiar to my non-accounting-trained eyes.

"This could take more than forty minutes," Rollins said.

"We'll stay as long as we can. Check the covers for anything obvious. I'm also looking at the first couple pages."

"Roger." Rollins flipped through a book. I constantly felt a pile or several of them would topple any second. We were playing Jenga with ledgers, Katherine Rodgers' life being the object of the game. I really didn't care if we knocked stacks over. Let Eisenberg know someone burgled his place; I didn't care what he thought.

Thirty minutes and some mound slippage later, I found a shopworn record book with "DR" on the front. A quick perusal showed sums I would expect a loan shark to handle, even if they didn't portend the financial struggles Rosenberg would encounter. A cooked ledger was still something—there was truth in fiction, after all. Rollins tipped a pile over and tried to recreate the chaos as best he could. "I think I found what we came here for," I said.

"Good," said Rollins. "My interior decorating skills are getting strained in this pig sty."

He walked to the door and opened it, looking around the small lobby. When he let me know, I came out, locking the door from the inside. We'd barely gotten back into the Caprice when Rich sent a text saying Eisenberg would be leaving Miss Shirley's. My quick return inquired about his financial profile. He didn't reply.

* * *

EISENBERG'S BOOKS painted a sunny picture of Rosenberg's financial situation. My printouts from the bank stated otherwise, and I knew I could get more given necessity and time. I set to working on it while I unearthed Marvin V. Bernard's business card. He answered promptly. "Marvin, I'm hoping you remember me. My name is C.T. Ferguson. We spoke at a funeral home a few days ago."

"Yes, of course. Is there something else I can help you with?"

I went over the details of the case, leaving out some stuff he didn't need to know but making sure he received a clear idea of the situation. "I'm trying to find the girl, and I think the records of a loan shark might hold some information."

"And you need my accounting expertise," he said.

"I do."

"I have an appointment in fifteen minutes, but their situation isn't nearly as dire as yours. I'll reschedule. Where are you?"

I gave him my address.

"I'll be there in twenty minutes," he said.

* * *

MARVIN READ through the book with his glasses pushed up on his nose and a studious frown on his face. His eyes moved across the columns at a glacial pace. I watched until I decided painting the wall and observing it dry would be more interesting. Marvin probably looked at every ledger this way. If he read a regular tome the same way, it would take him a long weekend just to get through Dr. Seuss.

"You mentioned some other documents?" he said after a few minutes.

"Yes," I said, "Printouts of bank statements."

"The police shared those with you?" Marvin arched his brows over his glasses.

"My cousin is a police detective."

He shrugged. "Must be nice."

I wanted to say it really wasn't, but I held my tongue. I handed Marvin the sheets. "Should be some more . . . arriving soon," I said. "If those don't paint the whole picture, the extra ones might help."

"It's an interesting picture so far." Marvin took the printouts and got back to work. I turned my monitor a little more away from him and went back to the rest of David Rosenberg's financials. It took a while, but Marvin the Torpid Accountant needed a while, so it all turned out well. I took care to make sure to erase my e-footprints, printed out my very illegally-obtained financial records, and handed them to Marvin. He took them without looking up.

I scanned the soft copies on my screen. Rosenberg made a few of those mysterious deposits, and they conveniently cropped up whenever he needed the money. I looked at the dates. One corresponded closely to the disappearance of Amy Horton. I wished I'd searched for this sooner. Could it have saved Katherine? I couldn't think like this now; I needed to find the link between Amy Horton's disappearance, the payout to Rosenberg, and whether any other money received lined up with other girls going missing.

I moved all the suspicious payouts into a separate document and printed it. Earlier, I located a few sites decrying Rosenberg. I went back through my history to find them again. With what I suspected now, those sites went from the bitter ramblings of people who dealt with a seedy loan shark to cautionary tales. Marvin Bernard's slow pace gave me all the time I needed to read a few websites, blogs, and local subreddits. I found stories of two more girls who vanished, and those dates lined up with deposits to Rosenberg's accounts, too. How did the BPD and BCPD miss this? Wouldn't they ask for warrants to look at his financials, considering his reputation as a loan shark? Or did they get denied because creeps like Rosenberg always have a friend in a high place?

Marvin still kept his nose buried in statistical pages, so I looked up the owner information for one of the websites and made a phone call. When a woman's voice answered, I said, "Is this Mrs. Driscoll?"

"Yes, who is this?"

"My name is C.T. Ferguson. I'm a private investigator."

"Oh," she said, "is something wrong?"

"I'm looking into a case involving David Rosenberg," I said.

She exhaled into the phone, and it sounded like she forced it through clenched teeth. "That bastard. What did he do now?"

"The same as he's always done, I suppose. During my case, another girl went missing."

"Oh, no. Her poor parents."

"I've been looking into some suspicious transactions in Rosenberg's financials, and I've lined a few up with the disappearances of girls."

"You're saying someone is paying him to kidnap the daughters of people who borrow money from him?"

"I can't make the conclusion yet," I said. "Right now, I'm following the money and seeing where it goes."

"Where is it going?" she asked.

"I'm still working on it, but I'm trying to learn as much as I can. Could I meet you somewhere?"

"Uh . . . sure, I guess. What area are you in?"

"Federal Hill."

"We're in Cockeysville. How about Spro Coffee in Hampden? Do you know where that is?"

"I'll find it."

"Twenty-five minutes?" she said.

"I'll be there. Thank you." We hung up. Marvin still studied and made occasional notes with a mechanical pencil. When he didn't need the pencil, he kept it behind his ear. "I have to run out and look into something else for the case," I told him. "How long do you need?"

"I want to make sure we get this right," he said. "At least another hour."

"All right. I'll be back as quickly as I can."

"I take it this is a *pro bono* gig?"

I smiled. "I promise you half of what my client is paying me."

A smile traced his lips. "I thought so."

* * *

I LEFT for Hampden right away. For the second time all month, I wouldn't be late for something unless it took forever to park in Hampden, which it often can. Thirty-Sixth Street—packed with shops, restaurants, and places like Spro—has been branded "The Avenue" to make it sound special. I never thought it needed the help, but the closest I got to a marketing class in college was mocking the people who took one. After a few minutes of driving around, I found a spot on a side street two blocks up and enjoyed a three-minute walk to the shop.

Past its purple rowhouse exterior, Spro looked like a lot of other coffee joints, only with more wood and paneling. The hipster count was consistent with other java shops, though the ones here dressed the part with more fealty. I walked past a couple girls trying their best to look like a new cast of *Jersey Shore*. They must have missed the memo.

I looked at the menu. It was about a quarter the size of Star-bucks, but the confusing ratio was inversely proportional. I settled on Experimental Dark made via French press and sat several tables away from the shore girls—or whatever they were. They regarded me like I'd been out of touch for a generation. I may as well have worn a velvet smoking jacket and puffed a meer-schaum pipe. I tried my best not to feel old well before my time. Handsomeness would cover the multitude of sins.

A few minutes later, a couple in their forties strolled in. Their

gray Ralph Lauren coats went with the color asserting its domi-
nance in their hair. They wore matching jeans and shoes you
couldn't buy at a mall. Both walked to the counter and ordered
coffee. Armed with a pair of drinks, they sidled away from the
counter and looked around. I caught the woman's eye and
inclined my head. She wandered toward my table, and her
husband followed. "You're C.T. Ferguson?" she said.

"In the flesh," I said, gesturing toward the empty seats at the
table.

They both sat. "I'm Sarah. This is my husband, Chris." Chris
gave a curt nod but made no move to put his coffee down and
shake my hand. I mirrored the same non-move. "Anything
involving Rosenberg concerns us."

"We know he had something to do with our Stephanie disappearing," Chris said.

"He probably did," I said. "I have to be honest: considering
the time elapsed, I doubt there's any chance of me finding your
daughter."

"I know," Sarah Driscoll said. She let out a breath and looked
down at her coffee before continuing. "She's gone. We've come to
terms with that. But it sounds like we can help spare another
family what we've gone through."

"And if we can get to Rosenberg, it would be good, too," Chris
added.

"Don't go and do something crazy, honey," Sarah said.

"The son of a bitch has probably vanished, right?"

"I presume he has, yes," I said. He had gone silent, and If he
were smart, he high-tailed it after we barged into his business.

"Well, if you find him, let me know. We were in a bad way
when we went to him. It's not the case anymore. We have money.
If some of it can buy him an early grave, it's money well-spent."
Chris stared at me, unblinking.

There was no wavering in his gaze. I took him seriously

because he meant it. He wanted Rosenberg's blood, and I couldn't blame him. "I want to find him, but right now, my concern is with finding the missing girl."

"Of course," Sarah said. "Is there anything we can do?"

"You could tell me what happened before your daughter was taken."

Chris sighed. He shook his head. Sarah squeezed his hand, and he returned the gesture. "We needed money. Banks didn't want to loan it to us. A guy I used to work with borrowed from Rosenberg and didn't have any problems. When my business started off slowly, we were forced to make some . . . reduced payments. We were trying, you know? We told him what was happening, and he said he understood."

"How reduced were the payments?" I said.

"Usually forty percent. Half when we could. We did it for five months."

"Rosenberg seemed OK with it?"

"He said he would have to add some money to the back end," said Chris, "but he wasn't giving us too much grief about it. No one came by and threatened to break our legs or anything."

"And then your daughter was gone."

"A week before her eighteenth birthday." Sarah said. She teared up. "We didn't get so much as a note from anyone. The police investigated for a while, but they didn't come up with anything."

"And Rosenberg still wanted his money?" I said.

"Sure did," Chris said. "We paid him off when my business started hitting it big. It ended a little ahead of schedule."

If Rosenberg got money when Stephanie Driscoll was kidnapped and then collected in full from the Driscolls, he was double-dipping. Why not simply kidnap the daughter as motivation? The Driscolls paid him off and still didn't get their daughter back. What happened to these girls? "I'm going to see what I can find out about all of this," I said. "I don't want you to get your hopes up, though. If there's information somewhere about your daughter, I'll pass it along to you, but right now, I'm looking for the girl who just disappeared."

"And Rosenberg."

I nodded. "If he's gone, then him, too."

"Make sure you keep us in the loop," Chris said.

"I will."

"Thank you, C.T.," Sarah said. She shook my hand. Her husband didn't.

* * *

I GOT BACK to my house to find Marvin Bernard waiting in the office chair where I left him. He'd closed the ledger book and marked the printouts with more lead than I could follow as I walked by him and sat behind my desk. "Looks like you've finished."

"I have," he said. "Mr. Rosenberg's empire, as it were, is a giant clamshell organization . . . 'shell' being the operative term."

"So the books are cooked?"

"To use the vernacular, yes. There are legitimate transactions in there, but some are embellished, made up out of whole cloth, or show deposits resulting from moving money back and forth."

"Why would Rosenberg need cooked books?" I said. "It's not like loan sharks are publicly-traded commodities."

"My guess is to sham a creditor or creditors who might see his finances," said Marvin. "Or maybe someone within his organization. I don't know, really. All I know is the books are falsified."

"Does he have any money on hand?"

"Some. More than the average person but far from a fortune."

"But he could pack his bags and hit the road if he felt the noose tightening."

Marvin nodded. "He has enough money to flee town and survive for a while. How long depends on a lot of factors."

"Those mysterious twenty-thousand-dollar transfers . . . I think they coincide with some kidnappings. Did you notice anything about them?"

"The ledger's details are not legitimate," he said. The hard copies you gave me show those sums came from an account marked THC. I concluded it to be The Hong Corporation."

The Hong Corporation. I knew of the name. Asian kidnappers. I hoped Rollins found some good information about human trafficking, and I wished even harder we wouldn't need it. "I'll need to follow the money," I said.

"If I were a forensic accountant, I could tell you more."

"You've told me a lot already, Marvin." I extended my hand, and he shook it. "Thank you. If I need more information later, can I call you again?"

"Please do. It's a shame what happened to that man and now his family. I feel . . . connected in some way. If I can help, I will."

"Great, thanks."

Marvin let himself out. I'd been handed a lot of information to digest, and as was becoming the norm, a lot of work to do.

* * *

I KNEW The Hong Corporation would be a shell company. If they were trafficking women overseas, I'd be playing the shell game for a while. I wasn't sure Katherine Rodgers could spare the time unraveling it would take me. While I started looking up some things online, I yelled for Rollins. He poked his head in the office door a moment later. "What's going on?" he said.

"I think the human trafficking angle is in play," I said, "as much as I wish it weren't." I filled him in on what I'd learned from the Driscolls and Marvin Bernard. "I know you did some research on it. I don't need the results now, but I want you to add something to it."

"What?"

"The Hong Corporation. I'm sure it's a fake, probably with as many layers as an onion. See how it fits with what you've found out about trafficking so far."

"And if it doesn't?"

"Then we know something, at least."

Rollins gave me a thumbs-up. "You got it," he said and walked away. I went back to my research. I quickly learned human trafficking was a multibillion dollar business. The fact gave me pause. In my time as a PI, I've gone after a few rich and prominent local assholes but nothing on this scale. Even if The Hong Corporation only handled a tiny portion of the sum, they could be raking in tens of millions. They wouldn't even miss the small checks they wrote to Rosenberg.

Hong maintained a negligible online presence, which was no doubt how they wanted it. Rosenberg owned a legit business he could point to; The Hong Corporation couldn't make the same claim. The ownership data for their website quickly proved to be a dead end. The email address listed as a contact bounced when I sent a test message. They needed to pay their web hosts, however, and they used a small overseas outfit called Brightstar Hosting.

Considering web hosting companies have a lot of valuable data in their systems, you'd think they would do a good job of securing it. Brightstar, for their part, had good if basic defenses, but my network mapping revealed an older Linux server they should have tossed out the window years ago. Pivoting onto that server took only a few minutes. Account information was easy to find. The Hong Corporation's hosting fees were paid by THC, LLC. This was like a Russian gift box. At least it represented new information. I searched for THC, LLC to see what I could find.

They had a similarly small online presence, but where The Hong Corporation was an obvious shell, THC added more appearances of legitimacy. I set a few scripts to run and left the room to get Rollins. I found him in the living room, frowning at a laptop screen. "Want to pay another visit to Rosenberg?" I said.

"Why are we going to see him?"

"We know more now. Maybe we can use it to our advantage. I'm mining for some data, and it'll take a little while."

"Sure, let's go talk to him."

I called Rich en route. He said he would meet us there.

* * *

RICH's blue Camaro pulled next to Rosenberg's business a couple minutes after Rollins and I arrived. We walked in and headed toward the back right away. Rosenberg's door was closed, and I didn't see any light spilling from under it. Jasper appeared at the end of the hallway and stared at us. If annoyed, afraid, or even alive, he did a good job of hiding it.

"Mr. Rosenberg isn't here," Jasper said.

"When did he leave?" I said.

"Mr. Rosenberg leaves when he wants. He wasn't feeling well."

"Guilt got him down?"

"I wouldn't know what you mean."

"Of course you wouldn't."

"Are you gentlemen interested in restaurant supplies?" Jasper gave us the fakest smile I'd seen in some time. "If not, I'm going to need to ask you to leave."

"You know where your boss keeps the girls?" Rollins said it louder than necessary and at a slightly higher pitch than normal. For a bodyguard, he seemed to relish his role in this case.

"Now I definitely don't know what you're talking about," said Jasper.

"We're going to find your boss," I said, taking a step closer to Jasper. He didn't move back. "We're going to find what happened to the girl, and all the other girls he's ordered kidnapped. When we do, you're going to go down with him, and I'm going to enjoy watching it."

Jasper's fake smiled faded into a scowl. "You should be careful with the accusations you make."

"Why? Your boss already tried to have me killed once. Didn't work out so well. Now he's turned tail and run. Maybe you'll be the one left holding the bag. He'll reward you for your loyalty by bailing on you. What a piece of work."

"You need to leave now," Jasper said, looking at each of us. "If you don't, I'll call the police."

Rich made no effort to out himself, and I went right along with it. "I think you'd have a lot more explaining to do than we would," I said. "But we'll go. Tell your slimy asshole boss we're going to expose him. It doesn't matter where he hides. It won't matter where you hide, either."

Jasper gave me a sincere smile this time. "I'm not going to hide," he said.

"Even better," I said.

CHAPTER 13

I KNEW ROSENBERG'S HOME ADDRESS FROM HIS FINANCIAL information. He owned a nice house but not a lavish one. It was a single-family dwelling, two stories, short driveway, vinyl siding, maybe fifteen hundred square feet. A middle-class family could have lived there, even with residential prices enjoying their gentle upward trend. When we arrived, the place was dark, and no car sat in the driveway or street in front of the house. Rollins, Rich, and I got out of our cars and walked up to the front door. Rich tried the doorknob. "Locked," he said.

"Detective, I think you're about to witness a crime," I said, taking out my special keyring.

"My vision is fuzzy," Rich said.

I got to work. Rosenberg had a lock and a deadbolt. They both looked new. Rollins and Rich did a good job screening me from the street. A couple trees in the front yard would also help hide what I did. If anyone got curious about it, Rich's badge would assuage their concerns, at least long enough for us to get in and get out.

Three minutes and zero goody-goody neighbors later, we walked in the front door. I've seen places which had been gently lived in and ones tossed by some miscreant—or the police—

looking for something. Rosenberg's house was a combination of the two. Entire rooms saw nary a piece of furniture or sign of past habitation in them, and others looked like someone lobbed in a grenade, closed the door, and laughed at the results. Boxes, papers, books, and drawers from dressers lay strewn about a bedroom and an office.

"Where do we start?" I said. "We don't have much time."

"He's obviously spooked," Rollins said. "He split. I don't think his people will give him up, if they even know where he is."

I looked through a few pieces of detritus on the floor but found nothing useful. Maybe Rosenberg took all the relevant stuff with him. Maybe he didn't have anything useful here to begin with. I didn't see a safe in any of the rooms nor any paintings whose sole purpose would be obvious hiding places for wall safes. Rollins was right: Rosenberg was long gone, and we weren't going to find him anytime soon. Sifting through the rubble he left wouldn't help. Katherine was still on the clock. I had to prioritize.

"You guys can stay if you want," I said. "I need to keep looking for Katherine. If we all stay here, it's not productive."

"I'll come with you," Rollins said. "Gotta earn my keep."

"I'll look around for a little while," Rich said. "If I don't come across something soon, I'll leave. Where will you be?"

I shrugged. "I have no idea," I said. Then Rollins and I left.

* * *

ROLLINS DROVE THE CAPRICE. I looked at some files on my tablet. Rollins said Rosenberg's people wouldn't give him up. We couldn't presume it to be true. I compelled toadies to flip on their bosses before. We needed someone who might know what was going on. Maybe nobody but Rosenberg knew where Katherine was, but someone surely knew to where Rosenberg absconded. I went through the payroll information and found Jasper's address. I gave it to Rollins. He said he knew it.

I called Rosenberg's business and asked to speak to Mr. Jasper Dexter, "my" account manager. This was the position invented for him in the payroll system. The pleasant-sounding girl who answered the phone said Jasper just left. I thanked her for her time, hung up, and told Rollins to step on it. Jasper didn't have a long drive to his house. I didn't want to give him a chance to get comfortable.

The Caprice surged forward. Rollins darted between cars, passed on the left and the right, and unlike me, never needed to use the shoulder. The Caprice was rarely still on the highway, and even when it was, I felt the potential for it to zig or zag any second. I rode in a coiled snake, handled by a man who knew its moves and anticipated making them. If I could afford to hire Rollins as my permanent driver, I would. I'd just be worried about him denting the Audi.

Thanks to Rollins, we got to Jasper's house in record time. He owned a newish plain end-of-group townhouse in Lutherville. I derived some satisfaction in Jasper's model being the smallest on the street. "Think he's home?" Rollins said as he parked the Caprice at the curb two doors down from Jasper's.

"Don't think so," I said. "There's no garage, and I don't see his car anywhere nearby."

"Let's look around back, then." Rollins padded around the left side of the house, and I followed him. The backyard lay framed by an ugly four-foot wooden fence. A small metal sign on it advertised the company responsible for building it. If I constructed the hideous thing, I wouldn't want my name anywhere close. I didn't see any lights on in the house, but the afternoon sun provided enough brightness we couldn't tell. Rollins broke his crouch long enough to spring over the fence, then took up a low profile again. I followed suit.

A row of flagstones bisected a well-maintained green yard unadorned by any accessories save a covered gas grill. We moved as quickly as our crouches would allow. Four concrete steps led to the white metal storm door. Rollins gave a tug, and it opened. While he held it, I tested the back door and found it locked. I took out my keyring and got to work. Jasper didn't have a very good lock; I cracked it in under a minute.

Rollins went in first. At some point, while I worked the tumblers, he drew his gun. I did the same and shadowed him in. We moved through a narrow kitchen filled with average appliances and counters years overdue for a cleaning. A closed door stood to the right of the refrigerator. Rollins ignored it and padded through a doorway into the dining room. Jasper needed new furniture. His dining table came from a discount store and must have been assembled by a discount laborer. No one hid anywhere. Rollins hugged the wall and peered through an arch into the living room. I stood beside him.

I didn't hear anything except my own heart beating. Rollins tore away from the wall and skulked into the living room. I crouched and went behind him. Jasper owned lousy furniture in here, too, but at least his slapdash TV stand propped up a nice big screen. Bookcases beside the TV held hundreds of DVDs and Blu-Rays. As Rollins and I nosed around in the living room, we heard footsteps on the front porch. Rollins pointed to himself, then the dining room—finally, to me and the front door. He moved into position in the next room as a key slid into the lock. I stood beside the door so Jasper swinging it in would hide me even better.

The key ground in the lock. The knob turned. Jasper opened it and came in. He held a few pieces of mail. Without looking, he grabbed for the door. Then he looked up and saw me. His eyes went wide in time for me to take a step into him and shove the .45 under his chin. All he could do was drop the mail. "Welcome home, asshole," I said. Rollins walked in from the next room, his gun leveled at Jasper.

"What do you want?" Jasper said. I couldn't see his face very well because of my gun forcing his head up. I hoped he looked scared.

"Katherine Rodgers," I said, "but I'll settle for your boss."

"I don't know who—"

"If you tell me you don't know who she is, I'm going to decorate the ceiling with bits of your skull."

Jasper pursed his lips. I felt his chin push into the gun as he tried to nod. "OK," he said, "I know who she is. But I don't know where she is."

"What about Rosenberg?" I said.

"Him either."

"You're not very useful for a man who has a .45 under his chin."

"I'm telling you the truth." Exasperation came through in Jasper's voice. I didn't care to hear it.

"A couple of Asian guys kidnapped the girl," I said. "Your boss must have hired them. You know anything about them?"

"If he did, he didn't tell me about it," Jasper said.

"Maybe you hired them," I said. "You look like you have Asian blood."

"Wasn't me."

I couldn't see a lot of his face, but I doubted Jasper. He or Rosenberg *must* be involved. "Give me something here," I said. "Where else would Rosenberg keep stuff? He have a warehouse anywhere? Rental property? Boarded-up snowball stand?"

"I don't know, I'm telling you."

"You believe him?" I said to Rollins.

"Not really." Rollins came into the room. "But I'm not gonna torture him. He's useless right now." Rollins moved beside Jasper and walloped him in the head with the butt of his gun. Jasper's head whipped to the side, and he crashed to the floor.

"Let's go," Rollins said. "We're still behind the eight ball. If the girl's been trafficked, she's running out of time."

We let ourselves out the front door.

* * *

* * *

I SAT across the street from Eliot Eisenberg's office with my laptop and a wireless antenna capable of finding a signal in the Marianas Trench. My guess was the residents of his building shared a connection, but Eisenberg's business did well enough for him to have his own. He wasn't smart enough to secure it very well, so his building-mates probably leeched off it. The answer to "who still uses WEP?" consisted of Eliot Eisenberg and the Amish. Wired Equivalent Privacy sounds like good security to people who don't know any better, and to people who do (like me), it makes breaking into a network easy.

Eliot kept his computer online all the time. Might as well get all the perks of your poorly-secured broadband connection. I poked around on his hard drive, looking for files on Rosenberg. Someone surely knew more about Katherine Rodgers, who took her, and where she might be going.

As I scoured Eisenberg's data, I munched pizza from Brick Oven Pizzeria and a hot pretzel from a nearby stand. All of it dropped to room temperature, but I didn't care; I just needed food to fill the gnawing hole in my gut. Finally, I found a hidden zip file labeled "DR" and copied the contents to my laptop. I hunted for some more Rosenberg-centric files, didn't find any, and made sure my e-fingerprints were gone.

I sipped some freshly-squeezed lemonade from the stand

(better than the pretzel at this point) as I looked over what I found. Eisenberg kept these simple. The ledger books were required to stand up to professional scrutiny if Rosenberg ever got audited or investigated. These files—safe behind a wireless network running outmoded security—did not need to obfuscate. I could see every payment made in exchange for a young girl. Their names were never listed, but Eisenberg listed them as "domestic commodity." I counted eleven such commodities over the last three years.

How come Rosenberg never faced charges for even one of these? As far as I could tell, no authorities also cared he was a loan shark. For whatever reasons, past police investigations couldn't make anything stick. Armed with what I discovered on Eisenberg's computer, I hoped to reverse the trend. After I found Katherine Rodgers. Eisenberg's files weren't helpful there. If Rosenberg told him the intimate details of his little kidnapping ring, Eisenberg had been smart enough not to save them to his hard drive.

* * *

IN ALL THE hullabaloo of the case, I postponed my search for a real office. The fact got punctuated by the man who stood in the doorway of my home-slash-workplace pointing a gun at me. He was Asian, Chinese to be specific, about five-nine and wiry. He bore no resemblance to a typical goon. I wondered if he was one of the men who took Katherine Rodgers. I wondered if I would get the chance to ask him. My pounding heart reverberated in my ears.

"No sudden moves," he said, stepping into the room. He had a small .380 semiautomatic trained on me. When I got home, I took the .45 off and put it in the bottom drawer of my desk. The two feet it would take me to reach the gun felt like a mile.

"What do you want?" I said. If I could inch my chair toward the drawer, maybe I could dive for the gun. Maybe I could do it without getting shot.

"You to back off," he said. He stared straight at me. I saw no emotion in his eyes. This was all business for him. Kidnapping, scaring someone, maybe even shooting them—all in a day's work.

"I'm a man of many parts," I said. "I take all kinds of cases because my name is out there so much." Using my right foot, I eased an inch closer to the desk drawer. My Asian friend didn't seem to notice. "I'm afraid you'll have to be more specific."

"You know what I'm talking about," he insisted.

"Pretend I don't," I said in Chinese.

He sighed. If I kept talking, the gun would get heavy in his hand. "You're looking for a girl."

"Aren't we all?"

He narrowed his eyes. I prepared to dive in case he opened fire. I needed to keep this guy talking, so he'd either get tired of holding his gun or so I could get to mine. What I couldn't do was push him to the point he decided bantering with me was no longer worth the aggravation. The expected value needed to favor me breathing at the end of this impromptu meeting. "You know the girl I mean," he said.

"All right, so I do," I said. "She got kidnapped. I was helping her family deal with a loan shark, so I moved on to her kidnapping."

"You need to stop looking." The gun remained steady. I inched closer to the drawer.

"I need to know she's safe. Her mother needs to know."

The Chinese man chuckled. It sounded hollow like he learned it in a bad movie years ago. "She is safe enough for now," he said.

"Just for now?" If I dragged the conversation on, maybe Rollins would come back. Or Rich. I'd take either one at this point. Hell, I'd take a random BPD officer coming to cite me for the numbers in my address being crooked.

"The girls have what they need."

If this were true now but not in the future, they must be on the move soon. "When are you transferring them?" I said.

"Why should I tell you?"

"You're holding all the cards here," I said. I gained another inch. "You have me at a disadvantage in my own office. You got the girl hidden somewhere I don't know about, and you have her mother sick with worry. You can't throw me a bone . . . maybe let me help her mother get one good night of sleep this week?" Appealing to the humanity of someone who would abduct a college girl as part of a human trafficking ring wouldn't count as my best plan, but I didn't see another play. Besides, I had a nonzero chance it would work.

I looked at the gun while the Chinese man studied me. I hoped he didn't peer too closely, or he might see my position changed relative to something on the desk or wall. "The girls go tomorrow," he said. "We have a few more to collect." His eyes never wavered from mine. I believed him. We had at least until the morning to find Katherine and the rest of the girls.

"I'll make sure the girl's mother knows," I said.

"Maybe I should tell her. Maybe my clients pay for an older lady. Has some experience."

"I can tell her."

"Maybe you're too nosy," he said. "You might keep looking even though you say you won't."

I surveyed my desk. I couldn't throw anything to stop this guy from shooting me. The turn in the conversation didn't favor my survival. My heart hammered harder. To my left, above where I kept the .45, stood a water bottle I neglected to put away yesterday. A few inches of water remained. "I'm going to take a drink,"

I said, pointing at the bottle. "Just so you know what I'm reaching for."

"I'll let you savor it," he said.

How nice of him. I scooted my chair down about a foot and grabbed the bottle. The drawer I needed was now within easy reach. I unscrewed the cap, took a swig, pushed my chair out with my butt, and dropped to the floor. I heard a shouted curse in Mandarin as I opened the desk drawer. The .45 felt cool in my hand. I flattened myself for a view through the kneehole as the Chinese man stepped forward. I pointed at his ankle and fired.

I'd never experienced such intense muzzle blast nor the sound of a bullet the size of a .45 smashing a mass of small bones before. Just before ringing took over my hearing was a noise akin to a series of sticks all being snapped at once, only with the volume cranked up to eleven. As if in a silent movie, the Chinese man's gun bounced once on the hardwood, he clutched his lower leg, and crashed sideways away from his weapon.

I stood, bent to pick up his gun with two fingertips, and set it atop my desk. Then I sat on the corner and looked down at him. Screams evidenced by his wide-open mouth gradually subsided as my hearing returned, but he effected major grimaces, and sweat covered his forehead and face. His breathing came in rapid gulps of air. I snapped a picture or two of his face with my phone.

"You're going into shock," I said. "And there's a good chance you'll never walk normally again." My voice sounded normal despite loud tinnitus; I hoped it sounded the same way to him. My heart stopped pounding, but my trembling foot told me adrenalin still coursed through me.

"You . . . shot me," he said in Chinese.

"You'll live. Assuming I call for medical attention, which I'll be glad to do as soon as you tell me where the girls are being kept."

"I don't . . . know."

I shrugged. "It's your leg. At least for now it is. Your choice." I tried not to look at the mess I'd made of his lower extremity or the mess on my formerly beautiful hardwood floor.

"I mean . . . it. I . . . don't . . . know."

With the twisted mask of agony he wore, discerning the truth from a lie proved impossible. He could have said anything to get help, so why not at least make up a location to get me to call 9-1-1? Instead, he said a few times he didn't know. I had to believe him, and I couldn't let him bleed to death in my office. Even my conscience has its limits.

I called 9-1-1.

CHAPTER 14

I BECAME ACQUAINTED WITH OFFICERS JENNINGS AND Brennan of the BPD over the past year. Whenever I experienced some incident requiring police intervention, they were the ones on the scene. They both nosed around the room as a crime scene technician took measurements, swabbed blood, and frowned like making faces was the crux of his job.

"You ever seen this guy before?" Jennings said. I shook my head. "Know why he came here?"

"When he pulled a gun and pointed it at me, I inferred the reason."

Jennings rolled his eyes. "Must be your private school education. I mean, why would he come here and point a gun at you?"

"Obviously, he doesn't like me for some reason."

"This dislike couldn't be related to whatever case you're working on?" said Brennan.

"Probably, but I don't know how he plays into the whole thing."

"Is there something you're not telling us?"

I put my hand over my chest and gasped. "Me?"

This time Brennan rolled his eyes. Jennings said, "What's your case?"

"Between me and my client," I said.

"You don't want to tell us?"

"Knowing what I'm working on isn't going to give you an epiphany."

"How do you know?" Brennan said.

"Because it hasn't given me one yet, and I'm smarter than you," I said with a smile.

They both closed their notebooks. "We'll let you know if we find anything important," Jennings said.

"Is he going to live?" I said. "He left a lot of blood on my floor."

"Paramedic thinks he'll live, but he could lose his foot. Forty-five slugs tend to wreck joints like the ankle."

"What do you care?" Brennan said. "Guy came in here and meant to kill you . . . or at least point a gun at you. Why do you care if he lives?"

"Because I'm not a killer," I said.

"And maybe because you want to know something more from him?"

"The living are more useful than the dead when you have questions."

"Not all of them," Jennings said. I couldn't argue.

* * *

HAVING UPLOADED the pictures to my desktop, I now ran them through the BPD's facial recognition program. They added it a few months ago, and I soon discovered it on one of my many unauthorized excursions onto their network. One of these years, they might try to keep me out. It wouldn't work for more than a few minutes, but I would appreciate the effort. In the meantime, I appreciated the access.

With no idea how well-known my Chinese friend would be, I

set the widest search parameters the BPD's software would allow. It would connect to a few federal databases. The process could take a while, so I went into the kitchen and whipped up a quick dinner. Gloria came in while I had the gnocchi boiling on the stove.

"Something smells good," she said, doffing her mink jacket and hanging it in my coat closet.

"Doesn't something always smell good in this kitchen?" I said.

She planted a kiss on me. "Yes, it does," she said with a smile. "What are you making?"

"Gnocchi and meat sauce with chopped sausage. Garlic bread is in the oven. I needed something quick."

"Why, is your case pressing?"

I filled her in on the details since the last time we talked. "We might have a day to find this girl, so I need to keep working, make sure I keep my energy up, and skip sleeping as much as I can."

"You're really dedicated to finding this girl."

"I don't want her getting sold into some sex ring and disappearing overseas," I said. "It might have happened with the other girls. We have a chance to prevent it this time."

Gloria looked pleased—maybe a bit proud? "No, it's good," she said. "I understand why you're doing it. I'm sure her mother is grateful."

"Right now, her mother is overwhelmed." I took the gnocchi out of the pot. Their fast cooking time made up for the sauce. I made two plates of the entrée and put the garlic bread on a third, then added two glasses and a small pitcher of tea to the table. Gloria sat after I did and inhaled the aromas wafting from the dish.

"Smells really good," she said, "especially considering how quickly you made it."

I ate garlic bread while I waited for the gnocchi and sauce to cool. "I had to shoot a man today," I said.

Gloria had started moving a forkful to her mouth and stopped. "What happened?" she said. "Are you OK?"

"I'm fine." I told her the details.

"It sounds like he'll live," she said.

I nodded. "Worse for the wear, but yes."

"He's the second crook you needed to shoot, right?"

"Yes. At least this one will make it." A couple months before, I put three in the chest of a man. He didn't make it.

"This is dangerous." Gloria grabbed my free hand. I looked down but didn't pull back. Concern creased her brows. "I'm worried about you. Loan sharks, maybe sex trafficking, and men trying to shoot you in your own home." She shook her head. "At least tell me you're getting an office soon."

"As soon as this case is over," I said.

"Good." She pulled her hand back and ate. We didn't talk much for the rest of the meal. After I cleared the table, Gloria stayed in the kitchen while I walked back to my office and checked the facial recognition software. It showed a match. Jiyang "Johnny" Chen was a hired fist and gun who worked for shady people like David Rosenberg. His sheet sported a few arrests but none for anything more than simple assault, and he never remained a jailbird long. Under his list of known associates, I found another Chinese name, someone he met in prison: Edwin Zhang. Maybe he was the second man who came to kidnap Katherine Rodgers. I took as good a picture of his face as I could and sent it as a text message to Zachary Rodgers.

A minute later, I got a return text: *Maybe. Measurements seem right and the eyes look familiar.* Good enough for me. I started looking for Zhang in the hopes he would lead me to Katherine Rodgers and whoever killed Stanley, which was the case I originally signed on for.

* * *

SOON AFTER I started my search for Edwin Zhang, Mouse called. I could use a shot of positive news. "Tell me something good, Mouse," I said.

"I think I can," he said. "Meet me somewhere. How about The Greene Turtle in Fells Point?"

"The Turtle's a move down from the steps of M and S, isn't it?" I liked the Turtle, but it didn't fit with Mouse's incongruous interest in looking upscale.

"A man's gotta do what a man's gotta do," said Mouse. "Can you be there in fifteen minutes?"

"I'll do my best," I said.

I made it in nineteen. Federal Hill and Fells Point aren't far apart as the crow flies, but as the car drives, complicating factors emerge. Afternoon traffic had picked up in Baltimore. It wasn't rush hour yet, but there were enough people on the road driving like assholes to do a close approximation. I got stuck behind a bunch of them, especially on Pratt Street. Once I got into Fells Point, parking was an adventure. I circled the block a few times before sniping a spot on Broadway.

When I got into the Greene Turtle, Mouse already occupied a booth as removed as possible from the happy hour crowd. I heard snippets of conversations about hot girls, bicycles, and mutual funds as I passed. At least they found one interesting thing to talk about. I slid onto the booth opposite Mouse. He nursed a whiskey-based drink stronger than the selection of beers he usually chose. Mouse inclined his head at me, and then his beady eyes flitted away as a comely young waitress appeared. Her Greene Turtle T-shirt struggled to hold her breasts in place, and I thought it could lose the fight any moment. I found her eyes, wondered how many people never did, and ordered an iced tea.

"Figured you could use a stiff drink," Mouse said.

"Maybe when the case is over," I said.

He pointed at his glass. "You want a sip of mine?"

"No, thanks." I shook my head. "I have a policy of never drinking after people nicknamed for rodents."

Mouse shrugged and took the sip he promised me. The waitress came, dropped off my tea, and asked if we needed anything else. Mouse ordered some onion rings, and she disappeared again. "I found out some stuff about your Chinese friends," he said.

"The friendship is strained," I said, "after I shot one of them."

"Wow."

"In my defense, he menaced me first."

"Who'd you shoot?"

"Johnny Chen," I said. "I'm currently looking for Edwin Zhang."

"Good," Mouse said, "he's the one I heard something about."

"What did you hear?" I said.

"He came here with a few other people," Mouse said. Rented some kind of a warehouse in Catonsville. Fake name and all. I heard he and his people had an agreement with Rosenberg. He gives them some pretty girls when he can't collect, and they give him some cash."

"Sounds consistent with what I know."

The waitress returned and dropped off Mouse's onion rings. They came in a stand with two dipping sauces. One was ranch dressing, but I couldn't identify the other. It appeared the color and consistency of Thousand Island dressing, which sounded repulsive on onion rings. Mouse bit a piece of the onion ring breading and let it cool before he dunked it in the mystery sauce.

"What's the other dip?" I said, jutting my chin toward the red-orange stuff.

"I dunno," he said, "some kind of spicy mayo shit. It's probably bad for you, but it tastes really good. You want one?"

Having lunched frequently with Joey Trovato, I was unaccustomed to being offered part of anything. I became good at picking my spots and swooping in to steal a morsel at the most opportune time. Mouse raised one eyebrow, which made me realize I simply sat and looked at him when he offered me an onion ring. "I need some rest," I said. "Sure, I'll have one." I took a medium-sized one from the basket and set it on my appetizer plate to let it cool.

"Where were we in the business conversation?" Mouse said.

I said, "You were about to tell me everything you heard about Edwin Zhang and his operation."

"I told you most of it already."

"You said he and his people struck an agreement with Rosenberg. Who are Zhang's people?"

"One's Johnny. I'm guessing he's the one you shot. He has one or two other guys. I didn't catch the names. Some Asian shit. His old man is here, too. Guiren Zhang."

I chuckled. "Name is ironic."

"How so?" Mouse said.

"Guiren means, 'valuing benevolence.' I don't think Zhang values anything close to it. I don't think he knows what it is."

"Doesn't sound like it."

"The name is familiar, though," I said. "I heard it when I was in Hong Kong."

"In hushed tones?" said Mouse

"Pretty much, yeah. I knew who they were. We were pretty bold hackers, but we didn't want to tangle with them."

"What about now?"

"Now we're going to have to tangle with them," I said.

CHAPTER 15

I TOLD RICH AND ROLLINS WHAT I'D LEARNED FROM MOUSE, and what I heard of the Zhangs during my time in Hong Kong. We sat at my kitchen table. Gloria went upstairs. I wanted her to go home, but she said she'd stay until the case was over. I made coffee for everyone, and we all sipped from our mugs. "Sounds like we have a problem on our hands," Rich said.

"A serious one," I said. "These people can't be taken lightly."

"How many men do they have?" Rollins said.

"I don't know. Mouse didn't say a number, only the people he saw or heard about. If they rented a warehouse, though, we can presume they brought enough to keep the place running."

"You mean keeping the girls in line."

I gave a grim look with the barest of nods.

Rich frowned and took a swig of his coffee. "We need to get police involved now," he said. "This is too big for us to take on by ourselves."

Rollins didn't say anything. I shook my head. "No," I said. "If they catch the police sniffing around, they'll pack up their operation, and we'll never find Katherine Rodgers. We have a chance to save her and however many other girls they're holding."

"We're not the Keystone Kops," Rich said. "We're not

bumblers. You assume the department getting involved means the Zhangs will find out about it quickly."

"It's possible they will," I said.

Rich slapped the tabletop. "I wish you'd stop supposing we're so incompetent."

"I don't, but we can't afford the risk."

Rich rolled his eyes until they came to rest on Rollins. "What's your take?"

"He's right, to a point," Rollins said. "You guys might not bungle it, but it's a high-risk, low-reward scenario. One badge not stowed away properly ends everything. I don't think it's a worthwhile risk."

"I can't believe you want to go after these people by ourselves." Rich threw his hands in the air.

"Not what I said," I retorted. "I'm saying we can't risk official police involvement."

"Because you've got us down as buffoons." Rich glared.

"No, but like Rollins said, one little mistake can be all it takes. Besides, the Zhangs are rich and careful. They may have paid off someone . . . or a few someones. We don't know who we can involve."

"So now the police are corrupt, too?" Rich shouted loudly enough for Gloria or my neighbors or most people in Maryland to hear. I couldn't back down, though. On some level, he knew I didn't think the cops were on the take, but now Rich was entrenched and defending his own.

"We're both saying the risk is too great, is all."

Rich seethed in his chair for a minute. "I'm going to call this in."

"No, you're not," I said.

He put both hands on the table and glowered across it at me. "Are you going to stop me?"

I stared back. "Yes."

Rich narrowed unblinking eyes at me. He gripped the end of the table hard enough to turn his knuckles white. I didn't waver. I understood his interest in protecting his own, but we weren't attacking them here. Finally, Rollins spoke. "As much as a staring contest between you two interests me, we might need to move past this."

"How do you suggest we do it?" said Rich, still not looking away. His left eyelid twitched.

"I agree with C.T. You're outvoted."

"Ah, democracy," I said. My eyes dried and stung. I wouldn't blink until Rich did, though. At least I fought for pride.

"Fine," Rich said, releasing a deep breath. "I'm outvoted for now." He blinked, and I did, too. It came as a relief. "I'll give it until sunrise tomorrow. We have a soft deadline for the girl anyway. If we're not pulling girls out of a crate by then, I'm bringing the entire BPD in on this."

"Fair enough," I said. His deadline gave us about thirteen hours.

"But the three of us can't take on the Zhang organization."

"I agree. It's why I'm going to call for reinforcements."

"Will I like this?" said Rich.

"I think so," I said.

* * *

I HADN'T WORKED with Captain Casey Norton of the Maryland State Police since Rich and I took down a shady veterans' charity in Garrett County. Like most cops, he didn't care much for me at first, but came around to see the value I added to the investigation. Now I counted on him wanting to help me off the books. I tried his desk first, then his cell phone. He answered, and I reminded him of our combined case-cracking.

"You still working out in the sticks?," he said.

I didn't know how to take his tone. "I'm trying to spread my charm and personality to the rest of the state."

"I'm sure you are. What can I do for you?"

I gave him most of the details of the case to this point. "We don't want official police involvement for fear of scaring these guys off."

"And they would either leave with the girls or just shoot them and find more somewhere else."

I hadn't even considered the more grisly option. "Yes," I said, wincing at the thought of telling Pauline Rodgers her daughter was dead. "We're trying to avoid either of those, but we don't have much time. We probably have until tomorrow morning."

"How do you know?"

"An informant," I said.

"This snitch tell you where the girls are?" Norton said.

"Unfortunately, no."

"So you want me to work off the books and help you find these girls?"

"We might need more than just you," I pointed out. "The Zhangs could have a lot of men. Right now, we have three. You'd make four."

"Given the stakes, I think I can rouse a few people to help me."

"Good. How soon can you be at my house in Federal Hill?" I gave him the address.

"Within the hour," he said.

"Drive fast."

* * *

AFTER I HUNG up with Captain Norton, I researched which management companies rented warehouses in Catonsville. It wasn't a long list. Finding one rented by the Zhangs was similarly quick. Property management companies didn't get targeted by hackers, so they only set up basic security measures. The Zhangs rented a warehouse at 5700 Executive Drive in Catonsville. With few occasions to explore Catonsville, I punched it up on a map and then pawed through my top desk drawer. I looked at my watch. If I hurried, I could make it.

"Rollins, you're with me," I said as I stood.

"Where are you going?"

"To check out the building," I said. "We need to know if the girls are there, or if it's just a place they're renting."

"Then let's wait for reinforcements," Rich said.

"No time. I want to get in while there's still a legitimate reason to."

Rollins stood ready to go with me. "So what's your legitimate need?" he said.

I flashed Rich a fake ID Joey Trovato made for me a while ago. "Building inspector," I said.

"You think it'll work?"

"I think it's our best chance." I told Rich about Captain Norton and when he and what reinforcements he could bring would arrive. "Wish me luck."

"I'm not sure I want to encourage you," said Rich.

* * *

I DROVE the Caprice like it was meant to be driven. Its souped-up V8 yearned for an eager driver and an open throttle. I provided both. All the way along I-83, onto the Beltway, Frederick Avenue, then Ingleside Avenue, I tore up the pavement, screeched the tires, and zoomed around everyone I could. I collected enough middle fingers to make the world's most morbid necklace, but I got us there in record time. Lights were still on inside.

"Wait in the car," I said to Rollins, "but be ready if I need you in there."

"How will you let me know?"

"I'll text you. Or you'll hear gunfire. Hopefully it won't be me getting shot."

"I'd feel better if I could go with you," Rollins said.

"Only have the one ID," I said. "I'll be fine. Just some smooth-talking and looking around."

"I'll be ready."

I went up to the front door. It was locked, so I pushed the buzzer. A voice crackled over the intercom a few seconds later. "Who is it?" Asian.

"Building inspector," I said.

"Building inspector? It's the end of the day."

"End of the day for me, too, pal." I took care to emphasize the Baltimore accent I always denied having. "I just want to do this job and go home. I'm in, I'm out, and unless you got shit falling down in there, everybody gets a gold star."

"Fine, fine. We'll let you in."

Ah, the power of social engineering. People wanted to be helpful. Sometimes, they merely wanted to be rid of you. Either way, the door buzzed a moment later, and I opened it. Someone turned most of the lights off already. The entry closing choked off some ambient light. I stood in a dim lobby. An unused reception desk sat before me. Everything else in the building was a window, hallway, or closed door. One of the interior doors opened. A Chinese man and a large white man walked through it. Both looked at me like they wanted to boot me through a window without opening it first.

"Building inspector," I said, flashing them the ID Joey made for me. If they called to verify it, I was cooked. I could only hope to get Rollins in here before they shot me. It was the end of the day, though, and I'd been convincing.

"Who ordered the inspection?" the Chinese man said. His accent was mild.

"New lease, new inspection. Them's the rules. I just play by them."

"You make us play by them, too."

"I'll be as quick as I can," I said. "I want to get home and open a beer."

The large white fellow smiled in empathy. The Chinese man stared steadily at me. He studied my ID like it contained a secret code. "Fine," he said after a moment of getting my pulse elevated. "Be quick. Ollie will show you around."

"Swell." Ollie led me through a different door than the one from which they emerged. Offices lined either side of a corridor stretching to the back of the building. I went into and out of each as quickly as I could while looking like I actually inspected something. I did the same in the two bathrooms at the end of the hallway. When I finished, Ollie led me back up the hallway, out to the lobby, then through another door.

"Odd the hallways don't merge," I said.

Ollie shrugged. "Ain't our building."

"Mine, either. Just another wonder of design." I wrote something on my legal pad to make him think I took a productive note. The rooms off this hallway could have been labs or served as a production area. The smallest was at least three times the size of the offices in the other hallway. While none were in use, I could see hookups for sinks, showers, and other industrial equipment. The girls would need showers; these rooms would work. I didn't see any evidence of recent use, however, and I didn't think Ollie would let me break out a fine-toothed comb. At the end of the hallway, swinging double doors looked back at us. I started toward them. Ollie coughed.

"Do you need to go back there?" he said.

"My title's not building-except-for-the-back-rooms inspector," I said.

He frowned. "I guess not. OK, come on." Ollie pushed the doors open, and I followed him. He went through another heavier door, and we walked into an industrial refrigerator. I got an ominous feeling about it and palmed my cell phone in case I needed to fire off a quick text to Rollins. If my phone got a signal in here. They'd filled the refrigerator with boxes, crates, and cartons of varying sizes. None looked large enough to hold a person. At least, not an intact person. I shuddered at the thought rather than the temperature.

I took more time in the fridge. It's easy to hide a secret panel, lever, or something to open an area a casual inspection would miss. I learned those tricks in Hong Kong, so I knew what to look for. I didn't find anything. After touring the refrigerator, Ollie led me back out through the swinging double doors into the hallway. We returned to the main corridor and then to the last part of the building. The final hallway opened into a large storage warehouse. There was enough room to play baseball inside, and the outfielders could check in delivery trucks during a break in the action.

One trailer sat waiting to be picked up by a truck. I walked to it during my inspection. While Ollie wasn't looking, I rapped on the side of it a few times. I didn't hear any noises coming from it. I made my way around it and rapped on it again. Ollie hadn't said anything yet. If they were keeping the girls in there, he might not have shown me the warehouse, and he certainly would have objected to my knocking on the metal trailer. Silence greeted me every time I rapped. I turned and headed toward the door. Ollie looked at me and pursed his lips.

"I gotta make sure stuff is sound," I said.

"Including a trailer?" he said.

"Comes free with the inspection. Besides, I can't resist

knocking on those things. I don't know why." I offered him a grin I hoped would disarm whatever situation might be developing.

Ollie shrugged massive shoulders and led me back out. "Everything looks OK?" he said.

"Looks good to me," I said.

"My boss will be pleased."

"I didn't catch your boss' name."

"Have a good night," Ollie said. He gave me a smile, one encouraging me not to ask again.

"You, too," I said, and I walked out, down the sidewalk, and back to my car. Rollins reclined on the backseat. If I didn't know better, I would have accused him of sleeping.

"Anything?" he said.

"They have the room to keep them here," I said, "but no girls."

"So this was a waste," Rollins said as I started the car.

"No," I said. "We know the girls aren't here. It's more than we knew before."

"You're optimistic."

"Sometimes, it's hard."

"This one of those times?" he said.

I nodded. "Very much so."

"You think they moved them already?"

"Maybe," I said. "All I know is the clock keeps ticking."

* * *

WHEN WE GOT BACK to my house, Captain Norton waited with two fellow state troopers. The first was tall and stocky with the same blond crew cut he'd probably been getting since he was eleven. The other was Hispanic, also tallish, and wiry. If I were a betting man—and I occasionally am—I would have taken the Hispanic trooper over the other one in a fight. Norton introduced them as Lance Bell and Jose Chavez. A round of handshakes later, and we were all caught up on who was whom.

Everyone drank coffee. Rich said he made a new pot. Maybe all the wretched coffee Rich choked down in the police station all day made him so generous with my Ninja and its interesting blends. He and Gloria might enjoy a weak coffee brew-off, and I would have jumped off the roof before judging it. I bucked the trend by fixing a mug of tea, and then filled everyone in on what happened at the warehouse.

"Any leads on where the girls are?" Norton said.

"None," I said.

"What about Rosenberg?"

"Can't find him."

Bell shook his head, but no one said anything until Norton spoke again. "Rosenberg's crew?"

"The party line is they don't know where he is," I said.

"You don't think they're involved in taking the girls?"

"No. I think Rosenberg farmed it out to the Chinese and collected a nice paycheck each time."

"These were all families who owed him money?" Bell said.

"I guess he thought the abductions would speed up payments."

"Did they?"

"According to his financials, no."

"You've seen his financials?" Chavez said.

"His accountant was forthcoming with some information," I said. It wasn't a huge lie. "I got it verified by someone else."

"And?" Chavez said.

"And he's barely staying afloat," I said. "If not for the money he pulls in from these abductions, he might have folded up shop by now."

"Be a damn shame," Norton said.

"It's more a shame we have missing girls on our hands," I said.

"Some of them have been gone long enough we'll probably never get them back."

"That's fucked up," Bell said.

We all nodded in agreement with his observation.

"What's our next move?" Rich said.

"Find the girls," I said. "We have to presume we're on a twelve-hour clock. It doesn't give us a lot of time."

"When we do locate them?"

"Once we know where they are and can be sure these assholes aren't going to kill them all, we can call all your cop friends and have a handcuff party."

"I like handcuff parties," Norton offered.

"TMI," I said.

* * *

ROLLINS LEFT to get some supplies and came back with two large bags on his shoulders. The first was a military-issue camouflage duffel. The second was black with pink highlights and straps. He plunked them both in my living room. It sounded like he dropped a ton of metal on the floor. I looked to make sure they didn't crash through the floor and wind up in the basement. "In case we have to do any heavy lifting later," Rollins said.

"I presume those are all legally owned and registered firearms," Norton said.

"They are. Too bad I left all the paperwork in my third duffel, though."

"I think it all looks in order."

"You said Rosenberg has an accountant?" Rich said.

"Yes," I said.

"And the accountant doesn't know where he is."

"So he says."

"You think he knows where the girls are?"

"Didn't come up in any of our conversations," I said.

"Might be worth finding out," Rich said.

"His office is in Fells Point. Why don't we go see where he goes when he leaves?"

Norton grinned. "We'll sit on his place. I like it. Bell, Chavez, and I will go. Give us the address. We'll let you know when he leaves and what direction he's headed."

"OK," I said. "I'll see if I can find out anything more about what the Zhangs are up to in our fair city." I gave Norton Eisenberg's business card. He called the number on the card and hung up quickly.

"Good, he's still there," Norton said. "Nothing like a hardworking accountant."

"And it's not even tax season," I said.

"This guy might be doing taxes for his cellmates when it's all over," Bell said.

THE ZHANGS DIDN'T LEAVE a lot of tracks. They rented the warehouse in Catonsville and a suite in a downtown hotel. The latter wouldn't be big enough to hold the girls, and a hotel made a poor place to stash a bunch of kidnapping victims. The Zhang family was as slimy as a newborn lizard, but I couldn't pin anything to them with what I found.

On a lark, I looked into Jiyang Chen. He had put down some temporary roots, renting a basement apartment in the county and buying his car from a local Carmax. He also formed a limited liability company with Edwin Zhang which professed to be in the shipping and receiving business. I imagined they told all manners of lies about what goods they trafficked if asked. I wanted to know if this shell LLC had any holdings.

The company leased a shipping container at the Port of Baltimore and a small warehouse on Key Highway. The container was not currently at the Port. Now we were getting somewhere. Rich perked up when I leaned forward in my chair. "What's going on?" he said. "Did you find something?"

"Maybe," I said. I explained what I found about Chen, the Zhangs, their phony company, and its local holdings.

"Sounds promising," said Rich.

"It does. The last thing we thought was promising turned out to be a dud, though." I kept looking into the shipping container and small warehouse. The warehouse lease expired at the end of this month with an option to renew, which no one yet exercised. The shipping container bore a bunch of paperwork, including what I guessed to be a bogus manifest, but it also listed a departure date of tomorrow morning. A little over half a day remained until someone oblivious to what he was doing would load the container onto a cargo ship bound for China. Then Katherine Rodgers and however many girls were stashed in there with her would never be seen again.

"You want to roll out on it?" Rollins said.

"Not just yet," I said. "We have a little time. Let's see what Norton and his troopers turn up."

Fifteen minutes later, Casey Norton called my cell phone. "Your accountant is on the move."

"Good. Where's he going?"

"We're tailing him out of Fells Point right now. Looks like he's headed down Light Street."

He could take it to Key Highway if he wanted to stop by the warehouse, or he could get to the Port easily from there, too. "There are a couple of possibilities for where he might go, I think." I said. I filled Norton in on my research.

"Looks like he's headed for Key Highway," Norton said.

"Let us know. We can be ready to move in a couple minutes, and it isn't far."

"I don't think he's going to the port." He paused. "No, he's not. He just turned into an industrial place. Looks like a rundown building for junk storage."

"Has to be it," I said. "Can you park somewhere you can keep an eye on things?"

"This isn't my first rodeo, you know," said Norton.

"I know."

"Are you on your way?"

"We will be in a minute." I hung up and told Rollins and Rich what Norton said.

"Let's roll out," Rollins said. "This is the most involved bodyguard gig I ever signed on for."

"But the most interesting, too. Where else do you get to take down Chinese sex traffickers?"

"It's a nice perk," he admitted.

CHAPTER 16

RICH, ROLLINS, AND I DONNED KEVLAR VESTS. ROLLINS brought enough armor for everyone, Norton and his crew included, and enough guns to make a militia envious. I packed my .45 with two extra clips and took another .45 and spare magazine from Rollins. I hoped the first gun and resupply would be more than enough. Rich borrowed a few handguns. Rollins carried a handgun and a small machine gun. I doubted he held my preference of not using it.

We repacked the excess into Rollins' duffel bags and loaded them into the trunk of the Caprice. I capitalized on the performance engine and made it to the warehouses on Light Street in a matter of minutes. Norton and his fellow troopers were parked on the street. I pulled the Caprice behind them. They wore their own vests, but each of them took a backup weapon in case things got ugly. Bell took a shotgun and smiled like he used one in a similar situation before. Norton chose his men well.

Once everyone was armed for war, we drove to the row of warehouses and parked near the entrance. Rollins scanned the front of the warehouse. "Drive around," he said. "Might help to know what's going on out back."

I drove to the rear. A large shipping container sat docked at the loading bay. No one milled around. "Looks like everyone is inside," I said.

"Hoped to catch a few out here," Rollins said. "Looks like we're doing it the hard way. Stop the car."

"Why?" I did even though I asked the reason I should.

"I'll find a way in here," said Rollins. "Don't give me a look. I'll be fine. A few of these assholes ain't getting the drop on me so easily. I want to make sure no one important bolts when the shooting starts."

"All right. Good luck."

"Thanks." Rollins got out and padded off toward the warehouse. I drove back around to the front.

"I hope he knows what he's doing," I said.

"He does," Rich said.

"You know him?"

"Never met him until recently. But I know of him, and I know people like him. Some of them aren't as good as they say they are. He is. Why he hires himself out as a bodyguard, I don't know, but you found a good one. He could be off leading a revolt in Burma or whatever they're calling it these days."

"I think it's Myanmar now."

"Whatever."

"I'm glad he's working for us," I said.

"Me, too," said Rich.

* * *

THE FIVE OF us walked to the door. We didn't encounter anyone. I found this odd but decided not to question our good fortune too much. "I wonder if they can see us approaching," I said, unable to resist being a wet blanket.

"I don't notice any cameras," Norton said.

"You might not be aware of good ones. And even if the people inside can't see what's on the camera, the management company might be able to."

"You'd think it would discourage them from shuttling a bunch of young women in and out," Rich said.

"Fair point," I said. "We are invisible."

"I wouldn't go so far."

We got to the door, and everyone flattened against the gray stonework. There were no windows along the front wall. If they didn't know we were here yet, they wouldn't know until we breached the front door. I tried the knob. It was locked. I took out my special keyring, which the four cops standing with me scrutinized.

"Would those be burglar's tools?" Norton said.

"They look like burglars' tools," Chavez added.

"I actually have a lot of keys," I said. "It must be the bad lighting out here."

Norton bent to look at the keyring as I selected the right tools for the job. "Must be the bad lighting," he concurred.

I slid a steel rod into the lock, then a tension wrench. Five tumblers reverberated at the end of the wrench. This was a good lock. The probe slipped a couple times, and I was forced to redo the first two tumblers. It took more than two minutes, but I popped the lock and put my keyring away.

"It's a lot faster on *NCIS*," Norton said."

"So are forensics," I said. "Funny how things get faster on TV."

"Someone's a little sensitive, I think," Bell said.

I appreciated the levity before we walked into what promised to be a pitched battle. "You have your professional reputation," I said. "I have mine."

Bell chuckled and brought the shotgun to bear in the next breath. Rich butted in front of me, drew his pistol, and put his hand on the door. I took out my .45 and noticed I'd been last to have his sidearm ready. These guys were professionals at this. As much grief as I gave them for being cops and playing within the system, I never lost sight of how good they were. While I held gobs of confidence in my own abilities, I'd been doing this for about a year. I was a cocky amateur.

Nice pep talk before walking into the warehouse, I chided myself.

Rich stood to the side and yanked the door open. Bell shouldered the shotgun and strode into the room. We were ready to go.

* * *

THE LOBBY WAS empty to the point not even a stray scrap of paper littered the floor. If we hadn't seen the container at the back of the warehouse, I might have guessed the Zhangs and company already packed up and moved out. One door led to the back of the building. It didn't have a window inside it. Rich went to it and listened, then moved away and shrugged.

"Want to try putting your ear to the ground?" I said, taking care to keep my voice low.

"If I thought it would help," said Rich.

I went to the door. If Rich didn't hear anything, I doubted I would. I tried the handle. It was locked, too. I crouched and broke out the keyring again. This was a simple door handle with a crappy lock attached. Whoever designed this building wanted to offend my skills. I unlatched it in well under a minute.

Bell stepped forward again, shotgun leading the way. Rich stood to the side and yanked the door open. A slender Chinese man in the process of lighting a cigarette looked up in surprise. His eyes went wide. The unlit cigarette tumbled from his mouth. He reached for a pistol. Bell pointed and snarled, "Do it! Pull your little pistol!" The Chinese man stopped. He looked at us, realized he was outgunned, and put up his hands.

"Be quiet, and we won't hurt you," I said in Chinese.

He frowned in surprise. Bell walked through and clobbered the Chinese man in the face with the stock. The crack sounded surprisingly muted considering the damage it did. Chavez had moved beside Bell and caught the man before he made further ruckus crashing to the ground.

At least we still maintained the element of surprise.

"You speak Chinese?" Chavez said.

"*Yo también hablo Español*," I said. Then I switched back to English and said, "But my Chinese is better."

"Good to know," Chavez said.

"A shame we can't stash this guy anywhere," Norton said, scanning the empty hallway. The first intersecting corridor connected in about twenty feet, and our corridor continued past it to a larger, ominous looking steel door.

"Just leave him here," Rich said. "We're going to lose the element of surprise at some point, anyway."

Norton bobbed his head, and we all moved out, creeping down the hallway. At the intersection, Bell peeked around and looked both ways. "Clear," he said in a harsh whisper. "A few doors either way. Probably offices."

"Probably empty," Chavez said.

"We can't presume," I said.

"And I'd rather not have our backs vulnerable," Rich said in support of my point. "I say we check them out. C.T. and I will go left. Two of you go right and the last man can watch the doors behind and in front of us."

"I'll watch the doors," Norton said. He jerked his head to Bell and Chavez. "You two go to the right. When in doubt, shoot."

"You got it, Captain," Bell said.

Rich and I went left. It featured three doors on either side and then dead-ended into a wall about forty feet ahead. "We'll start on the left," Rich said.

"Why?"

"Because left is always right." Confusion must have shown on my face. "I learned it from D&D," Rich elaborated with a smirk as he stopped, held his muzzle up, and jerked his head at the door. I tried the knob; it was unlocked. I turned it and pushed the door into the room. Rich went in, his gun at the lead. I filled the space behind him. The room looked empty and Rich confirmed the fact a moment later. The next room was similarly bare. As we walked away, I heard noises from the room at the end. It sounded like a woman's voice, yelling at a high pitch.

"You hear her?" I said to Rich.

"I hear something," he said.

As we walked closer, the noise grew clearer. "No! No! No!"

I sprinted the rest of the distance. Rich ran on my heels. We got to the door. I threw it open and brought my gun to bear. I will never forget what I saw next. Eliot Eisenberg, his pants around his ankles and his shirt bunched at his waist, had a young Chinese girl bent over a desk. They both turned when we burst in. Eliot's eyes went wide. The girl kept crying. Her ruined mascara and makeup made it look like she cried inky tears.

Eliot turned toward us and started to say something, but I strode to him and kicked him in the groin as hard as I could. He doubled over immediately. I drove my knee up into his face, snapping his head back and sending him to the concrete. Even though he covered his genitals with his hands, I stomped on them and kept at it until Rich grabbed my shoulder and pulled me away. "Tend to the girl," he said.

I nodded. The girl's eyes were puffy from crying, and one angry bruise already formed on her face. Blood trickled down her legs. Her feet barely touched the floor. She lay against the desk and stared at me with wide, fearful eyes. "I'm not going to hurt you," I said to her in Cantonese. Behind me, I heard Rich punch Eliot Eisenberg. I hoped he would shoot him.

Between sobs, the girl said, "Please help me."

"I will." Rich looked up at me after socking Eisenberg in the face again. I hitched my head toward the girl and stepped to the hallway. Bell and Chavez exited a room.

"Down here," I said.

They trotted to us. I stood before the door and blocked them from getting past. "There's a Chinese girl inside, maybe sixteen. We walked in on her being violated. She's going to need an ambulance."

Chavez took out his cell phone and turned away to make the call. "What about the guy?" Bell said. "He's going to need a bus, too."

"He can wait," I said. "Besides, if we leave Rich in there with him much longer, he might need a hearse."

"I'm sure Rich has the situation well in hand."

"I'm sure he does, too."

We waited in the hallway until Chavez finished making the call. "Bus is on the way," he said. "Now we're official. This isn't off the books anymore."

"We'll do what we have to do," I said.

CHAPTER 17

RICH STAYED WITH THE GIRL. CHAVEZ GUARDED OUR BACKS
as we stood at the ominous doors at the terminus of the main hallway. Like the others, these held no windows, and I could tell at a
glance they were made of sturdy steel. Their locks would be
good. I took out my keyring and got to work. It took over two
minutes, but I popped the mechanism on the right-hand door.

"Where did you learn lockpicking?" Bell said.

"Hong Kong," I said, "where I perfected my Chinese."

"So you learned the language and became a burglar."

"You're glossing over a lot of interesting stories," I said.

He chuckled, and in the next breath, the mirth melted from
his face in favor of a grim, determined look as he readied the
shotgun again. The next person who looked cross at him wouldn't
get the benefit of a warning. "Good to go when when you guys
are."

"You have our backs, Chavez?" Norton said.

"You know it, Captain," he said.

"Rollins is probably inside already," I said. "For all we know,
these assholes might all be dead already."

"We'll proceed as if they're not," Norton said. He crossed to
the other side of the door and jerked it open. Bell went in first

with me following. Norton moved in after me as the door swung shut. He caught it with his foot and let it close quietly.

The warehouse was a large, mostly open expanse. To either side of us, loose hallways defined by slapdash partition walls held production offices. The rest of the tiled floor looked free and clear. A loading dock bisected the back wall, and a trailer had been backed in. A few Chinese men, along with an American or two, pushed some young girls around. No one took notice of us yet. Bell edged up along the right-hand partition. Someone saw us then and shouted out an alert in Chinese. The shouter went for his gun. Bell blasted him. Blood ran from several holes in his body as he toppled to the floor.

I hugged the left wall and Norton advanced behind Bell. A slender Chinese man ran around the partition wall with a gun pointed at me. I squeezed off two rounds, one into the right side of his chest and the other into his left collarbone area. He sagged into the wall and crumpled. I backed up a step and started past the production offices to make sure no one plotted an ambush there. Rollins moved into the hallway from the other end. He held up his hand at me.

A gunshot rang out, then another. Both hit Rollins. He staggered backward and slid to the ground. His gun fell from his hand and skittered away. I took off at a run. A tall Chinese man with a wispy mustache walked out of the office, holding a gun on Rollins. "How did you find us?" he said in mildly-accented English.

Before Rollins could answer, the Chinese man noticed my advance. He whipped his gun around. I went into a feet-first slide. He finished turning and fired twice. I slid toward him and pulled the trigger as quickly as I could. My first missed, but then four .45 slugs took him in the upper leg and body. He rocked back, dropped his gun, and collapsed to the floor.

Rollins lunged and grabbed his gun. He looked behind me up

the hallway as I put another clip into the .45. I looked at the dead Chinese man. He bore some resemblance to Edwin Zhang in the thin nose and triangular jaw. He was also the first man I killed who didn't threaten my life. I inhaled deeply and let out a breath as the fact sank in. I defended Rollins. If I hadn't, the gunman would have killed him.

"How are you?" I said as I paused next to Rollins. I kept an eye on both ends of the hallway as he dragged himself to a seated position.

"I'll be OK," he said. "Vest took the slugs." Rollins pulled his shirt open and looked at the two mushroomed bullets embedded in his armor. "Knocked the wind out of me, probably cost me a rib or two. But I'll be OK . . . thanks to you."

"I guess it was my turn to be the bodyguard," I said.

"Rollins smiled. "I'll be nice and not charge you for today."

I held out my hand and helped him stand. "Sounds fair."

* * *

NORTON and I fanned out on the left side of the room; Rollins and Bell took the right. Only a few stragglers remained. I heard the shotgun go off once, but no one Norton and I encountered offered any resistance. Chavez came into the warehouse. Then he and Bell herded the remaining assholes into a corner and held them there at gunpoint. I walked to the cargo trailer. It was a medium red with a few markings. The fasteners had been engaged.

Thankfully, they didn't require any special keyring voodoo. Norton approached behind me. He and I raised the levers and swung the rear panels open. Norton produced his flashlight and turned it on. A few LED lights stuck on the walls of the trailer provided dim illumination. All told, about two dozen girls of varying ages were in the trailer. A few American, but more were

Chinese, probably the children of immigrants. All of them stared at us with wary eyes, and a few backed away and trembled. I didn't want to imagine what horrors some of these girls experienced from the Zhangs and their cronies.

"I'm Captain Norton of the Maryland State Police," Norton said. "You're safe now. We're here to rescue you."

I translated his words into Chinese for the Asian girls but managed to paint myself as the rescuer at the start of the message. To the translator go the spoils.

"We have an ambulance on site already and more on the way," Norton said. "More officers and counselors are on their way, too." He held out his hand and beckoned the girls forward. "Why don't you all come out of there?"

None of them moved at first. I spied Katherine Rodgers in the back. She might have been the oldest girl in the trailer. A bunch huddled together near the back. However long they had been here, they learned to rely on each other. All men did was hurt them in ways I didn't want to think about but already witnessed from Eliot Eisenberg. We needed to get them to trust a couple of men—at least long enough to leave the trailer and receive medical attention.

"Katherine," I said. She looked up at the mention of her name. "Your mother misses you. I told her I would find you. She's very worried. Why don't you come out of there?" She looked like she didn't recognize me for a minute. Then she bobbed her head and came forward. Her first few steps were dicey, but she found her footing on the cold steel floor and walked to the door. She took the last few paces in a run and threw her arms around me.

"How did you find me?" she said. "How did you find us?"

"It's something of a long story," I said. "But we're here and you're safe now."

Once Katherine came out, the other girls trickled into the warehouse. They shied away if Norton or I tried to help them.

Katherine assisted a few of them into the warehouse and onto chairs Rollins, Chavez, and Rich brought from the offices. A slew of paramedics descended on them, accompanied by several state troopers and officers from the BPD.

"Where's Eisenberg?" I said to Rich.

"On his way downtown," Rich said. "He's trying to claim police brutality."

"What did you say?"

"I said you weren't a member of the police department."

"To my eternal gratitude."

Rich smiled. "I also pointed out he only slipped and fell into my fist three times. It could have been worse."

"I doubt he'll see it the same way."

"Fuck him," Rich said. "He's lucky I didn't kill him."

"Considering what's likely to happen to someone like him in prison," I said, "I don't think he is."

"Good," said Rich.

I SAT IN KATHERINE RODGERS' room at St. Agnes Hospital. The attending doctor already called Pauline. I didn't think anyone should leave Katherine alone at the moment, so I waited for her mother. Katherine lay on the bed and stared at the ceiling. She didn't seem interested in talking, and I didn't want to push her. The TV provided background noise over the beeping of monitors. I didn't recognize the show.

"Some girls had it worse than me," Katherine said after a couple minutes, shaking me out of my intense counting of ceiling tiles.

"All of you had it pretty bad," I said. "I'm sorry this happened to you."

It was hard to tell from my angle, but I thought her quivering chin inclined. "There are two people I can blame, and one of them is dead." She paused. "I hope the other one ends up that way, too."

"So do I."

"Do you know where he is?" she said.

"Katherine, you should rest," I said. "You've been through a lot. Don't worry about him."

"I'm going to worry about him, dammit. He's the one who told them to take me, who allowed them to lock me in there with those other girls, who let the men . . ." Katherine's voice dissolved into sobs. I stood and grabbed the small box of tissues on the table beside her bed. She took one and wiped at her eyes. I set the box beside her on the bed. "Thanks," she said after a moment.

I sat again. "You're welcome."

"Part of me is curious how you found us. I thought we were goners. They kept saying we were leaving soon, that we'd never see our families again." Katherine stopped and cried a little more. She pulled another tissue, wiped her eyes again, and blew her nose. "Then the other part of me doesn't care. You found us, and we're all safe. Why dwell on it?"

"It's a good question."

She turned her eyes to me for the first time since I'd sat in the room. "Which part should I listen to?"

"The part not wanting to dwell on things," I said.

"I think you're right."

I heard a shriek from the doorway and turned. "My baby girl!" Pauline said and dashed to the bed. She leaned down and embraced Katherine, squeezing her like a wrestler going for a bear hug—or a mother who thought she might never see her daughter again. Both shared a good cry for a couple minutes. When it tapered, I stood and started for the door. Pauline put her arm out and stopped me.

"Thank you, C.T.," she said. "Thank you so much."

I patted her on the shoulder and smiled. "You're welcome," I said and walked out. They should enjoy their happy reunion by themselves. Besides, I didn't know where David Rosenberg was, and still didn't know who killed Stanley Rodgers. At least Katherine was safe, but the original case still stood before me, pointed a finger, and laughed. A few minutes ago, I advised Katherine Rodgers not to dwell on things. I planned not to take my own advice this time. Solving Stanley Rodgers' murder was the case I signed on for, and despite the happy reunion in room 412, I hadn't made much progress on it from the beginning.

Rich called me as I left the hospital. I drove downtown.

ELIOT EISENBERG SAT in an interrogation room. He clutched an icepack to his groin. It dripped onto the floor occasionally. I hoped they would make him clean it up. After watching through the window a moment, we walked into the interrogation room. Eisenberg's right wrist was handcuffed to a bar on the desk. He scowled and appeared surprised at us, managing to pull both off at the same time.

"You're not an investor," he said to Rich.

"Actually, I am," said Rich, "just not with you."

"Shoulda known."

"So raping and sodomizing girls is your cut of this sex trade ring," I said.

"Yeah, so? All those girls, right there. How could I not?"

My answer was ready to go, but I didn't see the point.

"You know, you kicked me a lot," Eisenberg said. He jutted his chin to his crotch, as if I'd forgotten planting my foot there a bunch of times. "I might be sterile."

"If I'd remembered my knife in the moment," I said, "I would have cut your dick off and fed it to you. Kicking you into sterility was the next-best option."

"I might sue."

"Good luck. I'm sure judges and juries are very sympathetic to pedophiles who rape girls captive in sex rings."

"Hey, I'm no pedophile," he said with complete sincerity.

"What was the girl, fifteen?" I said. "Statutory rape makes you a pedophile."

"Let's move on," Rich said. "This isn't getting us anywhere. While I would like to crucify you, the state's attorney is willing to make a deal if you give up Rosenberg and all other major players above you in this sex slave trade."

"What kind of deal?"

"Up to her. It depends on how good your information is. If the feds get involved, the deal expires."

"Minimum security?"

Rich and I both laughed. "You're doing hard time, you prick," Rich said. "How much and how hard is up to you. The clock's ticking. You wanna talk?"

Eisenberg sighed. He grimaced and crossed his legs. The puddle under the ice pack grew. "I don't know where David Rosenberg is," he said after a moment.

"So no deal, then?" said Rich.

"What do you mean?"

"You say you don't know where Rosenberg is."

"Because I don't."

"Have a good guess? Anyone else up in the chain you can give us?"

"I don't know where he is. If he's gone into hiding, I don't know where. There was no one else I reported to." Eisenberg's mouth twitched a little when he said it. I didn't have to look at Rich to know he saw it, too.

"You're sure?" Rich said.

"I think I know who I fucking reported to," said Eisenberg.

"And it was only Rosenberg?"

"Yes, only Rosenberg." I saw the small twitch again. "If he doesn't want to be found, you're not going to find him."

"Won't stop us from trying," I said.

"You'll be wasting your time."

"It's mine to waste, and I'll be doing it out here, while you'll be the one getting raped in prison."

Eisenberg frowned. "That's not funny," he said.

"It's a matter of perspective," I told him.

It was late when I left the station, and I hadn't slept much the last couple days. On the drive home, I looked forward to climbing into my bed and resting for about twelve hours. If Gloria were there, she would understand. My ringing cell phone interrupted my thoughts. Caller ID showed it to be Joey. What did he want at this hour? I figured there was one way to find out.

"C.T., I might have some information for you," Joey said, "but I don't think you're gonna like it."

"Oh, fuck. What now?"

"Can you meet me? I got a table at Della Notte."

I already passed it on my way home, but turning around would be easy enough. "All right. Give me five minutes."

Whatever Joey wanted to tell me didn't sound encouraging. I drove fast and made it in four minutes, plus an extra to find a parking spot. I left the Caprice directly in front of a fire hydrant, entered the restaurant, and saw Joey in a booth along the left wall. He waved, and I walked to him, and slid onto the opposite seat. He'd already got a soda, an order of fried calamari, and a bowl of Italian wedding soup. True to form, Joey worked over the squid first.

"Glad you could come out," he said.

"I'd had my fill of slimy pedophile accountants," I said.

Joey blinked. "One more reason to hate accountants, I guess. You want anything?"

"Not really. It's been a long couple of days. I want to get home and go to sleep."

"Still working on the same case?" Joey covered a nervous smile with a quick intake of calamari. I could never watch him eat for long.

"Yeah, just wrapped up the mess spiraling out of it," I said. "Now I still have to figure out who killed Stanley Rodgers."

"And you think things still point to David Rosenberg?"

"Looks like it."

Joey winced. Normally, I might have capitalized on a moment like this to snag a bite—I never got many chances—but I wondered what discomfited Joey so much. "What's going on, Joey?" I said.

"I set someone up earlier today," Joey said, lowering his voice. "He paid double the normal rate. Got him out of town in a hurry. Great work for a quick job, if I do say so myself."

"You just did."

"So I did." Joey flashed a quick, awkward smile again. He looked like he was smiling for his senior prom photo after realizing he hated his date.

"And this is significant to my case and my evening how?"

Joey sighed. He took his napkin from his lap and set it on the table. Now he was getting serious. Joey didn't abandon eating posture unless serious shit was going down. "I didn't realize it at the time, but the guy I helped was Rosenberg." He finished the sentence with a wince, like he expected me to hit him.

If I hadn't been so surprised, I might have.

"What?" was all I could say after a moment of mentally watching my case vanish down a drain.

"I didn't know who he was. I swear."

"Joey, you've been doing this work for a few years," I said.

He indicated yes. "About three and a half."

"In this time, you've helped people get away from Rosenberg."

Another head bob. "I have."

"And you knew who "DR" meant when I had no idea," I said.

"Right, I did."

"And despite all this, you didn't know what the area's biggest loan shark looked like?" I heard a couple conversations around us stop and felt eyes on me. Joey noticed it, too.

"Keep your voice down, will you?" he said. "I told you I didn't know—"

"Oh, I heard you," I said, pounding the table. "I just don't know when you became such a fucking idiot."

"Now wait a—"

"You get blinded by the fact he paid double?"

"Will you keep your voice down?" Joey whispered.

"No. Nobody knows who you are, and nobody gives a shit." I drew a breath. "You and I both fall on the right side of the line, but you're over it this time." I rested clenched fists on the table-top. "Where did you send him?"

Joey frowned. "I can't tell you. Professional ethics."

"Professional ethics?"

"Yes," Joey said, wincing at my continued refusal to talk quietly. Several people followed our conversation with interest. All we needed now was some jackass to tweet about it, or—worse —livestream it. "I'm sure you understand."

"Oh, I understand," I said. "I understand a man is dead, and his family still grieves. I *understand* the family got torn apart when his daughter was abducted as part of a sex ring. I *understand* I and a few others just busted up the ring and saved quite a few girls, though not before some of the higher-ups took some free samples. I know the man you just sent out of the state is responsible for everything I've said."

"I told you I didn't know who he was."

I stood, grabbed Joey's bowl of hot Italian wedding soup, and dumped it in his lap. He recoiled in the chair but didn't stand. "Here's what I think of your professional ethics. Fuck you, Joey. When you realize how bad you fucked up, let me know. Until then, go to hell."

Before Joey could answer, I stormed out of the restaurant. I got curious looks from the entire staff. I ignored them.

CHAPTER 18

WHEN I GOT HOME, GLORIA WAS IN MY BED, ALREADY asleep. She stretched across enough of it to encroach on my half. Sometimes, I can sneak up and wake her with a start when I sit on the bed. Tonight, I was too tired to bother. She startled awake anyway, but it happened when I walked into the bedroom. She recovered from her initial surprise and said, "Welcome home" in a voice sounding far more alert than I felt.

"Thanks," I said. I wandered into the bathroom to attend to my nightly rituals, emerged, and changed into my pajamas. I felt tired enough I almost slept in my clothes, but I had been uncomfortable in them for a while. It was the case more than anything, but still, I wanted to sleep in clean comfort. Gloria smiled at me as I sat on the edge of the bed, then lay down. My head sank into the pillow, and I let out a deep breath. Gloria put her hand on my chest. I smelled her perfume as she leaned closer and kissed my neck. For the first time since we met, I rebuffed her advances. I couldn't scrub the image of Eliot Eisenberg violating that poor Chinese girl from my mind. Gloria said she understood.

I doubted it.

* * *

IN THE MORNING, I awoke before Gloria. I did this despite being weary from the past few days and going to sleep later than she. As I pondered the grand unfairness of circadian rhythms, I walked downstairs, fired up the coffee machine, and set some breakfast things out for Gloria. Then I called Gonzalez.

"I was wondering when I'd hear from you again," he said.

"I thought I heard eager anticipation in your voice," I said.

"Did you?"

"I'm used to hearing it from a lot of girls over the years."

"Great," he said. "Today's my day off, you know."

"Then you have no excuse not to meet me for breakfast."

"You buying?"

"Sure," I said. "Where?"

The line went silent as Gonzalez thought about it. "Towson Diner. Remember where it is?"

"Yep."

"Forty-five minutes," Gonzalez said. I was about to point out he'd tried to tack on the when to the where, but he hung up before I could.

I went back upstairs. Gloria was still asleep. I got dressed quietly, wrote her a short note, left it on her nightstand—I actually thought of it as *her* nightstand, which both gave me pause and made me smile—then left.

* * *

GONZALEZ OCCUPIED a booth near the back when I got there, late as usual. No one sat within a dozen feet of him. The Towson Diner wasn't very big, and the rest of it looked moderately crowded. I slid in opposite Gonzalez and gulped down half the glass of water waiting for me on the table. "You order yet?" I said after wiping my mouth.

He shook his head. "Just the coffee. Waiting for you."

A middle-aged waitress who looked like she'd done this her whole adult life approached and took our requests. Gonzalez asked for pancakes with double bacon and a bagel. I ordered a western omelet, wheat toast, and coffee. The waitress returned quickly with my coffee and put a fresh top on Gonzalez's. I added some sugar and cream and tried a sip. Perfectly mediocre.

"It's better than precinct coffee," Gonzalez said.

"Damning with faint praise," I said.

"What's the latest on the Rosenberg case?"

"You BCPD cops are all business," I said. "Don't I get any small talk for buying breakfast?"

"Sure," Gonzalez said with a grin. "Go, Ravens. Now tell me about the fucking case."

I caught him up on the happenings over the last few days. His expressions indicated he followed, and he looked impressed when I told him about the sex trafficking organization we had broken up. If he felt left out about not getting cut in, he didn't show it. "Rosenberg is gone," I said in conclusion. "I don't know where."

"We don't know, either," said Gonzalez. "We had a man watching him and his place. He hasn't seen him anywhere. Cell phone goes to voicemail. Our informants never knew much about him . . . still true."

"I guess he figures the heat will be on now."

"I guess."

"What about his people?"

"The ones we think were part of the loan sharking business have gone, too. The legit employees in his store are still there, far as we can tell."

The waitress brought our food and refreshed our hot and cold drinks. Gonzalez buttered his pancakes like a man defying his doctor's mandate to reduce cholesterol, then added enough syrup to dare diabetes along with heart disease. I cut my omelet in the meantime and added a pinch of salt and a few dashes of pepper.

"What's your play now?" Gonzalez said after eating a bite of his pancake death traps.

"Not sure," I said. "I guess I hope to find Rosenberg or one of his key people."

"How are you gonna do it?"

I ate a forkful of my omelet and washed it down with coffee. In all my excursions to the Towson Diner, they always made a good western omelet. Their coffee hadn't improved over the years, but it was good enough to keep the Towson and Goucher kids caffeinated for their exams. "The less I tell you about my methods," I said, "the less you can criticize me for them."

"And the more plausible deniability I have."

"Ooh, fancy term for a humble public servant," I said.

"I watch TV," Gonzalez said.

We each enjoyed more of our dishes. I noticed some college kids, girls mostly, come and go with interest. Gonzalez did, too. We detectives needed to remain vigilant and keep an eye out for evildoers. After we both ate most of our respective breakfasts, Gonzalez said, "You got Rosenberg's accountant, right?"

I grimaced. "Yeah. Caught him sampling the merchandise." A shudder overtook me.

Gonzalez noticed and offered a sympathetic wince. "Bad?"

"Worse."

"What's going on with him?"

"Right now," I said, "he's being held on a litany of charges. I think the BPD and the state's attorney are hoping he'll flip on Rosenberg, but there's no sign of it. He claims he doesn't know where Rosenberg is."

"You believe him?"

"No."

"What's his motivation?"

"If Rosenberg is as ruthless as his reputation suggests, Eisenberg probably doesn't want to get shanked in the exercise yard."

Gonzalez nursed his coffee. "Maybe. I get the feeling there's something else at play here."

"You mean besides the girls being abducted for sex?"

"Yeah. I don't know. Call it cop's intuition . . . whatever."

"I'll see what I can find."

"I'm going to do some digging, too, when I'm not working the case folders piling up on my desk. Maybe if we both shake the tree, something will fall out faster."

"Here's hoping," I said.

WHEN I ARRIVED HOME, Gloria was awake, sipping coffee, and watching a cable news show, her preferred morning viewing. She rarely talked about the events of the day, but at least she kept up with them. I tried to when a case didn't have me too busy. Since I wanted to be busy as rarely as possible, I thought of myself as well-informed, but these past few days had done nothing for such an image.

"Did you fix anything for breakfast?" I said.

She grinned around her mug of coffee. "Just a bagel with butter and jelly. I don't do well in your kitchen."

I could have pointed out she fared little better in her own, but it felt uncharitable. Gloria had been raised with a cook in the house. She was probably lucky she knew how to boil water. "I ate at a diner," I said, "with Gonzalez."

"You've done a lot of diner eating lately."

"Yeah," I said. "I've been to this one so often recently, I feel I should know all the staff by name." Gloria grinned. "Enough about my eating habits, though. How was court?"

Gloria took a deep breath and followed it up with a long swig of coffee. "Difficult," she said, "but I got through it. I told about what he said, about what happened to me." She paused. "Then I stuck around. Other girls testified, too. They . . . he . . . did more to them. I was disgusted. I wanted to leave. But I felt like . . . a part of something. We were taking this bastard down. All he could do was sit there and frown."

"Great." I leaned against the wall. "I'm glad you did it. You're getting justice. All of you should be proud."

She showed a wan smile. "All we did was go and tell the truth."

"If telling the truth were so easy, people would do it more often."

"That's true," said Gloria.

"You did important work," I said. "That asshole's probably going away for a long time."

"Is this how it feels for you?" Gloria said after draining her mug.

"Hard to say. I try not to work within the system as much as I can. It's too . . . bloated. Inefficient. But bringing down a criminal always feels good. It's very satisfying."

"Do you think you'll close the book on these criminals soon?" Gloria stood, walked to me, and kissed me on the mouth.

"I hope so."

She gave me a mischievous look and kissed me again. "I hope so, too. I'm feeling a little neglected recently." Gloria pouted for my benefit. I couldn't help but find it sexy. Of course, I found most things she did sexy.

"Tell you what," I said. "Let me start making it up to you."

She took my hand and led me upstairs.

* * *

LATER, I sat in my office, staring at my monitor and waiting for a bolt of inspiration to strike me. Gonzalez said we would both be shaking the tree. At least he knew how. My leads evaporated when Rosenberg and his crew split town with Joey helping the big man bid adieu. I scratched my head; why would Joey do something so dumb? No point in dwelling on it. When all else fails, follow the money. I took a fresh look at the financials of everyone involved.

I started with Rosenberg's payroll. Once I obtained the relevant information for all his employees, legit and otherwise, looking for their financials would be time-consuming but uncomplicated. I compiled all the employee information, found their accounts, and set about breaking into them. Some took longer than others, but within an hour and a half, I got all the results I needed. Sometime during the process, I heard the TV in the living room fire up. Gloria changed from the news to some movie filled with sappy dialogue. I steadfastly avoided being dragged to many chick flicks over the years, so I didn't know it, and I didn't pay enough attention to it to make it into a soundtrack.

While I compiled financial data, I looked for what I could on the Zhangs, as well as Johnny Chen. They only held overseas accounts, except for dummy books they created for their shell corporation. Rich said the Caton Avenue warehouse would be combed over, even though he didn't sound optimistic about finding anything usable. I'd hacked into Hong Kong banks before, but it was while I lived there. The Chinese reacted quite unfavorably to our little ring when they discovered it. I felt tentative about doing it again and decided to wait until I really needed it.

I ran Eliot Eisenberg through my system while I tiptoed around Hong Kong and found both personal and business accounts. I wanted them both, and in about fifteen minutes, I secured my information. This would take a while to sort through. I wondered if I would need Marvin Bernard again as I printed everything. Thick wad of paper in hand, I leaned back in my chair and pored over everything.

Before long, I chided myself for not getting and examining Eisenberg's complete financials sooner. His secondary personal account listed payments of five thousand dollars right around the same time Rosenberg received money for the abducted girls. The payments came from something called the JZD Corporation. I guessed it to be another shell company, and some quick looking around gave me strong hints it was. JZD claimed to be a consulting business for international relations. This firm listed no executives I could find and boasted of no testimonials.

I looked up who registered the site's domain. The name jumped out at me.

Jasper Z. Dexter.

He was Rosenberg's lackey. At least, it appeared this way. Why did he have the website for a shell corporation bearing his initials in his name, and why was he paying Eliot Eisenberg? Those weren't the actions of a flunky. I called Rich. "We should talk to Eisenberg again," I said when he picked up.

"I just finished washing the slime off from before," Rich said. "Why should we go back?"

I told him about what I discovered. "Doesn't sound like a crony to you, does it?"

"Not in the least," he said. "Can you meet me in a half-hour?"

I said I would.

CHAPTER 19

THIRTY-FIVE MINUTES LATER, I FOUND RICH SITTING ON THE corner of a desk near the interrogation room. Both he and the older male detective he talked to made a show of looking at their watches as I approached. "Parking was bad," I said as a cover story.

"The hell it was," Rich said. He stood from the desk corner. "You ready to take another run at this asshole?"

"I might need some Lysol afterward."

"You and me both," said Rich. He opened the door to the interrogation room. Eisenberg sat cuffed to the desk like before. Rich and I sat opposite him.

"Didn't have enough fun the first time?" Eisenberg said.

"You given any thought to the offer?" Rich said.

"I told you what I know . . . or what I don't know."

"My people are preparing reports. A couple of those girls were from out of state. Means you and your friends kidnapped women and transported them across state lines. The feds are going to be all over this in an hour or two. Time's running out."

Eisenberg shrugged. "I answered your questions."

"How about some new questions?" I said. "Like, why did you

get payouts from a shell corporation called JZD right around the time Rosenberg got his from the Zhangs?"

Eisenberg's calm and vacant expression quickly turned into a frown. Color made a slow drain from his face. "How do you know about those?" he said after a couple minutes.

Rich stared at me, too, but I knew he knew how I came into the information. "I got a sneak peek at your financials," I said, "and found those payouts interesting."

"They were legitimate expenditures for services rendered," Eisenberg said.

"To an obvious shell corporation whose website belongs to your buddy Jasper," I said. "All a little too coincidental."

"What went on?" Rich said to fill the gap in the exchange when Eisenberg fell silent. "Why was Jasper paying you?"

Eisenberg looked around the small room. His eyes darted between Rich and me, then around the room again. "The deal still good?"

"If you talk quickly," Rich said.

"Jasper was the brains behind trading the girls. He said he had connections, and having their child kidnapped, would pressure people into paying what they owed to Rosenberg."

"If it was only a pressure tactic, why the payouts?" I said. "Why the trafficking ring?"

"The first couple girls were just pressure. Someone would snatch them, the parents would miraculously double down on their payments, and the girls went home."

"Unmolested?"

Eisenberg closed his eyes. The negative wag of his head was slight and brief, but I saw it, and I knew Rich saw it. "After a while, Jasper decided to use his connections. Family, I think. He said we could make some money for ourselves."

"Why pay Rosenberg?" Rich said.

"His business was our backbone. You'd be amazed how many

people get in with a loan shark, and you'd be more amazed how many of them can't get out."

"And a lot of them have kids," I said.

"Right," Eisenberg said and gestured with his free hand. "Sometimes, they wanted to put their daughter into some hoity-toity private school or pay for college. When conventional loans failed, they ended up borrowing from Rosenberg."

"And when they fell behind in their payments, their daughters would disappear," said Rich.

"A son or two, also, at the beginning," Eisenberg said. "Jasper said he had some clients with . . . different tastes. But girls trade easier and for more money, so we just focused on them."

"What about Rosenberg?" I said.

"He didn't really want to be involved. Said he didn't mind having someone's knees broken, but shipping their daughter overseas to get fucked by some sheikh wasn't his thing. The money changed his mind. He needed it."

"You and Jasper were siphoning off the till," I said.

"Jasper's idea. He bled a little here and there, put it toward the Zhangs to keep those channels open. Sometimes, we'd need to pay off some flunky somewhere."

"So Rosenberg was getting paid with his own money," Rich said.

"More or less. He was getting old. Didn't have any heirs, *per se*. I don't think his heart was in it as much. Been that way for a couple years."

"So he collected from you assholes here and there and didn't think much about it," said Rich.

"Yep. We had enough delinquent clients with girls the right ages to make it worth his while."

"And the police never caught on?" I said. Rich frowned at me.

"Different jurisdictions," Eisenberg said. "The girls were far enough apart in age, looked different, came from different backgrounds." He looked at Rich. "Your people like patterns in crimes. We didn't really have any. It made things tough to follow."

"So you chose your targets to minimize police attention?" Rich said.

"Of course," Eisenberg said. "We weren't stupid. Not everyone with an . . . eligible daughter, if you will, got targeted. It would have been too many, made it too easy for the police."

"You say you don't know where Rosenberg is," Rich said.

"I don't."

"Where's Jasper?"

"Don't know, either," Eisenberg said. "He disappeared when the ring got busted."

"You have any prearranged plans in the event something like this went down?" I said.

"Not really. The plan was we'd try to contact each other when we could. If he's tried to contact me, I wouldn't know about it in here."

Rich and I looked at each other. I shrugged. Rich nodded. We must have looked like a pair of geniuses. "All right," Rich said, "I'll make sure the state's attorney's office hears about your cooperation."

"What about the feds?" Eisenberg said.

"We'll do what we can."

We left the room. "What are you going to do now?" he said, sitting on the corner of the same desk. The other cop who sat there was gone.

"Try to find Jasper," I said. "He looks like a more important player than Rosenberg at this point."

"You still working with Gonzalez?"

"Yep, I'll tell him what I learned when I leave."

Rich pulled an earnest expression. "You need an extra hand, let me know."

I looked at him. "Awfully generous. You're already bucking for some kind of commendation."

"If I don't get my ass chewed out for going off the books."

"I think Sharpe will understand."

"I don't work for him, but I think he will. Anyway, I meant it. Call me if you need an extra hand. I know Gonzalez. He'll be OK with it."

"All right," I said, "I will."

* * *

NOT LONG AFTER I got home, a knock sounded. I was in my office looking into some things. Gloria, sitting in the living room watching some other chick flick, was closer and walked toward the door. I grabbed the .45 and dashed into the hallway. "Don't answer it, please," I said. "Let me."

Gloria stopped and looked at me. I had the .45 behind my back. "Do you know who it is?"

"No, and that's why I want to answer it. While I'm working a case like this, I think it's best. Until I get a real office."

"All right," Gloria said. She stepped aside but didn't go back into the living room. Whoever was outside knocked again. I walked to the door and let the hand holding the .45 fall to my side. Gloria hadn't seen it yet, but she would soon enough. I unlocked the three locks, grabbed the knob, and opened. Instead of putting my head out, I let the muzzle of the .45 stick out. Now Gloria saw it; I heard her gasp.

"I'm not armed," Joey said, "unless you count the food."

"The man who ate Judas," I said. "I might want to shoot you anyway."

"Can I come in?" he said. "I feel bad about the Rosenberg thing."

"You fucking well should," I said, scowling at him.

"I get it. I do. Now will you put the gun away and let me in?"

I poked my head around the door. Joey stood on my doorstep with a plastic bag crammed full of fragrant Italian food. "Where'd you go?"

"Your favorite," he said.

"Chiaparelli's?"

"You have another favorite?"

I smiled. "Just wondering if you remembered correctly." I opened wider. "Come on in."

Joey stepped over the threshold. I held the .45 at my side now and locked up behind him. He saw Gloria and smiled. "Hello, Gloria."

Gloria walked to Joey and, to my surprise, gave him a hug. He seemed surprised, too, but wrapped his free arm around her. "Hi, Joey," she said. "It's good to see you." She looked at the bag. "Anything for me?"

"I'm sure there is," I said. "Joey usually eats for three. Maybe he can cut back to dinner for two tonight."

"I'm sure we'll find something for you," Joey said.

"I'll set the table," I said.

* * *

AFTER WE ATE our late lunch, the three of us enjoyed a bottle of Malbec. Gloria sensed Joey and I had some matters to discuss, so she excused herself. Somewhere, a chick flick went unwatched, and Gloria had to rectify this sin. Joey and I sat at the table, both admiring the view afforded by her small shorts as she walked down the hall into the living room. I took a sip of wine, and Joey raised his glass to me. "So you two making it official?" he said.

"I don't know," I said. "We really haven't discussed it."

"Why not?"

"I don't know." I watched my reflection twist as I swirled my wine around in the glass. "We're . . . OK with the way things are, I guess."

"Are you dating?"

"I don't know," I said. I paused. "Not in so many words."

"But you're not playing the field?"

I shook my head. "Haven't even tried in a few months."

"Is she playing the field?"

"I don't think so."

"So you're dating," Joey said.

"Who are you, Dr. Phil?" I said.

"Just wondering. You seem happy around each other. I saw the way you two would smile at each other during lunch." Joey grinned. "I haven't seen you act that way with a girl in an awful long time."

I downed the remainder of my wine and set the glass back down. Tiny streams of dark red droplets descended to the bottom and coalesced into a small pool. "I feel good when I'm with her," I said.

"Then tell her," Joey said. "Don't give her the chance to go looking."

"Did you come here to offer relationship advice," I said, "or for some meaningful purpose?"

"You don't think I can give good relationship advice?"

"Not when your first and only love is a meatball sub."

Joey chuckled and shrugged. "You got me there," he said. The humor fell away from his face. "I realized I was on the wrong side of things when it came to Rosenberg."

"About time," I said.

"I probably should have realized it right away. Maybe the bigger paycheck blinded me. I don't know. But I know what you've told me he's involved in, and I don't want to hide someone like him. I've helped sinners and saints disappear, but he'd be something else again."

I nodded. "So what are you going to do about it?"

Joey took a folded piece of paper out of his pocket, set it on the table, and pushed it to me. "This is the identity I created for him and his new home address."

I picked up the paper without unfolding it. "What am I supposed to do with it?"

"Get him arrested," Joey said. "Have him shot. I don't care. I just wanted to clear my conscience on this one."

"Sounds like you have."

"Yes. Are we cool now?"

"I might have to make a few extra fat jokes for a while," I said after a few seconds of thought.

"An acceptable penance," said Joey.

* * *

AFTER JOEY LEFT, I looked at the paper. David Rosenberg now went by the name of Jeremiah Edelstein, and he'd moved to a house in Portland, Maine. I didn't feel like driving or flying to Maine in the cold months to look for him, especially if Eisenberg told the truth, and Rosenberg had been more of a figurehead than anything. I called the Driscolls.

"Chris, this is C.T. Ferguson," I said when he answered.

"Who?"

"I met you and your wife for coffee in Hampden recently."

"Ah, right. How are things going? Have you found that son of a bitch Rosenberg yet?"

"No, but I know he's fled the state, and I know where he went."

"Sounds promising. Is this something you're willing to share?"

I have never fancied myself a killer. It's impossible to work as a PI in and around Baltimore without having someone point a gun at you. On the occasions I've needed to kill someone, it was because either my life or someone else's was in immediate danger. I couldn't simply kill someone out of spite or because it was more convenient, nor could I admire those who did. If I gave Rosenberg's information to Chris Driscoll, I suspected he would have Rosenberg killed. This was no different than me doing the job myself. Sure, he was a bastard, but did he deserve to get killed for it?

Then the image of Eliot Eisenberg raping the poor Chinese girl leapt back into my head. Rosenberg had been a willing participant in kidnapping girls to use them in the sex trade, and who knew how many had been violated by someone in his crew before being sold overseas?

"Mr. Ferguson?" Chris Driscoll said.

"Sorry, I got lost in thought for a moment there," I said. I gave him the information. I didn't ask what he planned to do with it.

CHAPTER 20

On my second lap around Federal Hill Park next morning, I noticed a Nissan Maxima newly arrived since my start. People leave their cars at curbs close to the sidewalks all the time; it happens. After my last encounter with the two gun-toting goons near there, I didn't want to take any chances. Running at a public place left me way too open in the event someone wanted to try again. Being paranoid didn't mean miscreants weren't hot after me, so I finished my run on the streets. I saw it as a win-win.

I broke off my lap and ran down Battery Avenue. The recently-parked car didn't move. From Battery, I could easily get to Riverside Avenue and then to my house, but I didn't want to lead any potential pursuers directly to my front door. I ran down Battery, picked up Warren, and checked for the Nissan. It was gone. I didn't see it on the road. I hung a left down William, running against the flow of traffic on the one-way street. Since my last jogging encounter, I packed a gun for my morning constitutionals. It was a Ruger .32 revolver, and it required a warmup jacket at least a half-size too big, but at least I could feel prepared if someone decided to take a shot at me.

When I ran past the intersection of Hamburg Street, I noticed the white Nissan coming up William. It was before nine on a Saturday morning; traffic was light, and I didn't have a wealth of places to hide. Southern High School and Federal Hill Elementary offered some protection, but I didn't want to run and hide in a school—even on weekends, teachers or custodians could be there. Of course, I didn't know the people in the Nissan meant to harm me.

I figured it out pretty quickly. The car squealed wheels and pulled to a stop at the curb about a hundred feet in front of me. Two men got out, one dashing across the street. I crouched behind the closest car and drew the .32 from the running holster—purchased from Amazon, of course—under my warmup jacket. The guy in front of me was open, but the one still on the opposite curb could hide behind vehicles, too. Depending on where he went, I could be a totally exposed target.

The one approaching shouted, "Like morning jogs, do you?"

"You from Rosenberg?" I said. I looked for the other and didn't see him. Shit.

"Don't know who he is," he said. The guy was short, slender, and probably shaved as a last resort. Rosenberg's people might have been goons, but they were more respectable looking goons. I believed him. He rewarded my belief by firing at me. Two bullets shredded the air and embedded themselves in the car behind me. Was he simply a bad shot, or did he intend to spook me from hiding to set me up for his friend? I felt very vulnerable. I scanned the other side of the street quickly. If I spent too much time looking there, the jackass in front of me could get the drop on me.

Another bullet whistled my way, this one hitting the front of the car I crouched behind. I decided this guy fired to keep me occupied. Now all I needed was find the other guy and shoot him before he shot me, while not leaving myself open to the guy up the street. As I scanned the cars across the way, I saw a flash of motion and heard a report. I ducked, even though it would be too late to matter.

No bullet approached me. The movement I saw turned out to be the other shooter. He staggered from behind a car, a spreading red stain on his left ribcage. He looked down at his gun, up at me, and collapsed onto the asphalt. Nearby cars stopped. People could always rationalize away gunshots, but a guy bleeding to death in the street was something else again. The cops would be here soon.

The one down the road stood to see what happened to his friend. He looked at me and raised his gun again. I steadied my .32 on the trunk and fired. My two shots whizzed past him on the right. He ducked, moved to his left, and raised up behind another car.

I heard another shot and watched a hole appear in his chest below his throat. He staggered, only to take another round a few inches lower than the first. Blood gushed from the hoodlum's chest and his gun fell from a hand which could no longer hold it. He sagged to his knees, then slumped forward. Past ringing in my ears, came screams and shouts from people stopped on the street. Then I turned around.

Rollins, holding a small assault rifle, waved to me from about a hundred feet.

* * *

LEAVING the scene would have been nice, but too many people lingered after witnessing what happened, so we stayed and gave statements to the police. Later, Rollins and I sat in my living room. He sipped a cranberry juice and club soda—the latter being an infernal beverage brought into my home by Gloria—while I nursed a coffee with a plus-sized shot of Irish whiskey. Gloria seated herself beside me on the sofa, silent since Rollins and I sat down, but her warm eyes glistened if the light caught them right.

"I paid you," I said to Rollins.

"Yeah," he said, "you did. But you saved my ass in the warehouse."

"So now you've returned the favor."

"I guess. Look, I'm a guy for hire, sort of like you, but I do different work. In the Army, I shot a lot of people because the alternative was much worse. But I'm not you. You haven't shot many people. You shooting someone to save me means a lot."

"I don't think body count is a factor," I said. "You popping those guys today means everything to me. The fact that you've killed more people doesn't matter." Gloria grabbed my hand and squeezed it.

"Maybe you could've gotten yourself out of that little mess," he said. "Whatever. You're doing good work, C.T. If I can help you along the way, let me know. I'll make sure to give you a good rate." Rollins smiled.

"You think the attempts on my life are over for a while?" I said.

"Depends on who sent those two today. You know?"

"I'm working on it."

Rollins regarded his drink. Its pink sheen matched the trim on his jogging pants, jacket, and shoelaces. He looked up at me. "You know why I left the Army?" he said.

"I can make a good guess."

He smiled again, but it lacked humor this time. "They didn't ask, but I told."

I said, "Good for you."

"You're not surprised?"

"Your outfits and the drinks you choose?" I grinned. "Let's just say you're not exactly stamping out the stereotype."

"No, I suppose I'm not. Did you know I have three to live down?"

"Three?"

"I'm black, I'm gay, and I'm Jewish on my father's side."

"A gay black Jew," I said.

"At your service."

"I went to college with a guy who was a gay black Hispanic Jew. He beat you by one."

"Bastard," Rollins said with a chuckle. "My being gay bothers some folks."

"Not me," I said. "Besides, you don't seem like the type to let it bother you."

"I'm not, really. It's just good to know."

"I suppose it is," I said.

* * *

AFTER ROLLINS LEFT, I called Joey, hoping he'd be awake by now.

"Hello?" he said, in a voice sounding like he'd survived a mummification attempt.

"I know you need your beauty sleep, but it's getting late," I said.

"It's not quite eleven."

"What if I needed a new identity at eight-thirty?"

"Then you'd be shit out of luck. What's up?"

"Find anything about Jasper?"

"No," he said, "nothing."

"Same here. I think it's time for a different tactic."

"Do tell."

"How would you like to play legbreaker once more?" I said.

Joey chuckled. "Are we going after a state senator's wife again?"

"A lower-profile target this time. I'll come by your place in an hour with brunch. Practice your menacing stare in the meantime."

"I'll give the showerhead quite the hairy eyeball," Joey said.

"Now there's an image I didn't need," I said.

* * *

I BROUGHT a bag of breakfast sandwiches and coffee to Joey's house an hour and six minutes later. He inhaled one of the croissant delicacies before I opened the bag all the way. I counted my fingers to make sure they were all still there. "Help yourself," I said.

"Thanks," Joey replied around a mouthful.

I sipped a vanilla latte and munched on a turkey bacon breakfast sandwich while Joey gorged himself amid bursts of looking for his best legbreaker suit. When I suggested he'd had over an hour to find the goddamn thing, he grunted something uncharitable at me past more food and coffee. By the time I finished eating and downed half my drink, Joey emerged in the necessary attire. His suit fit snugly in just the right spots to suggest strength and malice. His narrow, opaque sunglasses made the scowling eyebrows above them look a measure more sinister.

"If you ever need a second job, I think you've found one," I said.

"The only problem would be if actual legbreaking were required," Joey said.

"Definitely a snag," I said.

With Joey garbed correctly, we headed for Rosenberg's business. His office manager, Shelley Hicks, had been with him long enough to know what her boss really did for a living. None of the other employees logged more than sixteen months but Shelley stayed with Rosenberg for seven years. Her financials also showed direct payments from Jasper. I hoped she knew where he was. Someone did. If it was Shelley, Joey's legbreaker routine and some clever fabrications would hopefully be enough to get her to talk.

I parked the Audi across the street from Rosenberg's supply company. We walked inside and headed toward the back offices. My dark gray Armani overcoat flared in my wake. Joey didn't wear an overcoat. Better to keep the tight suit jacket on and maintain the legbreaker illusion.

A young woman at the back looked up at us. Her throat bulged and contracted as she gulped. Joey kept his sunglasses on. I took mine off, slowly put them away in their case, gazed on her, and smiled. Joey stood beside me, arms folded, the suit jacket straining at his chest, midsection, and upper arms. "We're here to see Shelley Hicks," I said.

The girl swallowed hard again. I almost felt bad doing this to her. She was the right age to be a recent college graduate, shared no connection to the seedy part of Rosenberg's business, and was easy on the eyes. "Um . . . do you have an appointment?" she said.

"We don't make appointments," I said.

"The people we represent don't do appointments, sweetheart," Joey said. He sounded like he stepped freshly out of a pizza shop in the heart of Brooklyn. Joey normally spoke with no accent at all, but he could fake the stereotypical Italian-American one when necessary. "Why don't you go fetch Miss Hicks for us?"

She looked at us a moment with wide eyes, then rapidly bobbed her head. "Yes. Yes, I'll do that." She scurried down the hall. Normally, I might have watched her walk away with some interest, but I couldn't now. The price we pay for keeping up illusions.

A minute later, she came back, still looking pale. "Miss Hicks will see you in her office," she said. "It's at the end." She pointed to the short corridor she traversed down and back.

"I thought she would," I said and walked past her along the hall. Shelley Hicks' door was open. We walked in. Two guest chairs sat before her plain and sparse desk. I didn't see any pictures of family or anything marking the office as belonging to a long-term employee. I sat in the left-hand chair and Joey took the right one.

"What can I do for you?" Shelley said. If we frightened her, she didn't show it. She'd probably seen worse from Rosenberg and his cronies. Or other scary types in the arrangement.

"Mr. Rosenberg skipped town," I said, "along with several of his . . . shall we say . . . important players. He was supposed to stay out of Baltimore City. He didn't." I gave a slow, negative shake of my head. "I understand Mr. Rosenberg wasn't making all of the decisions of late. You know what I'm talking about?"

She looked at me for a few seconds, then Joey. She stared at him longer, sizing him up. "I know what you mean," she said after a moment. "It was unsavory, what they did."

"Why'd you stick around, then?"

"They paid me well enough." She shrugged. "I don't have any children, so sympathizing or empathizing with the parents wasn't going to happen. I guess I was the perfect person to know about the whole thing."

"We're trying to find Jasper," I said.

"We understand he'd been the brains for a while," Joey said, still affecting the accent. I didn't think we needed the legbreaker act at this point, but we couldn't stop in the middle of it.

"Mr. Rosenberg became indifferent a while ago. Jasper . . . branched out and picked up some revenue we needed. Mr. Rosenberg went along because he got a cut."

"So I've heard," I said. "Jasper split, too?"

"I presume so," Shelley Hicks said. "He left me an irregular note."

"You've been involved on some level since they started kidnapping the girls?" I said.

"I've known about it. I never helped with a kidnapping, if that's what you mean."

"What I mean is . . . Jasper and them paid you all along this process. Now they cut and run when the heat is on and all you get is a note?" My hands splayed to show I understood her plight. "They're doing you wrong."

She looked at me again. "They are," she said. "I've kept my mouth shut about the loan business, this mess with the girls, all of it. I admit they've paid me well over the years, but now this?"

"You're dealing with scumbags, lady," Joey said. "The people we associate with wouldn't do you so wrong."

Shelley Hicks seemed to weigh her options. "What is it you're here for?"

"Jasper," I said.

"He left me a note with a phone number. Said he would have it for a while and then get a new one. He didn't say where he was going."

"It would help if you could let me see the note," I said.

"I'll do you one better," she said. "I'll make you a copy."

And she did.

CHAPTER 21

I dropped Joey off at his house. He said he was upset at not getting to play the part more, but he would get over it. When I got home, I took out the copy of the note Shelley Hicks made for me and dialed Jasper on my office line with a recorder attached.

"Who's this?" he said in a rather rude way of answering.

"A man you can't kill," I said.

"I guess I'm not trying hard enough, then. But you'll have to be more specific."

"Have a lot of people you're trying to kill?"

"Can't keep track of them all." I heard sounds in the background, like someone talking at regular intervals without excitement. "Why don't you tell me who you are?"

"C.T. Ferguson."

"Ah, the detective. You took a shit all over our operation in Baltimore."

"Our" operation? "So big a shit you and your boss both needed to split town like cowards."

"My boss?" Jasper's voice rose. I heard agitation setting in. "My boss? Rosenberg wasn't my boss. We made it look like he was because he had the reputation, but he'd become . . . what do you call it . . . a paper tiger? The accountant and I ran pretty much everything."

"Loan sharking, too?" I said.

"Rosenberg was involved there. Met with the marks and all. And he could still act ruthless if someone came to see him. But I think he just got older and didn't care as much."

"So you decided to branch out?" I said.

"We wanted to make up the money he wasn't bringing in anymore."

"You don't mind telling me all of this?"

Jasper laughed. "I'm half a world away from you," he said. "I won't have this phone in a few days, and you couldn't trace it anyway. What do I care?"

"You'll care when this whole mess swallows you, too."

"What are the odds?"

"Better than you think. Eisenberg is a day or so away from getting his comeuppance in jail, and I happen to know where Rosenberg went."

Silence. I heard the background noises again. They weren't clear enough to make them out, but I could play the call back later and amplify specifics. Something sounded familiar in them, like I'd been where Jasper was right now. "Congratulations. You found two Jews who couldn't hide very well. I'm a little better at it. You're not finding me. My family will protect me."

"Your family?"

"The Zhangs," he said, laughing again. "We have reach. We have power."

The Zhangs. Jasper Z. Dexter. Now it made sense. I never looked deeper into Jasper to find his middle name. I should have made the leap or at least the presumption. Because I didn't, Jasper might get away. "I thought you looked Asian," I said after a few seconds of self-flagellation.

"Not everyone sees it. My grandmother was born a Zhang. I took it as my middle name when I turned eighteen."

"Wanted the keys to the kingdom?"

"I guess so," Jasper said. "I knew what the family did, and I wanted access to it. They wanted a bigger presence in America. Win-win."

"How deep was your family tied into Rosenberg?" I said.

"Not past me, and what money they'd toss at him for sending along a nice girl to pick up."

"So they won't mind terribly when you get hauled away."

"I almost like you," he said, adding the laugh I came to find annoying. I would have preferred fingernails on a chalkboard. "What happened to those two guys I sent for you?"

"I'll send flowers to their funerals," I said.

"You will?"

"No." He didn't even seem fazed the two men were dead.

"Oh, well," he said. "I guess you win the battle. I'm over here, winning the war."

"For now."

"For good." I heard the background noise again, a little louder this time, along with a bunch of people talking and milling. "Hey, it's been fun, but I need to go. Places to see, girls to kidnap, money to make. You know how it is."

"I know several urban philosophers noted a direct correlation between money and problems."

Jasper laughed again. "Yeah, but they're dead, aren't they? I'm not. There's the difference."

"One more thing," I said. "Stanley Rodgers."

"What about him?" Jasper said.

"Who decided to kill him?"

"I did. Eisenberg and I convinced Rosenberg. Rodgers used to be somebody. We figured it'd be easier to get his girl with him gone."

"Who killed him?" I said.

"The two guys we sent after you the first time."

"Nice to see you didn't bother upgrading the help," I said and hung up. I'd had more than I could take of Jasper and of this case as a whole.

* * *

GLORIA POPPED her head into the office when I finished. I loaded my sound editing program. "Is this case almost over?" she said.

"I think so," I said. "I hope so. I only need to find the slippery son of a bitch who fled town."

"You know where he is?"

I loaded the file of my recent call into the program. "I'm not sure, but I think I'll be able to figure it out."

Gloria walked into the room. Her gray sweatpants, which I could never believe she owned, fit her loosely but exactly tight enough to pique my interest when she walked. She wore one of my Ravens T-shirts over them. Somewhere along the way, Gloria was loosening up. She would be loath to admit she dressed like the common people (even if her sweatpants were made by Hilfiger), but I noticed and smiled.

"What?" she said.

"Nothing," I said. I played my call with Jasper. Gloria walked behind me and watched over my shoulder. I felt a shudder run down my spine. Working with someone looking over my shoulder always bothered me. In Hong Kong, I was compelled to learn more independently than my fellow hackers because I hated feeling eyes behind me. I fast-forwarded a bit until the background noises became easier to isolate.

Gloria watched me tweak the controls, turning up the normally extraneous sounds and silencing the main track. When

I clicked the Play button, we heard the isolated ambient noises. It was a mechanical woman's voice, speaking Chinese. "What is it?" Gloria said. "Japanese?"

"Chinese," I said. "Mandarin. She said the train to Beijing would board on platform number three."

"So this guy is in a train station in China?"

"Yes. I think I know which one, too, but I want to see if he's headed for Beijing." I advanced the track closer to the end of the call, when I could hear people milling about. This time, we heard the voice again, a little louder, advising travelers to let other passengers get off the train before they got on and thanking them for taking the train to Beijing.

I had him. "He's going to Beijing," I said.

"Great," Gloria said, leaning down and looking at my computer screen with interest. "Now what are you going to do?"

"I have to tell someone."

"Who?"

"Ideally, I should tell the Chinese police."

"I thought they didn't like you very much."

"They don't." A brief flashback to my days in the Chinese prison forced a deep breath. "The feeling is mutual, though I have an idea."

* * *

LATER, Gloria and I walked back to my car after dinner at Chazz, which Chazz Palmentieri opened in Baltimore several years ago. I didn't know how authentic the touches of Brooklyn were; I simply liked the food. Gloria did, too, but I think she preferred the wine. The bottle we shared cost three times as much as our entrées. I don't know if its price made it good wine or not.

I pulled the car onto Eastern Avenue when Rich called.

"Why the hell am I getting an email from the Chinese police?" he said.

"Maybe you should read it," I said. "The Chinese are good at explaining themselves."

"I did read it. They thanked me for my information on Jasper Zhang Dexter and his sex trafficking ring." Rich paused. I heard a familiar tone in his voice, like a parent talking to a rebellious teenager. It was a mix of scolding and resignation. My mother frequently used it throughout my teenage years and still brought it out from time to time. "Did you break into my work email account?"

"I wouldn't call it breaking in," I said. "More like walking in through a door someone left ajar."

"What the hell do you mean?"

"It's not like the BPD practices good password security."

"Which makes it OK?" said Rich.

"Look, I found Jasper. I knew what he did. I knew where he was going. I also knew I couldn't exactly call the Chinese police and report what I knew. They'd tell me to go to hell."

"I like them more by the minute."

"So I reported it under your name. I sent them a nice long email with what I knew and a recording of a phone call between me and Japser. You told them you got the tip from a CI, by the way. They don't have the same laws about taping conversations we do."

"Amazing," Rich said. "You never learn, do you?"

"What are you complaining about?" I said. "You sent the Chinese police information they're going to use to find Jasper and bring him down. They might even get his family. Do you have any idea how huge this is? Your bosses will get a good report on you, and you'll have yet another commendation you got because I dragged you into it, kicking and screaming."

Rich sighed. "Fine. We'll see how this plays out."

"It's going to play out with the commissioner shaking your hand at a podium and you owing me another dinner."

"It'd better. In the meantime, I've already changed my password."

"Yeah, passwords always stop people like me," I said.

* * *

THREE DAYS LATER, my cell phone ringing on the nightstand woke me up. My bleary eyes read the clock at 8:22. I felt Gloria stir beside me as I reached for the phone and answered without even looking at the caller ID.

"Coningsby, it sounds like I woke you," my mother said. Note to self: check next time.

"Because you did," I said.

"Well, you should be getting up soon anyway."

"Schools are closed on account of snow."

"Very funny. Your father and I noticed an article in this morning's paper. Richard got a commendation for helping the Chinese police put a major slave trader out of business. He mentioned you helped a lot in the case."

I smiled at my mother's use of "slave trader" for sex trafficker. "I guess I should be expecting some calls from the press," I said.

"You should, dear. There are a few who always talk to you after something like this. What's that pretty one's name?"

"Can we talk later, Mom? I'd like to get some more sleep before the media blitz bowls me over."

"If you must," said my mother. "Your father and I are going to wire twenty-five thousand to your account today. This was a major coup, Coningsby. Be proud."

"Right now, I'm focused on being tired."

"Be proud later, then. Have a good day, dear."

"You too, Mom," I said, and hung up. Gloria still snored softly beside me. I returned the phone to the nightstand and fell back asleep after a minute or two of deciding what I wanted to do with the money coming my way.

* * *

THE SAME NIGHT, I took Gonzalez to dinner at Kobe Japanese Steak House in White Marsh. He helped a lot more than Rich on the Rosenberg case, and I didn't want him being unhappy about Rich getting the credit for it.

"I was a little salty when I first heard about it," he said over sushi.

"It's the way I needed to do it," I said.

"Why?"

"When I finished my master's, I decided to travel the world. I didn't want to work, so why not travel? I hit a few places in Europe, then made my way to Hong Kong. I ended up staying there thirty-nine months."

"You must have liked it."

I enjoyed another piece of my eel and avocado roll. Gonzalez got some roll with cream cheese in it. I fought the urge to vomit in my mouth a little. Cream cheese is perfectly acceptable on a bagel, but it has no place near raw fish. As we ate our sushi, the hibachi chef came out, lit the grill and set up the show. "I fell in with a crowd of hackers," I said, lowering my voice. "I knew a lot already, and they showed me a bunch more." I stopped to watch the hibachi chef make his knives twirl, dance, and gyrate as he prepared to cut the vegetables.

"You got caught," Gonzalez said matter-of-factly.

"We all got caught," I said. "I spent almost three weeks in a Chinese prison. Eventually, they sent me home and made it clear they didn't want to see me again. So I couldn't exactly call the Chinese police and tell them what I found."

"You could place an anonymous tip."

"No. With all the information I put together, plus the phone call I'd recorded, I couldn't. The reason I used Rich instead of you was because I could break into his email in about thirty seconds."

Gonzalez chuckled. "I was wondering how someone who didn't work the case much knew everything about it."

"Mystery solved. No hard feelings?"

"Nah," Gonzalez said. He raised his stein of Sapporo to me. I raised mine, and we clinked glasses. "The important thing is the ring got shut down. Your cousin might have gotten a shiny plaque, but I'll take a dinner here instead."

"I think he gets a cash award, too," I noted.

"Rub it in, why dontcha?" Gonzalez said.

* * *

LATER, Rich sent me a text. Someone in the Chinese police told him Jasper got shanked in prison. His survival was tenuous.

I thought about Rosenberg, living under an assumed name in Maine, if in fact he still lived. I refrained from contacting the Driscolls since I gave Chris the information. I didn't know what, if anything, he did with it, and I didn't want to. On some level, he knew this, and I didn't expect to hear from him or his wife again.

Gloria went home earlier in the day. She was going out of town with her family tomorrow and needed time to pack the fourteen suitcases she would no doubt take with her. I looked at her side of the bed, a little amused I now thought of it as her side. The bed felt empty without her. When we first met, I didn't think I would like her much outside of the bedroom. Over time, we grew closer, and I came to understand her. Now I missed Gloria.

Maybe I would take another case.

END of Novel #3

Hi there,

This book featured the worst criminals C.T. has dealt with so far.

Will he be able to save an innocent man when the threat is much closer to home?

C.T. has enjoyed a so-so relationship with the police thus far. When it all goes south, can he still work with Rich to find a killer? Find out in *Already Guilty*!

THE END

Do you like free books? You can get the prequel novella to the C.T. Ferguson mystery series for free. This is unavailable for sale and is exclusive to my readers. Visit https://bit.ly/CTprequel to get your book!

If you enjoyed this novel, I hope you'll leave a review. Even a short writeup makes a difference. Reviews help independent authors get their books discovered by more readers and qualify for promotions. To leave a review, go to the book's sales page, select a star rating, and enter your comments. If you read this book on a tablet or phone, your reading app will likely prompt you to leave a review at the end.

The C.T. Ferguson Crime Novels:

1. The Reluctant Detective
2. The Unknown Devil
3. The Workers of Iniquity
4. Already Guilty
5. Daughters and Sons
6. A March from Innocence

7. Inside Cut
8. The Next Girl
9. In the Blood

While this is the suggested reading sequence, the books can be enjoyed in whatever order you happen upon them.

Connect with me:
For the many ways of finding and reaching me online, please visit https://tomfowlerwrites.com/contact. I'm always happy to talk to readers.

This is a work of fiction. Characters and places are either fictitious or used in a fictitious manner.

"Self-publishing" is something of a misnomer. This book would not have been possible without the contributions of many people.

- The cover design team at 100 Covers.
- My editor extraordinaire, Chase Nottingham.
- My wonderful advance reader team, the Fell Street Irregulars.